I0784038

RESERVED

Other Titles by Hannah Marie.

Solivagant

Mama

HANNAH MARIE.

Reserved

Other editions:
Hardcover ISBN 979-8-9910586-2-9
eBook ISBN 979-8-9910586-3-6

https://hannahmarieartwork.blog

This is for my parents: my first teachers.
My siblings: who teach me every day how to love.
Friends who become family.

And that little girl with pigtails, whose favorite color is purple.

Acknowledgements

I have several people to thank for my debut novel:

To my family and friends, especially those in my writing groups, who listen to me muse out loud and try not to laugh.

My early editor, Laura Ross, who saw this manuscript before it bloomed.

My final draft editor, Nicole Fegan, who helped find the heart in my story.

My teacher friends, who patiently listen any time I randomly spout out new ideas.

"It has been a terrible, horrible, no good, very bad day.
My mom says some days are like that. Even in Australia."

– *Alexander and the Terrible, Horrible, No Good, Very Bad Day*
by Judith Viorst

Cold sweat, bad dreams
I try to tell myself that it's gone
The nightmare will never come again
But nothing is as it seems

The night stalks me like a shadow
Grabbing, relentless, ignoring my screams
I can't get away and I fall, helpless
Is there any hope for tomorrow?

I have a beautiful girl
Two of them, who give me hope
I will keep on for them
Them alone—no one else!—they are my world

Present Day.

This must be a dream. Someone screams directly above me, shaking me from sleep. I jerk to a sitting position, smacking Ed in the face. He groans and turns over, a hand raised to protect himself from another unintentional slap. I can only see the glisten of his eyes as I slide out of bed, offering, "The girls!" as an explanation while I shuffle barefoot down the hall. There has to be a better way to deal with night terrors, but I haven't figured it out yet. Eight full days. Eight very long nights.

When I step into the dark room, a tiny silhouette sits frozen in the middle of a twin bed. The second bed is completely empty. "Where's Penny?" I ask the shadow and the figure points to the corner of the room, creepy in the wavering light, reminding me of the third ghost of Christmas. The second child must be under the bed. Small wonder. I huff, regretting for a second that I read the classics to the children. The moments that stick with this new generation make me shudder. Like...never mind that now. I feel old when I start thinking like this. The forties have nearly crept up on me; it's time to let go of childish ways.

Only now, there's this child. And not just one, but two. I glance at Kelly's face before ducking my head under the bed.

"Penny, honey." I try to soften my voice with little effect. Adrenaline is winning. "Was it another dream? It'll be okay. Do you want me to turn the light on?" What do I do in this situation? As an answer, the small girl pushes herself farther away under the bed. There will be no snatching at her now as I had hoped. I can almost see her eyes shining back, looking like a creature from the deep, which I assume might be close to the terrors this little one has been experiencing daily in dreamland.

And in waking, for that matter. I allow bitterness to creep in, just for a second. What was *she* thinking?

"Come on out. It's okay. Let's go." My verbal prodding toward her does no good, and even though I'm only on my hands and knees for a short time, maybe ten minutes, my limbs complain that it's longer. Middle age is coming. Still, I ignore my body's stiffness and lie on my stomach, placing my hands under my chin like I'm merely peering into a fort. "You know, this isn't a bad spot," I comment. "It has some good airflow," I point to the darkest corner, "and I think I saw a unicorn scurry under here last night." My voice is all sweetness and I've entered into a child's world, where vegetables are lollipops and bears are friends. I can do this nurturing adult thing! All it takes is a sense of coolness and the right tone. I chuckle to myself at my unusual composure, reminding me of my husband. The whimpering is getting softer, right? "I once saw a swish of a tail, and I think she likes to rest under here. Have you ever seen her?"

Nothing.

"Well, Uncle Ed tells me that if we have a unicorn under our bed, it only brings happy dreams. The bad dreams can't get around all those clouds and sunshine and rainbows."

Did she nod?

"But anyway, the unicorn is a shy creature, so she won't come over here if she sees someone is in her cave. She likes her space."

Another nod.

"Do you want to get out so that she can come back to live here?" Penny shakes her head and frustration rises in my chest again. The calmness that I had built up quickly evaporates. Impatience wins. "Penny, we have to move! We can't stay here all night. You'll get hungry."

Right on cue, Ed's voice rises from the space above me and his loud voice emanates kindness. Always my Ed. "Penny, I've got your favorite: Chocolate! Chocolate chunk cookies. Do you want to bring back some for our unicorn friend? I think she'll only take it from *your* hand because my clunky feet will scare her." Not a sound, but I see a kid's foot move. I nod at Ed, silently willing him to continue.

"Could you help me get it out of the box? I think it got stuck in a corner."

Penny nods in the dark, but not a word. That's our girl.

"You'll have to come out and help me. Kelly will come with us, too." He bends down next to me. One of my legs is now fully asleep. He reaches a hand under the bed, crouching with a peculiar expression. Penny crawls out and looks at Ed's hand, her face unreadable. She doesn't take it, but does have a slight grin as she crawls out toward the kitchen.

I pat him on the behind and whisper, "I want to be like you when I grow up." I stand and Edmond follows suit, but not before whispering to me, "I think I pulled a muscle from that squat."

"What are we doing?" I shake my head, unable to smile at his lightheartedness. He just looks at me before following the girls.

DEIRDRA

Present Day.

Curses soar through my head. Not now. But ironically, *now* is all I have.

The pen scribbles my thoughts faster, but they only draw a simple outline of the giant swirls of emotion in my mind. I can't pin down enough words. My hand waves around as if to form sentences; feeble attempts to create poetry like I always have. I always take to that resource, attempt to clarify my thoughts and figure out the problem. My early expensive education does me no good. Not when I have a life to keep. I must keep moving. The words *have* to come! They have to!

Nothing significant. It's hopeless. She is hopeless.

My mind is broken. And it is my fault! I am the evil genius behind this grand disaster! Eventually the words come in a torrent of accusations. They don't stop. Around and around. Never-ending punches to my gut which I must expel or they will eat me up inside. But the words on the page come out differently than I planned. The crumpled paper taunts me as I squint through my tears, those words good for nothing. Well, not nothing.

It's an easy solution.

Besides, the paper's already been worked on and reworked many times.

Once more won't hurt.

Then I'll quit, for real this time. I have to focus, to get these words out of me. They are the real demons. I tear off the edge. I am broken. Just this once. Again. No harm done.

Right?

Alexia

[A little before] Present Day.

In the hours before my life turns upside-down, I follow the same routine as always. I wake up at the same time every day. Exactly 6:05am. This is just enough time to put on a pot of coffee, set Ed's overnight oats on the counter, and shelve any extra dishes from last night's dinner. Ed maintains his health kick, but I surmise that my morning coffee routine will never change. I'm a notorious creature of habit and the simpler for me, the better. Normal veggies are good enough for me, though my love for a good steak Edmond sizzles on the grill most definitely keeps me from going vegetarian. After a wonderful dinner with my husband and movie on the couch, we both tumble into bed, ready for a night of sweet dreams.

RING!

I jump out of dreamland and roll over toward my husband. Ed is dead to the world. The clock beside the bed blinks 2:17am. Too late for a sane person. Too early for a safe person. My hand reaches toward the disturbance and I clear my throat.

"Hello?" My voice cracks. I swallow and blink, my effort not affecting the darkness in the slightest.

"I need you."

The voice on the other end urges me to think. My mind is mud. "What? I..." My usual automatic reply is blurred in fuzziness.

"Alexia. I need you! Get over here now!" My sister. Why can't she just figure some things out for herself?

"Deirdra? What—" My voice is more convoluted than normal.

"I can't do this. I just—" Fast breathing and laughter in the background. Anger surges through me. And where are the girls? She's probably high. The only answer to what would have given her the gall to ask a favor in the middle of the night.

A sigh. What else is new? "Why are you calling me, Deids? Now's not the time—"

My heart races, matching the rhythm of the other line. Determined, I lay aside my natural reservations and kick Ed from his sound sleep while deftly pulling on my tennis shoes with one hand. I nod into the darkness and tie my shoes, yelling into the phone before hanging up, "I'm on my way!"

"What's that?" Ed asks.

"My sister." I might start yelling or crying if I say more. There. What else do I need?

"What does she need? You haven't heard from her in, what…?"

"Yep, that's about right. It's about time. And it sounds bad." I slam the door on the last bit of normalcy that my life is ever going to have.

The house is small and austere on the outside, but when I step into my sister's residence, I note that the walkway is swept, as is the kitchen floor. There are very few things hanging on the walls, but everything seems to be in its place and swept to perfection. Even the kitchen table has a bowl of fruit. Well, a bowl without the fruit. An attempt, anyway. I glance to the room on my left and see the same theme. Everything is neat, but very little within sight, except for the essential furniture. No trinkets on the dresser or extra toys on the floor. Can they afford toys? Surely, I'm allowing paranoia to cloud my judgment. But then again, what do I really know about Deirdra's life situation? Absolutely nothing! And whose fault is that? I wonder how I'm going to break the ice.

My sister steps into view, her arms crossed and not making eye contact. Instead, she glances down the hall more than once. It doesn't take much imagination for me to wonder what is in those nooks hidden in plain sight. Deirdra's paranoia is palpable.

I can't help it. "What? Like I'm going to turn you in?" I quip. Deirdra stares me down now, but no hello emerges. "So?" Not a good start, but at least I'm not yelling. Ed is still the cricket on my shoulder. Deirdra finally does make eye contact and smiles a little. I take a step closer and pat her on the side of her arm. Not a huge gesture, more like a hug deflated. "It's good to see you." Lame.

"I have a favor to ask, Sis." It is a quick request, the pleading evident. Here goes. The favors. She used to ask for lots of these and they were never good. How many lives has she already ruined? How many are hidden in these closets? She has never been good at cleaning up her own mistakes.

"It's not one of those big favors, of course," Deirdra rushes. Sure. "You'll like it. I need you to watch the kids. Just for a little bit. Maybe a week or so."

"What are you into?" My suspicion overrides courtesy. After all, we are still virtually strangers as adults and she's asking her long lost sister to watch her kids? Who is she kidding?

Before I can protest, Deirdra continues. "I am looking for a job. It's out of town. There are several...interviews, um, that I have lined up. I just need you to keep them for a few days. Oh, c'mon! What are a few days between sisters?"

Bingo. I've hit the nail on the head. It's convenient, so she calls up her sister, someone proficient in doling out favors. "Why now, Deids?" Two can play at this game. "We haven't talked." No need to elaborate. Deirdra hangs her head. I spot tears in the corners of her eyes. Probably fake.

"You're right. It's unconventional. I only called you because—" She sobs completely, ignoring the makeup running down her face. "Dave just left, for good this time, and I can't hold it together. You said you'd always be there for me. Is that not true?"

The words hit me like a slap. "I'll have a spot for you. Always here." That was a promise we had repeated over and over growing up, especially in the tough teenage years. Right before Kelly. And then Penny. As we grew into adults, growing apart, I still meant it, but it has become more metaphorical, just something recited silently. A knife twists in my gut, but I jump when a little face with a pair of eyes peeks around my sister's leg.

"Who are you?" a little voice asks. It seems more curious, not shy, even though she is half hidden behind her mom.

"This is your Aunt Alexia, Kelly. She's going to be the one to watch you while Mommy is gone."

"Oh." The girl moves from around Deirdra's leg but just stares at me, smiling nervously. Accusations plague me behind the smile. Pictures or the occasional phone call would have been good. I barely even know these children! My own blood. My planning brain kicks into overdrive. How are we going to do this? We need a list of steps, a contract in writing, something. But these are my nieces. How does that even work?

"Let me get Penny." Deirdra places a hand on Kelly's back. "She's a little more shy than this munchkin here. Penny! Where are you?" she yells up the stairs.

"She's in her room. Coloring," Kelly's voice chirps, bird-like, half excitement and half nervous energy, her bare feet dancing on the hallway linoleum.

"Kelly, can you go get her? And make sure your things are ready to go. Don't leave your room messy!"

Present Day.

My heart does one of those leaps, trying to say what my mouth can't. I make sure that I fix everything in my room, perfect and in place for when I come back. When that happens, when my Mommy is ready, everything is going to be just how she likes it. I straighten the pillows again. One more time. They always seem to be in a different spot after 'mares in the night. Maybe with the bad thing gone, they will go, too. But what about Mommy?

"C'mon, honey. Here, I can help you with that." I've never heard those words before from this lady who isn't Mommy and I pull my hand away without looking at her. I want to hug my little bear, but I can't find him. I run over to my closet. He has to be here. I throw clothes everywhere. He might be hidden underneath. Maybe the dresser. I pull things out, but he is not there. My bed is empty and where he normally sits, there is nothing. All my clothes are on the floor. Not neat anymore and I breathe fast. When Aunt Alexia touches my arm, I yank it away. No! She can't help me. I'm supposed to do this like a big girl. I don't yell at her, but I want to. I don't look at her, either, because I don't want to read her eyes. I close mine.

"Hey, look what I found!" Someone says. My head moves over to the doorway when I hear the voice I don't know. A man.

"And this is your Uncle Edmond, remember?" Mom points. My uncle, with a big smile. He looks past my aunt and my mad face. I don't want to stay with them. Then he sees, and his smile kind of goes away. He has my bear! That thought is the only one I have when I take it away from his hand. He says something happy, but my mind blocks. I have my bear. I have my bear. I have my bear. It is safe.

That means I am safe.

"Are you ready?" he asks.

No. No I'm not.

He doesn't hear my words because I don't say them.

Present Day.

"Okay, we can use the sewing room downstairs for one of them." I glance at the girls, laughing as they chase each other in the open yard. I sigh and turn back to the issue at hand. Their rooms. I rushed out so quickly this morning that I was unable to arrange anything. "That would be perfect because of that bathroom right outside. The other can have the room at the bottom of the stairs." The list in my hand starts out as bullet points of supplies to get, and a few lines down it works into scribbles, cross-outs, and side notes.

- Beds, tables, lamps, closet space.
- Do we need to buy more clothes? Send them?

- School supplies and research neighborhood schools? Registration?
- Contact mom every day? Every other day?
- Does she even want us to call her?

"Not the old sewing room, Alexia."

"What? It's ginormous! Perfect for bunk beds."

He doesn't even bother using my pet name, so he must be serious. "Well, where else would you put them?"

"The room off the kitchen. They'll even have their own bathroom." Ed continues in his soft voice, which signifies that he is trying to persuade me. I won't be persuaded. "It has that large window but doesn't get too hot because the sun only comes in early morning. We can get blackout curtains if one of them are sensitive—"

"Is," I correct him, but he ignores the interruption, already caught up in one of his projects.

"—and maybe a night light in case one of them is scared of the dark. Well, maybe a couple night lights and we can put one in the bathroom, too..."

"Look, I have a list!" I wave the nearly obsolete pad in his face. His voice trails off and I'm rushing out of our bedroom and hurrying down the stairs. It's a two-hour drive from here to Maddington, but if the traffic is good on a Saturday morning, we could probably make it in one forty-five. While I'm pouring out the cereal for our daily breakfast, disappointed that we don't have bananas but cutting an apple instead and putting it on each of the two empty plates, my mind is spinning. Two girls in the house? Is everything up to date? When was the last time anyone even slept on that bed? Should I get new pillows? Edmond appears behind me, his presence—and silence—dispelling some of the anxiety that threatens to creep up.

He pops open the toaster and plops two warm pieces of bread on each plate. I place the plate on top of my monthly fitness goals. Secretly, the warm toast with honey is my favorite part of our routine breakfast.

"Thanks, hon." I give him a quick kiss and grab my plate. I wander over to the back window.

Another new routine.

We have a big enough yard, that's obvious. But are we going to manage two little ones?

"We can do this, Al. It's just for a little while," Ed encourages and rubs my arms. He's always been able to read me well.

"How? These girls don't know me! It's been, what, five years?"

"Not quite."

"What am I supposed to tell them? That their mother dragged them across the state to get away from their big, bad aunt? What if they're afraid of me?"

He shrugs. "Well, at least they'll talk to *me* while they're here." I want to punch his arm, but a smile creeps to my face just the same. He always has that effect. He plays with some hair that has fallen down from my messy bun. I put so much work into my hair, and yet it refuses to stay in the hair tie. "Don't worry. It will work out," he assures me.

"How?" I demand. "How is this all going to work out? There isn't any sort of plan for when your grown adult sister decides to play hooky! Who knows what these children have seen? Am I going to be just one more failed attempt at redemption?"

A screaming voice interrupts my thoughts. I race outside to check on the two little ones. Deids mentioned that Penny has some issues, but I really don't know what to expect. Apparently her finger is caught, and Kelly is bent over her, singing a silly song. Instead of calming her, the singing seems to further aggravate Penny, who's waving one arm in the air to keep her sister back. If she just gives a yank with her other arm, she would probably be free, but she is huddled down, frozen.

"Penny, hon, you'll have to get your finger unstuck," I start to explain. But Penny shakes her head and the wailing intensifies.

"She's not listening to me sing. She's not listening!" Kelly cries. "But it always…" A gasp. "The song always works!" The child's eyes spill over and her volume increases.

Two girls crying and two adults staring open-mouthed. This must be a sight for the neighbors. I can imagine the coming days: "Hon, get the popcorn! That crazy family is out again!" For a second I have a flashback of what we went through as kids. Then I have an epiphany. Maybe whatever I did to help their mom calm down might work with them. The screaming continues, so I jump in, to the tune of "If You're Happy and You Know It."

"If you've got a hurt finger, clap your hands…If you've got an awesome sister, stomp a foot." All the motions get her focus off her finger and I have a chance to step in and yank out her hand.

I brace for a moment of gratitude, only it starts another round of blood-curdling screams, and Penny adds, "No!" At least she's saying something.

I sigh and convince the girls to come in for pancakes. Kelly rushes over and embraces her sister and Penny grudgingly allows it. I can't help the thought that emerges in my head that second. Is Penny possessed? But in that moment, as I watch the two sisters, I can only think that they are two people on Earth who need each other.

What kind of task have I said yes to?

DEIRDRA

Present Day.

A gunshot? That has to be my girls. I run outside, but nobody is in the yard. The street is as quiet as ever. I frantically look around for someone. Anyone! One of my neighbors has just turned, shutting the door to her house. "Where are they? The girls—" Then I remember. My girls aren't here. They are with my sister. She has them. Because she's better at this than I am. The one of us who has never raised a child in her life is watching my two little ones. A twinge of bitterness creeps into my body and I use that to propel me back into the house. I collapse on the bed for more sleep, something I can't ever seem to get enough of. Just a couple of days, that's all.

Restless sleep comes. Dark.

PENNY

Present Day.

Okay. It's time to get ready! I scoop up two more spoonfuls of oatmeal, leaving a couple bits of apple. A perfect end to the meal. I POP the last pieces into my mouth and chew, listening to the crunch. Apples are such a yummy fruit! I want to say it to Aunt Alexia. My thoughts come out more like, "Ah," and I seal my lips, staring at my bowl, now empty. Staring. It's a word like scaring. But I am the one trying to scare more food into my bowl. I can't explain myself to her.

"It is pretty good. Do you want any more?" she asks. I give a "no" shake of my head as Aunt Alexia takes my bowl away. She uses the soapy water and I put it on the towel next to the sink. It CLINKS but not very loud. We will come back later anyway and will put up the clean dishes after they've air-dried. I like the sound of that word. Air-dried. It is like a puff of cloud enters the house and blows a wind around the kitchen, somehow making the dishes dry by magic. I run upstairs to brush my teeth. It's my first day ever going to church, and my stomach feels like a nervous wave. What's it like?

We enter the church. Huge, big doors like at Aunt Alexia and Uncle Ed's house. I move my eyes around. Lots of space. Right now it's just a little bit of people, but lots of chairs are in the big room over there. Also pictures and sayings are painted on the walls with pretty clouds and flowers and a large cross hanging off to one side, but the words aren't the same as my mom writes. I don't know what it says.

"Let me show you where we're going, Penny," says Aunt Alexia. "You have your own class." Class? Like school? "You're going to meet a few people who are around your age. Our neighbors Mr. and Mrs. Carter, too." She gives her hand like she wants to touch but then stops. She shows me the hallway with her hand, giving me lots of room to walk with her. She smiles. I like that. But I am more worried about what is coming and I can't smile. I follow, my feet moving slower and slower.

Aunt Alexia points at pictures on the wall. "This is the birth of Jesus, who was the Son of God. This is a picture of Moses parting the Red Sea, one of the miracles for the Israelites. That one over there is a picture of Jesus blessing the little children. Like you!" I smile because she's looking at me, but I don't understand. "Miracles," "Israelites," and maybe "blessing" I know, but the man is not moving, like TV. One of the kids in that picture looks at me. And that other one, too. What do they think? Are they wishing I would say something? Am I supposed to smile back? All of Mommy's pictures are mountains and song people, not any pictures like this. I don't want to shake in this new place. But I am. My arms and my legs. Deep breath. We move like a parade. First her, then me, then two other people with really little kids.

I don't know how long I'm sitting here before I hear a soft voice right next to my ear. "Penny, are you okay? It's me, Mrs. Carter." I move my head away. The teacher can't talk to me. But she is sitting right next to me. Not close enough to actually touch me. Nope. But she's sitting close enough to whisper so that only I can hear. It's like our own little secret. I don't answer, but I do stop the tears, sniffling a little bit. Using my shoulder is a good way to clean off my face. "Do you want to come hear the story?"

I know exactly what I want to say. "No." I make myself even smaller with my legs and I try to disappear out of the room. I miss Mommy and I want to go home! My real home! She leaves and I wonder how much trouble I will be if I secretly get out of the room. If it were Kelly or one of the other boys in class, my one smiling friend in particular, I bet they would. Trying hard as I can to squinch into a smaller ball, I look over my knees to see what is going on. If an adult looks at me, I pretend not to see. No way I'm letting them talk to me.

One of the kids says, "Can I go give her a cookie?" She bounces up and down while she talks. If I ignore all of this, maybe it will go away and I'll be back at my house. The teacher must have told the bouncy girl that she could because quick, quick, she is by my table. "Here you go. I thought you might want a cookie." The bouncy girl tries to place it on my knees, but I don't let her.

"Just leave it there." The teacher points her finger down, tapping an invisible floor, and she says to the bouncy girl to come back.

Just thinking about these people–all these people! I'm going to throw up.

Even when I was littler, Mommy would say, "Sh-h-h, I have a headache."

Or when we were in our imagine land. "Now make sure, Kelly, that you don't wake the neighbors."

"Penny, don't get that out. It's scratching the counter." I just wanted to help. But I know, kids shouldn't do adult jobs.

"You girls don't get too rowdy, now." And we couldn't play too loud.

When I was really, really littler, Mom was with everyone else, people who came over to the house every time. She yelled at us. She was mad at someone. Us, mostly. 'Cause when you yell, it means you're mad.

Don't move too fast, just be quiet. Don't say anything.

I tried to just do what I was told when I was really little. That way I got a smile, or sometimes a story at night. Mom got mad a lot, especially when other men were with us. I liked it better, just us. Sometimes those others would yell at her, or us when we got too loud. Mom would yell right back, and that usually meant the other man would leave. Mom's yelling wasn't so bad then. So I learned not to say anything that would make someone look at me. Not to speak. Not to move. And sometimes, not to breathe. I got really good at breath-holding.

When we are driving home after church, nobody speaks. I like the quiet, but I know something is wrong with the silence when Kelly tries to say something. Both Aunt Alexia and Uncle Edmond just nod their heads. "Great! I'm so glad!" Then nothing else. They always ask questions, and now they're silent. When adults are silent for a long time, they're either sleeping, studying, or mad.

"An ostrich's eyes are bigger than its brain!" Kelly shouts.

Uncle Edmond makes a funny noise with his mouth, but then turns around in his seat while Aunt Alexia gives him a look. He says, "Where in the Bible did you learn that? Did you study Noah?"

"Nuh-uh!" She smiles at him, but then gives me a pouty look when he doesn't say anything else. We drive the rest of the way without anything. We don't even have any music to listen to. It's great. When we are at the house again, Kelly jumps out and runs ahead of Aunt Alexia, who tells her she can use the spare key to open the door.

Uncle Edmond helps me out. I don't go fast because it's a big car. Really tall and I have to jump to get down. Uncle Edmond has my arm and helps me stand like I'm supposed to. I look eye to eye. He knows I am saying thank you.

He smiles.

I go after my sister and Uncle Edmond calls my name. I stop, but don't look at him. Maybe I'm in trouble now and he'll start yelling. I should have gotten out from under the table. My body shakes a little. "Did today scare you? When you went into that room with those kids?" He walks around and I can see his face. I won't cry. I never want to cry with adults because they'll get mad. But I nod once and look at the ground. The tears are on my face. "I'm sorry." His voice sounds super quiet. Not mad. "I didn't know that it was going to scare you that much, but maybe next time I can come with you for a little bit? Or maybe the teacher can give us a coloring paper and we can work on it together?"

Really? I can color it exactly how I want? There won't be any of those loud kids? I shake my head. No way, no how. I won't go back. Not at all.

Uncle Edmond looks at me. What does that look mean? "You don't want to color with me?" I open my mouth. I want to say how, but nothing comes out. "Well, we can figure out something. What about for now let's just go inside and see what Kelly is up to?" We walk a little bit. "Hey, Pen?" Eyes meet eyes. "You know that you are a great girl, right?" I look down. I don't know what to do with those words. "Really. I mean it."

"Ed, hon, the guinea pig got out again. I think he just went under the shed and the newest mama cat is chasing it!"

"Whoops, guess we'd better get in there!"

We walk-run for a moment before he stops me again. "You have been through so much already. Just because you don't like meeting new people doesn't mean that you're weird. It's just uncomfortable. And you know what? It's okay for you to say that you need the comfort of being with us. Because that's already waaaaaay outside of your comfort zone." His hands are wide, like a plane. "That's okay. You are doing good, Penny, and I hope that it gets easier for you. Someday you'll decide to do something different and your aunt and I will be like, 'Whoa!' when that happens." He makes his eyes really big and does something funny with his mouth when he says this. He has his hand on my shoulder for a little bit, then moves it with a smile. We walk toward the house again. Together. It's been an okay day. Even this. I don't want it to stop soon.

"Let's try something. Which one of these books do you like? One of them is *Peter Pan*, one of those classics your Aunt Al likes. And this one here is *Charlotte's Web*, about some farm animals and a special, surprise friend."

That night, we read a little bit before bed. "Well, what did you think?" Still not ready for words, but I use my head to show him it was good. "Maybe we can do this again?" Before he gets off the bed I take the book, not to keep, but I put it right on the table by the bed. Next time we say night-night, we might read more.

I stand in the middle of my backyard but it is super big, bigger than now. It is nighttime and there are super tall trees all around me. I am really little, not like I am now. Something makes a noise behind me, but when I turn, there is nothing. Nobody. The trees disappear and I am in the middle of snow, but I'm not cold. I take a step and try to say something, but my voice doesn't work. Maybe it's tired. My mind takes a step, but I don't go anywhere. Just deeper and deeper in the ground. In the white. My legs start moving faster and someone calls my name. "Penny! Penny, wait!" That voice! I know that voice! Mom is crying, and she is almost screaming, like the day that we left our house. I have to find her. But she's up there, where the top of the hole is. My foot is stuck. My foot—I jump as hard as I can and run up the side. Faster. Faster. And my legs hurt more and more.

When I wake up my legs still hurt, like I was really running in my sleep.

"Who's Alma?" Kelly stands in the middle of the room. I was talking when I was asleep, too.

My head falls to my pillow and I look at the star on the ceiling. Aunt Alexia and Uncle Edmond would only let us put one star each. One of these days I'm going to visit one of those stars and I'll be famous there. Everyone will talk about my beautiful paintings.

Kelly plays with the measure stick that we put up right after we got here. How long ago was that? And Kelly's shoulder leans against where my growth mark is. I have gotten six inches bigger than when I came that first time! Uncle Edmond says that he's going to start calling me Beanstalk. Or Jack. He says that because this boy Jack had a beanstalk that grew tall and almost touched the stars. Instead there was a castle. Maybe one day when I'm big I will build a castle and have everyone live with me! All my family.

Stars.

I wonder if Mommy sees the stars, too.

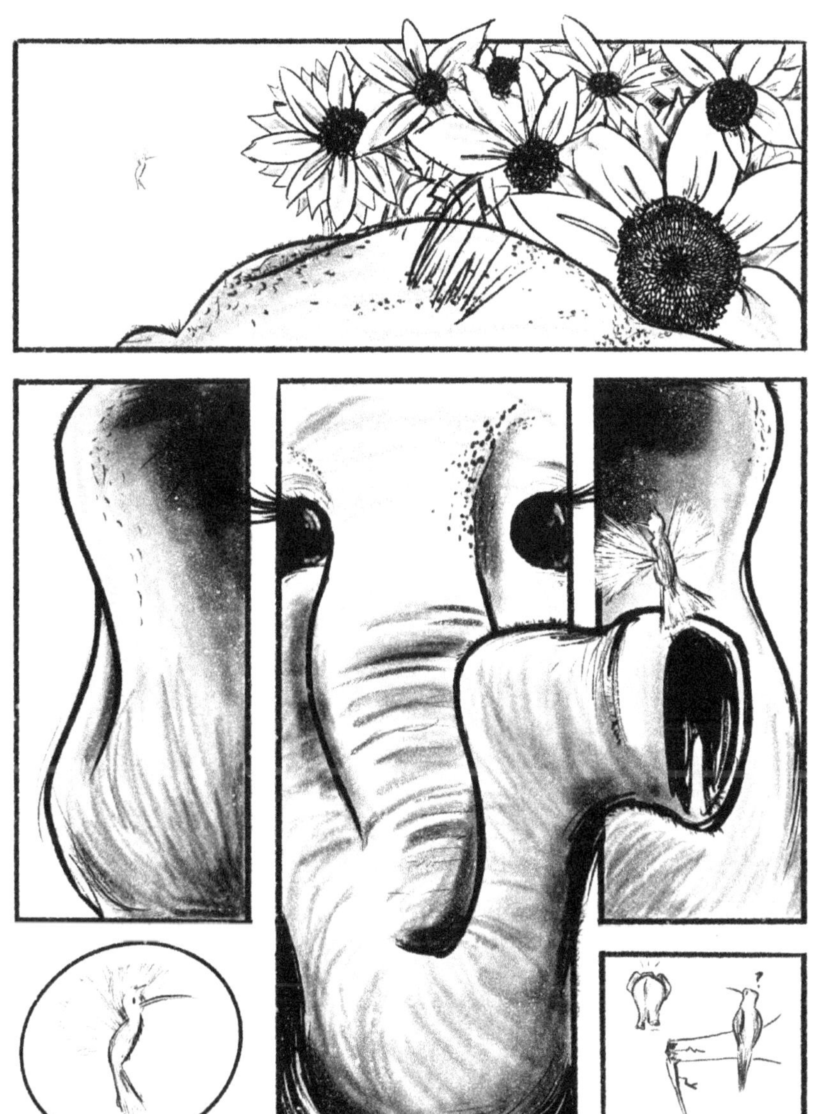

DEIRDRA

Present Day.

I gasp, pulling myself out of the water of my nightmare. The images flashing before me of sleeping under a bridge don't compare to the sheer terror of drowning while I'm still alive. But it wasn't a hand pushing me down. More like convincing me to follow. Instead, I had watched in disjointed horror, as if I were someone else. The hand that first beckoned this "temporary" life had brought me further into the depths of the river, luring me to join their murky darkness. It is tempting. Maybe my girls would be better off without someone like me in their lives—more than once this has pricked me. I am better to live on as a friendly ghost, the spirit of an idea that once was with my girls safe in the cocoon of Christianity, a bubble of ignorance. And yet. Yet there remains a sliver of something in me, like a song not yet written, of a life that ushers me into something glorious that I could find in one of Kelly's books.

The words of one of my songs echo into my thoughts, urging me to stay and, oddly enough, moving me into a direction I can't even fathom at this moment. A takeout menu is the closest available object. I write through the haze.

You must run, fly (soar?) And twirl all around everywhere (WHIR-WOP)/So get out there and give everything you've got because (TAP-TOK-TAP)/Others need you (DEE-A-DOO) to bring all of it (DIR-A-THWACK)/Your best self. (BOOM!) It's true! Don't be something useless sitting on the shelf

I sing it out loud to myself, dancing around a little with each of the onomatopoeias. It's dumb, but the sounds first came to me when Penny was a baby and her colicky lungs did nothing but wheeze while my tiny baby screamed. Kelly was already a little mother back then but was beginning to get frantic. I was beyond that. All I could do was just sit and scribble in a corner to drown out my hopelessness. I had tried everything and there was no more money. Nothing was helping that night. Something within me welled up and I had jumped to my feet, looking for something, anything, to keep my girls happy. I started to recite notes, scribbles on the breast pump instructions, singing a random, made-up tune, the not-yet-existing music to the lyrics. Then when I reached the end of a phrase, I jumped up and down and started adding the WHIR-WHOP and DIR-a-THWACK as I made funny faces and hand motions. Kelly laughed through her tears, a big, belly laugh that I couldn't ignore.

Moments like that are what surface, even in the unconscious of my dreams. Water is not enough to keep me down, though sometimes the lightness of the cooked H seems something close to that. I hold my broken guitar and sing out, ignoring the popped A string. The music pierces the night. I sing through tears, wishing my girls were with me, dancing to my nonsensical lyrics in the living room. "Hands in the air! Feel the rain!" I make a sound, only seeping through my teeth. "It's there." It's just me. No one else. And there is no one else to turn to. It takes me away from my troubles for a moment. There is nothing left in me to give. Despondency settles around me once more, a friend in the midst of hopelessness. It might not be comfortable, but it is familiar and I can use something familiar. It almost feels safe. I want to feel something I have not felt in years, really since I stepped foot outside of Kelly's father's residence. Life then was unknown, sure, but it was something that I was choosing, to live a better life for my kids. Is this better? I have done everything I can. Since that time, my mind has never quite allowed me to go back there. I brought this on myself. At times I want to run away for real, not just a couple days. But something is keeping me anchored to my spot, with the bruises and all. I just can't quite put my finger on what "it" is. Is it enough to pull me out of this hole? I went back to that man a week later.

I am just as weak.

The menu falls to the floor.

Alexia

Present Day.

She's in one of her moods again. Don't engage. Focus on the positive. "It's okay, Penny." Penny just slapped me for touching her arm. I thought we might try cooking again because that seemed to go well last weekend. But when she reached for a breakable measuring cup, I was afraid she'd drop it. I shouldn't have touched her, but I did, and the second I snatched it, she flailed out at me. I felt panic surging up to my heart, but I didn't let it get to me.

Deep breath, I tell myself. Think. I need to get on Penny's side. I want this little one to see that I will not cause her any more pain. Any more? Yeah right.

A voice inside me reverberates in my head, like that old pinball machine at—what is the name of that pizza place? The voice mocks me. I've never struggled with confidence, but something about these children makes me doubt everything I've ever been taught.

"You can do it, Sweetie." Encouraging voice. Breathe again. "Just use the cup to get a little flour out of the container." I make sure my hand is close to Penny's. Pointing where she needs to go, but not touching her. Will she listen? The girl peeks over the container, drops the measuring cup into the flour, and pulls it out with a quick tug, throwing flour everywhere. A puff of fine flour flies over my face. I cough, way too dramatically for a few specs and Penny drops the cup on the counter. She wipes her hands, fruitlessly trying to clean them.

She doesn't like getting dirty. Tears. I do the first thing I think of. I put my hands, palms up, under Penny's and rub gently. "Here. I'll help you clean them. Now let's use this towel. It will help get the flour off your fingers." I grab a towel hanging over the oven and hum a nonsensical tune. Act calm and not hurried. I am learning that music soothes her, most of the time. It's hard to know the right timing! For anything, really.

Pretty soon, her hands are mostly clean, though I can't say the same about my cabinets and kitchen floor. No matter. I check myself, making sure that I am calm and add, "Would you like to try again? Just do it gently this time." Penny shakes her head and pushes at my arm again. I think that might mean it's my turn, so I scoop out flour, trying to even it out as much as possible, but not even scraping it flat with a knife. Another habit down the drain since these kids. I pour the heap of flour into the bowl and then another. *This is for Penny*, I keep telling myself.

Glancing down at Penny, I see that her frown has disappeared, but she is still solemn as she watches the process. "Do you want to help me pour this one out?" I try again but there is that head shake again. I nudge the cup toward my niece. "Here. It's easy. You can do it." I still hope to see progress. It doesn't happen much, but in an inspiration, I tilt the cup to the counter and allow a small pile to fall onto the surface. "Look," I say quietly, noting that her eyes are already following my hands, curious, but unsure.

"You can draw in the flour." I touch my fingertips to the edge of the flour pile, completely ignoring my own inbred philosophy of not playing around in my own cooking. Breaking all the rules today. Then I touch it again. I run my hand flat against the counter and widened the area of the flour-covered counter. I forgot how amazing flour feels. It brings me back to my own childhood and I have an idea. I poke twice into the layer, one dot next to the other, then drag my finger across the small area. It makes a poorly-done, but still recognizable smile. "There's a smile, just for you, Penny! He's happy to see you!" I'm no artist like my sister, but the effect is priceless. Penny glances at me with something in her eyes—that sparkle of curiosity. What can I do to make this child smile? I want to see it more than just that once.

Penny points at the flour. "Go!" she says. This surprises me. What is she talking about? Does she want me to leave? I'm not about to give up that easily.

"Look at this. Can you follow what I'm doing?" I try to straighten my finger so that I am pointing tight as the tip of my finger touches the tabletop.

Will she try it?

I suggest with a nod that Penny can try with her own hand, but Penny just shrugs and hides her hands under the table. Maybe it is the texture. I file this concept in the back of my head as a mental note to ask Penny's teacher about suggestions for alternate play ideas.

She waves her hand, as if to correct me and say with her body language, "No, Aunt Alexia, you do it like this!" We spend the next ten minutes with her pointing and me building flour castles. With my hands. And it's more than just a little fun. The new challenge: Find what she likes to do. My new thoughts on breaking some of the rules? Completely worth it!

PENNY

Present Day.

Aunt Alexia comes into the room so early! I'm awake, though. My sleepy didn't come last night and I lay down looking at the ceiling during the dark time. I heard something outside, something bumping against the window. I kept saying to myself it's just a tree, it's just a tree, but my brain wouldn't listen and it was too dark to see what it was. A dark blanket laid over the Earth. I'm going to pretend that the noise is my little hummingbird tapping on the window with its mouth. That's not so scary. My mind does more happy thinking when it can see the sun.

Aunt Alexia pats my leg under the blanket but I move back.

"Let's get going!" she says. "I've got breakfast on the table." Her thumb points.

I turn my face to the wall. Pretend not to hear.

"Okay, take your time, little one. Unless you want something to eat. I'll have Kelly come and check on you in a little while."

I should mind my aunt. Mom always said that. Minding adults, I always should. I know I should. I like staying with her and my Uncle Edmond. I like this bed. It's so soft! I bury my face in the pillow so my face is all smooshed into it and the hummingbird *POP* s into my head. When Aunt Alexia leaves, I move out of bed super slow. Then slower. I'm a snail leaving its shell. I pick up the big pencil and paper I put by the bed last night and draw. I like crayons better 'cause they fill in empty spaces. Prettiest colors only. But this is all I have here. We had some drawing lessons in class at school and Teacher told me to use shapes to make things. Sounds easy! Okay, so what shapes make a hummingbird? I want to draw my friend. First, a circle for the head, then another circle for the body. No, that's not right! Think! Think! Think!

My head hurts from banging it on the desk. I erase all of it until the paper is almost white—but it's not, really. It's kind of messed up. I try again. A circle is too fat for the body, so then a square, but that's bad, too! Maybe just two lines? Ugh! I hate my drawing! I should show Kelly.

Carefully now, I pull a line from the circle for the mouth. Then a flower on the side. Okay. I like drawing flowers 'cause they're easy. Just a circle with more circles, circles, circles all around the outside. My circles aren't perfect, but my teacher told me they don't have to be. Do my best. Some look like little eggs, the kind baby birds would POP out of. I am working so hard I ignore all of everything.

"Penny!" Kelly makes me jump and we both laugh a little. "Aunt Alexia has breakfast ready." I wait. Today is not a talking day, not for me. My mind is still on my picture and my eyes are on Kelly. "Well, if you don't want food, can you come down to keep me company?" she asks. She tells me Aunt Alexia is worried and we need to cheer her up. Bring my drawing. I don't let her take it.

I will.

Aunt Alexia is eating a bagel with cream cheese when we come downstairs. I forget that I'm not hungry. "Wow! Is that for me?"

I shake my head. It's not for her to keep. Just to make her smile. I know it's hard for even Aunt Alexia to understand me. My mouth doesn't want to listen to my brain. Like I have two different brains. One wants to say everything all at once, and the other says, Nope! Don't say anything or all my secrets will get out. It's like that cartoon of the TV roadrunner, the one we would watch before coming here. We saw it in our house. With Mommy. I want to do that. To disappear in a big dust cloud and get away as fast as I can. The roadrunner never has to say anything except

BEEP! BEEP! and he is fine. I can do that, too, just watch.

I push Aunt Alexia away from me and away from my picture. My words are still inside me. Quiet is winning. She doesn't say anything, but I know I'm in big trouble.

Never push people. Never hit. I hurry my fast feet to Kelly.

"Penny was drawing this picture, and I told her you'd like to see it," Kelly tells Aunt Alexia. "I told her it might make you happy."

Aunt Alexia's face doesn't look mad now. "Kelly and Penny," she says, "I'm happy because you both are here! It's wonderful to have you in our house." She picks up the phone on the counter. She's smiling when she hits the numbers. "How is Mom, is she feeling better? When can we go home?" Kelly asks. But there's no answer. She doesn't talk. She frowns, but doesn't say anything except, "You know what, girls? I think we should all drive down to your house to see if your mom needs anything. Maybe she's still not feeling well."

Kelly keeps eating. I jump up to go, but a noise is outside. My hummingbird! No, that's just my head. Only in my drawings. From a story Mommy told us.

"What kinds of stories do you like to read?" It's like Aunt Alexia knows my mind. I look at my hands. "Mommy reads you bedtime stories, right?" Kelly almost shakes her head but then says, "Well, kind of. There was that one time, but mostly, she just reads to us when we're sick or something, or if she just got mad at us for being bad and then she feels sorry. She sings us songs! Lots of silly ones, and sometimes sad ones. She makes them up. If she doesn't have work the next day, we stay up and tell stories. Then she says we need to have 'silent time' and to leave her alone, after she's been with

friends." For this part, she waves her fingers in the air like Mom and Aunt Alexia laughs. Did Kelly just do something funny? "That, Cute Girl, is called air quotes. Well, how about this?" Aunt Alexia starts. "What if we stay home this morning and do some reading together? Then we can go get some lunch and take it over to your mom."

"Yes!" Kelly grabs my hands.

"No!" I pull away. It feels *really* not good. My hand doesn't want touch right now. But I don't know how to say all that 'cause then she moves, and she'll be mad, so I try smiling. Kelly laughs, like Aunt Alexia. Reading with her sounds like fun. I turn my smile to her. Kelly starts dancing and Aunt Alexia doesn't tell her to be quiet so that the neighbors won't get mad. She dances with us, too! She dances and dances, then falls on top of the couch. "Whew! You kids tire me out! How about if I tell a story and you draw pictures to go with it? Penny, I see you like to draw birds, so I'll tell a story about birds. Kelly, for you, I'll include some dogs and cats, okay?"

"The chicken, too?"

"Yes, Barb can be in it, too."

Deirdra

Ten months ago.

"You could have done so much with your life!"

Look at that. She can't even meet my eyes, so I yell toward the back of her head. "I did!" I grab my children—*my* children!—too rough by the shoulder. Kelly releases a tiny squeak and I loosen my grip. My anger can't get the better of me, not now. She rips into me again.

"You were constantly making up those annoying songs and skipping around with a paper in your hand, or writing lyrics in the dirt. Why didn't you just do that?"

It's not like I didn't try. But the girls were growing, and we could only live on ramen for so long. "I didn't want to spend five years of my life doing something that wouldn't pan out!"

"Argh!" She screams in frustration. "Don't you get it? You could have made more of yourself. You would have been someone!"

"I wanted to sing. I really did. But after so long...I got sick and tired of the boos on the stage." I counted off with my fingers, "The early morning hours, little pay, and going home with no food in my stomach." My voice cringes in sympathy at the recollection.

"Not much better now," Alexia snorts.

I don't say anything. I can't reply. I turn so that she can't see my tears. The silence is too much. Roars in my ears. "I can do it. I can—"

"You can what? Go beg on a street corner?"

"I've already done that. I'm an expert at pulling at the heartstrings of others."

"Why doesn't that surprise me? You even got that guy of yours caught up in it."

"Leave Dave out of this!" I don't tell her we aren't even talking. Not for months now.

"Why? Why should he not be included? You've already ruined your life. You don't need to drag him down with you."

"If I had everything you had, I wouldn't be so high and mighty as you! At least I can have kids!"

That silences Alexia for a moment after a sharp intake of breath. "What made you the way that you are?" she hisses. "I wanted to take care of you."

"Oh, yeah, you took care of me!" I laugh sardonically. "Until it was too much for you. Then you just left me to rot, right when I needed you."

* * *

"No, it's not a good time, Al." She has some nerve. I didn't even get a week to stew.

My sister protests on the other end. "C'mon, Deirdra. I'm not asking for much. Just—"

"Well, it's a lot for me. I can't do it right now. I have..." The papers crisply sprinkled with treasure in front of me nudge me toward my pressing duties. I can't get caught. "I just can't right now. That's all. I'll think about it." I hang up before second guessing. She can't come. The poorest excuses in the world won't stop my sister from asking questions, but it will keep her away for now. It's time. I've got to get out.

"Mommy, why are you mad at Aunt Alexia?" Penny's quiet voice slides up behind me. *I can't.* I spin around, already on edge.

"Penny, you don't understand!" The tension stretches me thin and I snap. My job hangs by a thread. My boyfriend doesn't believe me. And these two kids need food to fill their bellies. My voice rises as desperation shoots through me. "You can't just go sticking your nose into my business. I'm the adult. I will take care of it." Kelly peeks around the corner, her mouth open for a follow-up question. "No. Just shut up! You're ruining it!" Kelly closes her mouth and Penny starts crying. My stupid voice runs on before I can stop it. "Shut up, both of you. Mommy has to THINK." I scream the last word into the darkness of the kitchen, the electricity long since snuffed out following another round of unpaid bills. I cry with my children. I yank Penny into her room and turn around to get Kelly, who has disappeared. I just need quiet. I close the door and go back to the kitchen. I don't hear either of their voices, not even Penny's whimpering. I won't hear it for a long time.

* * *

"Welcome back, my dear Deirdra!"

There is something behind his smile that I don't trust, but I have no choice. At the moment, a job is superior to the desert of homelessness. Sleeping on couches doesn't cut it. I'll save up again, and I'll need to figure something out. I have to. Soon. Besides, the man standing in front of me has connections, which will help my prospects. At least it should. The desert of possibilities—or, rather, impossibilities—stretches before me. I am the only one who can figure out a way through. No one will help me. I grab my children by the hands, one in each, and march through the door. It's just temporary. Until I can get on my feet. Then I can be a respectable mom. Here goes nothing.

Penny

Present Day.

A bright light hits my face. Like a billion fireflies. "It's Mom!" Yes! I jump up and Kelly squeaks, "Mom is here!" We race to the front door, running into each other as we hit the closed opening.

"Scoot back! Your mom needs room to come in," Aunt Alexia says. She pretends like she's going to get us and we run away. Little cockroaches.

Mom opens the door and we all hug. Kelly doesn't let go, and her arm is on top of mine. Instead of feeling Mom's arms, I feel her hands push us both away, moving funny, like she can't walk right.

Oh.

Kelly starts telling what we did that night. "And then Uncle Edmond got caught in the door when we were playing hide and seek! Well, no, he didn't exactly get caught in the door—"

"I just couldn't get up! I was stuck for a good ten minutes behind that door." Uncle Edmond laughs. I go over to the corner closet. It's time to hide.

"How'd you...um..." Mommy looks like a ghost. She doesn't say words like normal. "...get in here?"

"Key." Aunt Alexia points at the window. She sent me and Kelly to look around the flowerpots and we finally found that other key! "Remember, you asked me to watch the girls?" Mom acts like she says something that we can hear, but no words. She almost sits, but she misses the chair and falls onto the floor. Mommy starts crazy laughing and laughing. "Deids, let's go lie down." She takes Mommy's arm, but Mommy doesn't let her.

"No!" she yells. "I'm not gonna...anywulsh. I came...get my girls." All the other words are mixed. Kelly moves toward me and Uncle Edmond does a 'come with me' signal. I ignore to watch Mom. What are we going to do? I want to go with Mommy, but something's wrong. She is never like this during the daytime.

Aunt Alexia takes one of my new drawings off the fridge for Kelly. "Hon, can you take Penny to her room and help her get ready for bed? And then you can finish coloring. If you get done you can turn it over and start working on the back."

Me and Kelly are upstairs when Mom starts to sing. She doesn't sound very good, like she's trying to make a noise. Kelly gives me my picture. "Here. I won't draw on it. I have one of my own." I nod and Kelly closes the door and I can't hear what Mommy says to Aunt Alexia.

Penny

Present Day.

"Meow! Meow!" I try to hear the tiny sound. Maybe it's still a dream. There! I jump out of bed. My head almost hits the window, but I don't see anything. There it is again. I run over to the front door and try to unlock it without anyone hearing. Mom will probably be getting up soon, but I don't hear anyone moving. It's okay. I go outside and follow the house wall, the one I pretend is my secret fort, to the part under my bedroom window. Nothing is different, even when I look at all the things. The tree. The fence. The butterfly on my shoe. I get close to the ground. I hear it! The meow is really big.

A dream wakes me after a restless night
A ghost or spirit haunts me; a fright
　　—ening thought, if the It
Is playing with my mind again. I shake
　　my head because it can't play
I play with words that mean nothing if
　　—my visions still pinch me awake
And I wake without clearly seeing a vision
Of where I am going
　　I shake my head.
No! I can't fall into this measuring contest.
Where I measure myself against here or there,
　　scares or HER.
And who walks in but HER.
I am proud, but pitiful because I have fall
　　—en in her eyes and I can't meet her measure
My sister with her bags of treasure.
"Why are you here?"
She has a key because I gave it. Me.
She brought meat and even pizza, loads of bread
　　I shake my head.
And begin to whine.
She pulls us out, into the sunshine.
"You need this. No arguing. It's going to be fine."
This must be a dream.

I use my teeny voice, "Come here! It's okay." I stick out my hands and wiggle to the little eyes and fluff, but the little kitten just looks at it. When I try to scoot closer it moves back. I try again, moving just inch by inch, and think about calling. It won't listen to me. It SKIT-SCATS under the bush and goes away to somewhere else I can't see. I call it and search hard, but I can't find it. Would Mom say yes to a cat?

When my school stuff is almost ready, there's another MEOW! Outside, nothing. But Mommy isn't home now and it's near go-to-school time. Kelly is in the kitchen and has a note. "Try reading it," she says.

I guess reading is better than talking. But not really. I can't get past the first word. "Gee."

Kelly takes the note to read with a loud voice. "Girls, I came in late. An—Aunt Alexia—"

"Oh! Her!"

She rolls her eyes at me. "...is going to bring you to school. Love you." Kelly says the "U" with a jump and I do know that word. Mom put U and not all of the word. Like she wanted to make it easy. We jump up and down, making sounds and Kelly says her AEIOU's song so we jump for them all. "E-e-e-e" is the best and Kelly tickles me.

Aunt Alexia does get us in not very long. Kelly runs out to get her before she comes in and hugs. I won't do that. "Hello, Sweetie! Girls, you know I love seeing you, but will you tell your mom to text me the night before, not in the wee hours of the morning?" She stops a yawn with her hand. "C'mon, get in the back. We're going to make a coffee stop before school so Aunt Alexia can stay awake. I'll even come eat lunch with you both!"

"Aunt Alexia, we have different lunch times." Kelly is right.

"Well, all the more reason for me to be there, Kelly. The time in between will give me a chance to chat with your teachers." Kelly does a not-happy sound and jumps in Alexia's car. I don't really like it when anyone talks to my teachers either. Aunt Alexia laughs and waves at me. I leave breakfast and get my backpack. I always need that. The cereal goes in a side pocket and I pat it. The last one. Kelly let me have hers. It'll be good for lunch. When we are driving to school I want to tell Kelly about the kitten. My eyes look on the grass and next to the corner. "Penny found a cat!" Kelly tells Aunt Alexia anyway. "Oh, that must just be a stray. There are lots of those around. Especially with the awful mice population everywhere right now!"

I hope she says more, but she won't. Population is a big word but I guess it means lots of mice. There were two mice running around the back porch. Kelly told me peanut butter on a mouse trap works. Mom did get some for us and there were two mice! Then I had a plastic bag and we put them in the dumpster out back. I smile when my aunt smiles back at me. Maybe we can.

After school is done, I run to the house. Is the kitty still here? Maybe she ran! But when I see the bundle on the porch, there you are! I grab the cat and hold it. I must have hurt it really because she 

makes RAWR-*Hissssssss*! and scratches. My arm has blood. I let the kitten go. She shouldn't have done that. I'm trying to help. Was I too rough? "Um, kitty." I get down and see the little paws under the bush. Almost hidden and I want to crawl under there. I don't want to scare the kitten, so I don't get up. "You hungry?" Cats would eat human food, I think. When it doesn't come out I go to the house to find some cereal. As much as I can fit into my hand. My hand sticks out and I do the don't-breathe thing. The cat peeks out its nose, then ears, and then its paws. I'm afraid it will go back. It eats one thing. It's working!

DEIRDRA

Twelve Months Ago.

"I've got Park Place!" Kelly throws up her hand and squeals in delight. "You owe me!" She leans closer to Penny and holds out her hand, waiting for payment.

"Woah, Kels! She's got it. Okay, Penny, do you know how to count this out? She needs two of these." I wave the two hundreds and think of the bag of H under my mattress. I didn't know where else to put it. All expensive things should be put under the mattress, right? At least, I've heard alternatives like that. The girls play in the closet, so that's out of the question. But there is no way they could lift the weight of the bed. Where can I get more? I've not got nearly enough. Surely there's someone else, or do we all think that? That there is someone else out there just like me.

But no. In reality, it's just me. And it always has been. If I want to find help, I'm going to have to do it myself. It's my job to protect these kids and I am going to have to figure it out. Only, I have no clue where to start.

PENNY

Twelve Months Ago.

In the dark. I watch Kelly get out of bed and I pretend I'm still asleep. She must be looking for Mom, but she comes back so fast. Kelly picks up the phone. "Mrs. Kenom? Hello? Hello?" She pushes buttons and tries again. She gets an old man twice, and he sounds mad, so after two calls, she stops and puts the phone down.

"Penny," she calls to me, "start getting dressed, okay? I'm gonna run over to Mrs. Kenom's. When I get back, I'll give the secret KNOCK!. Come down and let me in." I peek out and she grabs her coat.

Kelly makes a noise and climbs the stairs. She waves her hand at me. She's not waiting. I'm scared. My self doesn't feel right. Like I'll lose her if she closes the door. Like Mom. I try to say something, but my voice is stuck, and the whispers that come out, Kelly can't understand. She makes one of those sight things. "Penny, we don't have time—" She walks around the room back and forth, back and forth. She looks at the ceiling, at me, at the door, and again at the phone. "C'mon," she says finally, and waves at me to follow. "Fine, you win. We'll leave the door open for a minute, since we don't have the key. I'm sure Mrs. Kenom will know what to do."

Kelly grabs my hand, ignoring my struggles to free myself from her touch. I'm curious to see where we go next. Kelly pulls me downstairs and out the door, which she leaves just a little bit open. "I hope she can help." Who is she?

* * *

"That's right. They're here in my house."

Mrs. Kenom has been on the phone for a really long time and she's made lots of calls. She watches me, but I stare right back. I can do that without her asking me more questions, 'cause she's on the phone.

"No. Okay, I can do that. Yes. Can you give that to me?"

Mrs. Kenom pulls out a paper and writes something. Then she puts down the phone and presses a button, making us hear the person she's talking to. Whoever it is—some man—is saying a bunch of numbers. Then, "Are you sure you're okay? We can come over there if we need to."

Kelly ignores when Mrs. Kenom looks at us, but I look right back. I am not understanding. She seems to have answers. "I just don't know what to do." Maybe not. Kelly's feet wiggle back and forth.

"No, that's okay," Mrs. Kenom says, and she starts talking. I can't really tell what she's talking about but I don't like the sound of it. Are we going? We have school! Mom will wonder where we are, why we're not home. Maybe no school? Yes! Then I can sit with my comics. Kelly's comics. And watch the puppy next door. She hangs up the phone and maybe whoever she was talking to will find Mommy. Maybe she's coming back. But Mrs. Kenom puts on a not-real smile, just top teeth as she looks at Kelly and says, "Well, girls, how about a little road trip?"

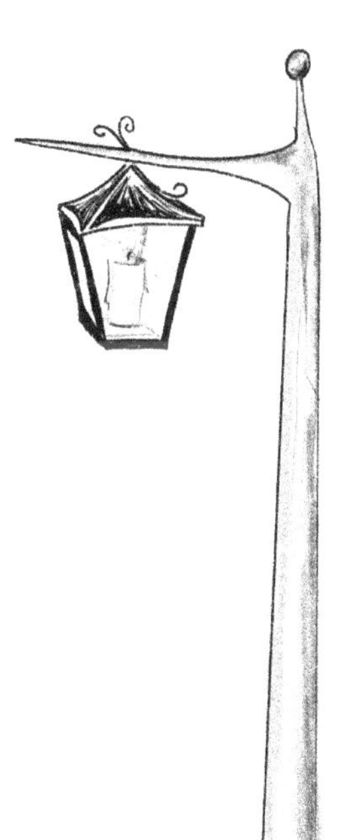

That tight feeling in my stomach comes back and makes me want to cry, but I know I can't while she is watching so I button my lips up tight. We all go back to our house with Kelly skipping in front. Mrs. Kenom touches my back one time, then two, which makes me walk even faster. I don't like running, but I do a

fast-walk because I really don't like to feel someone touching me.

"Did you leave the door unlocked to come over to my house, Kelly?" she says.

"Yes'm, because we didn't know where the key was, and—we were kind of in a hurry. Um…" She turns in circles, stops, and turns the other way.

"Kelly," Mrs. Kenom says. Her voice gets louder. "When did you last see your mom?"

"Before bed last night, Mrs. Kenom. She told us a story and then said she had to work today."

"Are you sure she didn't wake you up for school? Maybe you just—"

"No! I'm telling you. We didn't see her."

Mrs. Kenom is making Kelly mad and she doesn't get very mad. Two tears down her cheek, which she wipes off. I see. Mrs. Kenom gets real quiet, but her face looks like she wants to keep talking. She points up to our room and tells us to get stuff. Clothes and books, like we are going to a sleepover. "Don't forget your underwear and maybe your…blanket or teddy bear. Whatever you like to sleep with. Just one backpack, girls."

"Mrs. K, are we going to leave?"

"No, Kelly. Not for always. We're just taking a trip to visit your aunt and uncle. You've probably met them before. Aunt Alexia and Uncle Edmond?"

Kelly's face makes one of those squnchy looks, like she's trying to push a memory into her head. "Yep, I remember Aunt Alexia. She has yummy good ice cream, remember, Penny? We like going to their house! We get to go there now, instead of school?"

"That's right for today, Kelly, You can stay there for a little bit until you, um, come back here."

Kelly twirls in circles some more. She doesn't hear lots that Mrs. Kenom's voice says without saying. But I do. Mrs. Kenom meets another grownup right in our living room. Kelly is quiet now as we sit, no twirls, waiting for something familiar. Kelly shakes her head when I ask her to tell me a story. We play with puzzles and I've almost got one built when the doorbell RING! and a tall lady in a pink shirt stands at the door. I stand on my knees to see better.

"Come on in. It's Trish, right? The girls are almost ready." Mrs. Kenom nods but I move to sit on the bottom of our stairs. "Girls, this is Mrs. Canadie," she says in a happy voice. Something is wrong and I don't know what it is. "These are the Bonner kids, Kelly here, and Penny."

It's not right. Mommy should be here. Where's Mommy? When I start crying, Kelly gives me a hug. I push her. They're taking me away from here! From Mommy!

Kelly starts singing, the notes soft and made-up words full of my favorite things. SHOO-WUMP! TOO-LUU! PWUAFF! Jumping, laughing, and making new drawings. She's good at that. I get quieter, and the tall Candy Lady gets on her knees, face to face with me. "It's good to meet you girls. I know this is really hard right now. I work in a place that makes sure that kids like you stay safe."

From what?

She must hear my inside voice because she says, "It's not very safe to stay in the house by yourself, without your mom. I talked to your Aunt Alexia this morning, and I'm going to take you over to her house so you won't be alone. Okay? It's a pretty long ride."

I hear Mrs. Kenom tell Mrs. Candy Lady, "This is not the first time this has happened, but most of the time she calls me or another sitter. Penny, do you have your bag?"

I say yes with my head. She is trying to push-walk us out the door, but Kelly says, "No! I don't want to go. We need to stay here and wait for Mom!" If Kelly doesn't want to go either, then we can do this together. I can do this! Something inside me wakes up, something that has been wound tight. Until now. I start screaming again, louder than my first time. But it doesn't matter what we do because the grownups get to decide and we're just kids. I don't want to be a kid. It's not fair. I want to be with Mom.

We get in the car and the lady makes us put on our seatbelts. Mrs. Candy Lady shows us the buttons for watching TV, but I act like I don't hear her. When we don't use it, she turns on the radio and starts to sing along like Mom sings. But it doesn't sound like Mom.

Kelly watches the Candy Lady then turns the TV on, so then she turns off the radio. Kelly yells over the cartoons, "When are we going home?" When the lady doesn't answer, she yells even louder.

"WHEN ARE WE GOING—" A big bump in the road. We both bounce in the air. Human basketballs. "HOOOME?"

Mrs. Candy Lady answers. I sit very straight and whisper in Kelly's ear, "What are we doing?" My whisper is a not-whisper because the TV is still loud.

At the stop light, she says, "Your mom is a little sick right now. She needs some time to get better. Then you can all be together. I'm sure it won't be long." When we don't say anything back, she keeps going. "Your aunt and uncle will be so happy to see you and have a visit while Mom is getting better! Won't that be nice? Like a vacation!"

When we get to the house, nobody comes out. The house is still. We are still. Maybe we can go home? The monster in my chest is back and my stomach moves in flip-flops. The lady gets out and walks around to my side. When she reaches for me, my arm hits her. Hard. Right in the ear. She can't touch me. The monster inside roars and I try to show her, just with my eyes. And now we're at this weird house—

"Let's go, girls." We follow Mrs. Candy Lady up a long hill to the house. It has a big porch, and a big door. I hope it doesn't have a big dog. A couple plants are perched next to the door. "Perched." A word I learned last week when Teacher showed us a picture of a bluebird sitting on a branch.

"Mrs. Canadie," Kelly asks, "Penny and I want to know how long we are going to be here." She always is good at reading thoughts.

"Oh, dear, I'm sure it will be just a short time."

I still don't understand why we have to come here at all. Mom isn't sick. The only one who has been sick, not yesterday, but another time, way back, is me. Mom talked about a party, not this day, so I'm sure nothing is wrong. I want a party with Mom, not standing on this cold, cold porch, watching Mrs. Candy Lady try to hold all her papers from blowing out of her hands, like a little kid trying to escape on a playground. PLOP! PLOP! SPLAT.

Someone walks up. The door squeaks open and a man stands there, real still. I stretch my neck to see behind him, but he's filling up the doorway. He's not big enough for a giant but it's like one of those story books. A darkness or wave in this house makes it look haunted though Teacher says there's no such thing as ghosts. I need to ask Kelly about ghosts later, and if she thinks they are real. She's read lots of scary stories and knows about these things. The man smiles and moves over so we can go in. I don't want to go in the haunted house, but Kelly does go, so I follow. Mrs. Candy Lady and the man talk for some time about grownup stuff. It's not time to eat lunch, but my stomach makes hungry noises. One of the tables in this big kitchen has red, fuzzy stuff and a white sparkle cloth, like Christmas decorations, but it's not Christmas. Not even close. Weird.

The grownup voices get softer, the way they do when they don't want kids to hear what they are saying. I can hear a few of their words like, "hurry," "stay together," "a-band-in." That last word is one I'm not sure about but I think it must be something bad. Mrs. Candy Lady bends down and looks down at me.

No talking. Is she mad? Sad? I get tired of looking at her and walk away. I don't care if anyone follows me. Kelly tries to look at something under the table, like she wants to hide there. Maybe I will, too.

"Penny. Kelly. I need you both to listen," Mrs. Candy Lady says. "This is your Uncle Edmond." The big man. He smiles. I don't. "He and your aunt are going to keep you here for a little while. This is your mom's family."

What does she mean, "Mom's family"? Aren't Kelly and me her family? She talks more, explaining all the new, but the explaining doesn't stay in my brain because I am trying to figure all this out. Everything is a puzzle! Another lady comes in the room who looks just a tiny bit like Mom, or maybe she doesn't. I think I know her.

"Hey, Pen!" she says. "Wow, you are so big! It's been a while since we've seen you!"

I don't say anything or move a muscle. Mrs. Candy Lady starts talking again about how we're going to stay here "'till your mommy feels all better." She tells Kelly, "Can you make sure Penny doesn't get too scared? Talk to her and tell her stories? And, Penny..." She looks at me. Again. This time I watch my feet. "I want you to listen to your sister. She's done a really good job taking care of you. You both can watch out for each other. But don't forget to have fun." Fun? How can we, not at home? She does

one of those one-eye blinks. "Your Aunt Alexia and Uncle Edmond will take awesome care of you."

Kelly nods and opens her mouth. No words come out. She has the same questions as me, probably. When are we going to go back? Is Mommy coming here, too? How long are we going to stay? The new Ant Lady bends down and says, "Penny, I'm your Aunt Alexia.

I'm so happy that you are staying with us for a while. Did Uncle Edmond show you our puppies?"

I don't say anything, but I like puppies. Just not big ones. Everything is kind of foggy and my brain makes it like I'm seeing this through the eyes of someone else. This can't happen really! This is a dream, right?

Kelly smiles at the lady but I don't think it is her real happy smile. The lady, I mean, Aunt Alexia, says, "Do you girls like animals? You'll have a lot to explore while you're here, and we have all sorts of critters!" Something in my brain does a remember and clicks right then. A little rabbit hopping around inside a house. Was that here? It was a small name, like "water" but not.   Aunt Alexia and Kelly go down a long hall and then another one and I go, too, not ready to leave Kelly. Enough leaving for the day. All through until I feel like I'm lost. But then we reach a large door at the back of the house. Like a garage door. Aunt Alexia talks the whole time, but I don't listen good, just looking. She says "rabbit" and I start listening again. "We used to have a rabbit named Walt who would wander around our house." That was the same as my remember! "Now we have a bunny named Buster." She finds one in a wire box with see-through holes and pulls out a big ball of brown and white. Kelly squeals as the ball of fur moves. That's a foot! It's the biggest bunny I have ever seen!

"I know, you're a big boy!" Aunt Alexia talks to the rabbit in a funny voice, like Mom uses when

she tells stories. "But you love people, don't you? Say hi to Penny and Kelly."

She thinks this bunny can talk! They do in stories, but not here. Well, maybe. Would he talk to me? Aunt Alexia talks in a low, sounding voice, like the bunny is talking. "Hi, guys," says the bunny voice. "I'm so happy you're here!" Aunt Alexia holds out the bunny and wiggles its paw toward us. Then she says in her own real voice, "Here, girls. Do you want to pet Buster? He likes it. Most rabbits don't."

I step back, shaking my head, but Kelly sticks a finger out to tap Buster's ear. When he doesn't move, I almost want to pet him, but he's gonna bite, I know it! I pull my hand back instead. I don't understand this. Why am I here?

DEIRDRA

Twelve months ago.

How does one win against an invisible enemy?

PENNY

Present Day.

I try hearing Uncle Edmond. He's being really nice, even though I'm not going to bed like I'm supposed to. He talks. About the rain outside, saying I shouldn't be scared even though I really am. A lot. We're at their house now until Mommy gets better. Just for a little bit. Another little bit.

"Rainstorms are important, Penny. They're God's gift to the world," he says and points to the big plant in the kitchen. It's almost as tall as Uncle, a leaf giant! "Remember that our plant friends can't grow without water, just like we can't grow without good food and milk!" I wonder why we have to have thunder and lightning with that. Why does God not explain? Uncle Edmond taps me on the nose. I don't mind this time. "I'll tell you a secret, Penny. When you smell the scent of rain, it means change is coming. That's my favorite part. We can't always make things happen the way we want them to, but nothing stays the way it is forever. Just like the weather changes. The rain reserves come down and then the sun comes out. Our lives change, too."

"Reserves?" I don't understand.

"Reserves are the extra. Things might be bad, but there are extra good things reserved, stored up, to come after the rain. Things the plant really needs to live. And when things seem really bad here, the one thing we know is that they'll get better."

From now on, when the thunder starts, I am going to try to forget about it and just—I take a deep breath, like it's coming right now—smell the rain.

"You want to go play with the goats before going to bed?"

Absolutely! Yes, yes!

* * *

The sirens. Red and Blue. Blue and Red. Mommy yelling at those fancy dressed people pointing at her, "Leave well enough alone! We have enough trouble at this house without you having to come stick your nose in it!" I hold my breath. "You have no right to tell me how to live my life! These are my girls! They are all I have." Then she yells at Aunt,

"Allie, please! You're family! You can't do this!" It's just a dream. Just a dream.

Mommy is sick. She is on the floor. There are bottles and white stuff and a spoon with a match thing. But she is fighting. She grabs at me and I can't move. Her hand goes tighter and tighter. I couldn't move even if I wanted to. She is strong, but her voice sounds funny, a growl like a dog, not Mommy. "I will hurt you if you come any closer!" At them. This part of my dream I really want to wake up. I know it's a dream! Wake up!

A police comes to us, but then stands. Mommy stamps her foot like those kids in kindergarten. I hear her crying, with her mouth open, and her tears are on my neck. "Please. You can't! I can't live without them! Please! Please!"

I scream loud and open my eyes in the dark. I am not outside with the police lights. I am here. At Aunt Alexia and Uncle Edmond's house. My neck is wet and my pj's are too. My fingers hurt because they are grabbing the sheets so hard. My breath is fast.

And it isn't my dream. I'm in a nightmare. I'm here. Not home.

DEIRDRA

One year and one month ago.

My eyes flutter open. I know that look—the shock and resignation in his face. My head pounds, and from the corner of my eye I recognize my own bed, but I don't feel the least bit safe. "What are you doing here?" My words come out sharp, but my need for information pushes aside our last fight.

"Don't try to move just yet." Dave has a voice that's more stern than I expect and his eyes bore into me. It's like he's trying to pull a secret out of me just by the look. Careful.

"How long have I—" I attempt to sit up.

"Wait, don't—" Too late as I vomit over the side of the bed.

After a couple shaky breaths, I lean back on my elbow. "Fever?"

He shakes his head. "Why don't you—"

"No."

"Meds and an empty stomach don't mix well. Don't talk right now. It'll take a while to feel yourself again."

"I know! I know! I screwed up." I stare at the chicken noodle soup he hands me. "I had to get out!" Alexia's patronizing warnings beat inside my head. Unwelcome melody, one of those tapeworms in my head. "But I try hard," my mouth insists before I get the chance to think. "I just...can't handle it sometimes. The job, the kids—" My arm waves through the empty air and I squeeze his arm. "I thought I did! Found a way to make sure my kids have what they need anyway. Now they have Alexia."

"You don't get it," he says.

"Hindsight and all that." I refuse to listen.

"They need their mother, Deirdra. They need their mother to be well and strong and...free! That's what they need. Alexia and Edmond can keep the girls safe for a while. They still need you to get better." I didn't realize until that moment how much he means to me. But I won't have it.

"I know. I try!" I protest. "But I keep failing. Then right when I think I have it, I fall again. I'm just tired of getting up, and then having to get up again and again. It's exhausting."

I start crying and try to sit up again.

"Careful," he warns me. Too late.

I close my eyes, holding one hand over them, as if warding off a headache. I forget for a moment Dave is sitting next to me. For how many minutes? Time seems to have evaporated. "I'll be fine. I'll be fine," I mutter, as if to myself. "I'm gonna do this on my own."

Silence.

"Dave? I need you to help me."

"I thought you didn't need me."

The jest stings. I grab his arm and lean out of bed, depending fully on him for a minute.

"Oh! You're up! I'm so glad you are feeling better." Alexia wraps an arm around my other side and they're both fully supporting the "patient." I hate it, but it can't be helped.

"What are you doing here?" I spit the words like poison. "Tell me, Alexia. What could you possibly want from me now?"

"I'm here to check on the kids. I've come to get them, Deirdra. The police came by this morning." She delivers this line with so much emotion shaking in her voice.

Whoa, that was close. I'm not steady at all. I push both away.

Dave says, "Listen, Deirdra, I found you."

"Why arc you cven here?" I spit back.

"I left my wallet here last night when I paid for the pizza. But, D," His eyes are accusing. I can't look away. "You were on the floor. You were completely unresponsive. The girls were scared out of their wits. The kids can't be in a situation like this any longer, Deirdra. They have to be in a safe

environment. What if you had been there all night? What if you had died, Deirdra?"

A bucket of cold water to bring me back to reality.

"It's just temporary, Deids," Alexia says. "It's until you're back on your feet. Until she gets help." She faces Dave. Then, turning back to me, she says, "We'll keep them until you can get yourself under control, and we can talk about the future."

It's almost like I become superhuman in that moment, my visible rage giving me an inhuman strength, surging through my body. I stand, though shaky, but my voice is as strong as I can handle, cutting into the stunned silence that beats by. "My own sister!" I scream. I hobble for the stairs, refusing help, and curses fly out of my mouth. I want to get away from both of them. "How could you do this to me? They need their mother! I'm taking them, now! I'm just having a bad day. It doesn't mean there's a problem! Where are they? Where?"

Dave and Alexia stand with open mouths, unable to answer. Good.

PENNY

Present Day.

No, no, no! My panic comes up to my throat as I see the tall, ginormous door. I love that word because it makes me think of a giant named Norman. Kelly taught me and I like saying it. But I don't love this. Worst thing ever. My hands shake and my legs, too. My new tennis shoes don't help. Aunt Alexia took us shopping when we came to their house last week. To stay for a long time. This is scary! More than scary. How many people are there? Do we have to stay at this new school? What if people talk to me? I can't breathe when I think of all the people looking at me. Asking

me questions. No, no, no! All of me wants to run, but my aunt's hand pushes me to move. Maybe I can still run. I try once, but an arm makes me still and Aunt Alexia bends down next to me.

"It'll be okay," she tells me. "I'll stay for a while. Until you feel comfortable." A boy is close there, beside the teacher. He gives his mom his backpack and stares at me. Big eyes.

The words don't come out but they are screaming in my head. No, it won't be okay! You are going to leave me, and I'm going to be here with all these people. Don't leave me here! Please don't! I even remember to use please. But Aunt Alexia doesn't understand any of my thought-words. My eyes aren't good at giving information because they have tears in the way.

The door. The lights. Aunt Alexia's wrist. Moving kids. Another adult standing with that smiling boy. I don't know her. I don't know him. I don't know this place. I start crying when Lady asks if I want to have breakfast. I get hiccups and my body shakes. I don't want to cheer up. My voice comes up in my head again and I start screaming. More than scared. I need out. I have to get out!

The room is noisy, though all the kids are sitting down eating or something. There was a birthday party months and months back when cousin Maci turned four. Same as today. My mom was there that day. The noise keeps going, covering all my sides, just like the classroom. It gets smaller, even when I close my eyes. I'm stuck here. Right now I don't know anyone. I won't fall, I won't run, I can't get a stain on my shirt. Can pencil stain my shirt? What will Aunt Alexia say?

Mommy slapped me once for getting my shirt all dirty. Kelly told me later it was the drugs and not her but I don't know. She isn't always like that. She did say sorry and started crying then and rubbed my face. She said sorry again and again. I know she was sorry. But I also know it was my fault. I just should've kept my shirt clean, and she wouldn't need drugs to feel better. When Mommy needs space, Kelly is there.

But she's not here today.

All of this moving in my head, two thousand times faster than usual, like super fast thoughts. This place is not safe. One rule for today: Keep my clothes clean. And now I'm in this class with the funny smells and the loud people.

Mommy's job is to get better and my job is to do school. When Aunt Alexia doesn't leave but stands far away, I don't cry lots. I can see the room, a giant classroom all filled with bookshelves, blocks, and tables. There are big papers pushed in the corner. School has been going this year before this. I don't know how long, but there arc lots of papers on the walls, lots of letters, and lots of things. I won't understand the new stuff. Everyone will already know everyone. They will already have friends and I am not one of them. I don't have anyone. Breathe. Like Mommy always says. A boy comes to me. The boy with big eyes. His curly brown hair moves in front of his smiley face.

I don't ever figure out what he tells me because I run toward the closed door as fast as I can. I use my fists over and over. It doesn't

What have I gotten myself into now?

He meanders in before she gets off at the store
A long day full of people and papers and more
A melted ice cream bar in lieu of flowers arranged neatly
Checking if she's free tomorrow and hoping she will be
She makes a little snort and tosses a folded sheet
A number left for him to dial; will he?

They both stand, not knowing what to say; to go or stay?
Awkward, like a teen. Then a single word: Dave
See you tomorrow with those flowers
Who knew words could have such power?
With a grin like a kid, he knows for sure
He'll see her again! Just wait.

change. Aunt Alexia is gone. She left when I wasn't watching her. "No, no, no!" I make myself cry this time, hoping that someone will see me. I squint my eyes as the tears come. She left! She left me alone! Just like Mommy! I scream again and again and a hand grabs me. Hard. She is still here! I cry out and turn to hug her, but it's not my Aunt. It's Teacher. My heart beats fast and I can't get air. My stomach gets tighter and tighter. Nobody can touch me! I've gotta stay safe! I pinch Teacher's fingers from my arm and push. It works. I have to think. Something else. I hide by a bookshelf. The closest safe place I can find.

No, no, NO! I can't stay here! I can't stay! Think!

My breathing gets faster. My eyes open wide as the tall lady, who must be the teacher, bends down next to me. She is touching my black backpack. One of the pockets gets stuck on something and an old pencil falls out. No! I scream this in my head, but nothing comes out. Just more tears. Now the hiccups again. I shut my eyes and pretend that I can melt into the shelf, to another world. Away from this terrible, unknown place. I can hide my face in my knees and cover my head with my hands. That's all I focus on. I push again and again at Teacher.

Then she's not there either. A long time goes by. I don't even know how long, or how I got here. Aunt Alexia needs to be back. I look hard at my shoes and feel books on the shelf push in my back. It hurts, but I try not moving. If I don't move, maybe Teacher will forget about me and I can just fall on the carpet, where no one will bother me.

Bouncy music comes from somewhere behind me. It's like the music is skipping down a sidewalk. Happy music. Like what I hear in my head when I'm happy. The teacher's voice sings and a CLIP, CLOP, CLIP. Her shoes are standing next to me. Teacher's voice keeps saying over and over that I need to join them or sit in a chair, or play

with Play-Doh, or—No. No. No. No way. No how.

I do not want to hear those things. My eyes stay on the floor, pushing her out of my head by thinking of my room, my bed, my pillows. Somewhere, anywhere away from this strange place.

I don't remember lots of that first morning of school. If I pretend it isn't happening, maybe it will go away. So I do it again. Every day my screaming keeps the kids away. Same thoughts. I don't want to be here. Why do I have to be here? Where is Mommy? I want to go home! Then the kids make a line, they don't come near me. One or two stare, but they follow the leader when Teacher says move. I forget to cry because they really look funny. Like a kid caterpillar. And I watch as the kids move one, then another out of the classroom. Am I leaving? Is Mommy coming? No, it's Aunt Alexia now. But she's not here, either.

My head doesn't want to listen to Teacher, but my loud stomach says yes. I don't touch the rope with big knots. Even that scares me. Most of them have trouble with the person in front. Why don't they just let go? But Teacher likes the rope. "For practice," she says.

A kid near falls in front of me and kicks my shoe. "No!" I scream, pushing with one arm toward the kid, and grabbing my foot with the other. This is my shoe. Mine! That kid can't touch it! Everything of mine is going home.

The cafeteria is loud. It never stops. There are students everywhere and they are not taking turns. A lot of them are sitting at tables all lined up in the huge place. Some kids hop down the aisle or wiggle under a table to get to a friend. I cover my ears. I don't want food anymore. And why can't we go home? I am alone with all these faces, jumping up and down, sitting up and down, looking up and down. It's too loud in here. My mind tells me over and over again. Home. Home. Home. I don't believe the teacher. She said we're almost done. She's not my mom! My mind says this, not my mouth. All day long.

I stay there with my food. Pizza. Macaroni and cheese. Turkey. This pizza's my favorite but I don't eat it. The class gets up again. Another kid takes the hard plate and puts it in the bin. Teacher says, "Thank you" really loud, but I look for Kelly. She's here, right? Why can't I find her?

The kid with curly hair says a joke. Or a smiling girl sits next to me. Or nobody does and I'm by myself. Then the kid with curly hair tells me a joke the next day and the next. And it does make me smile. Just when no one else can see. Now when I look at the clouds, I do see a bunch of cotton candy, too. The boy is looking at me. He smiles before my eyes go back to the floor. Aunt Alexia says that it's been mostly six months here with them. My other family. They might be family, but it is not the same. Will things get the same again? A super fear fills up in me.

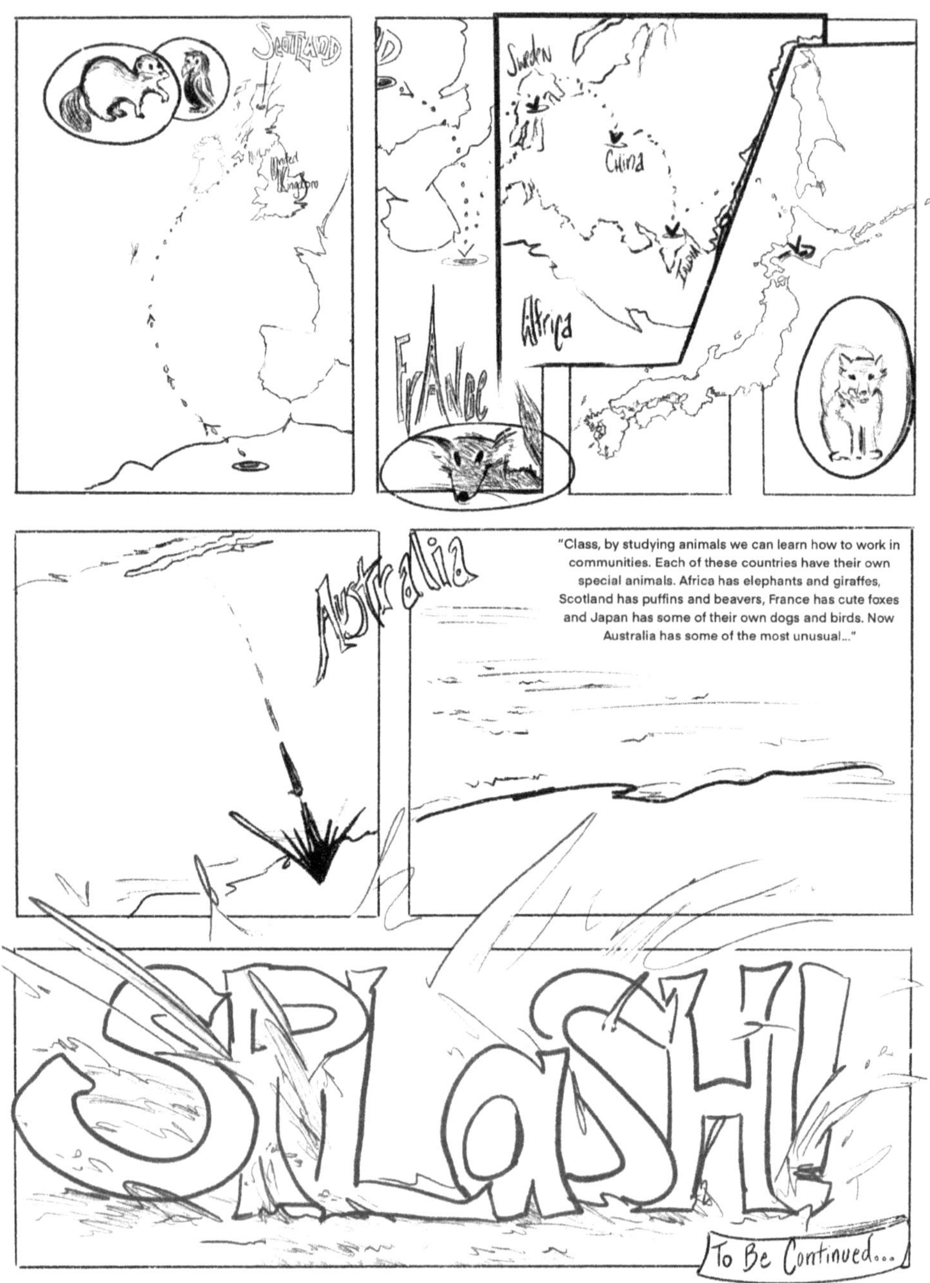

SCOTLAND
United Kingdom
Sweden
China
Japan
Africa
FrANce
Australia
"Class, by studying animals we can learn how to work in communities. Each of these countries have their own special animals. Africa has elephants and giraffes, Scotland has puffins and beavers, France has cute foxes and Japan has some of their own dogs and birds. Now Australia has some of the most unusual..."
SPLaSH!
To Be Continued...

DEIRDRA

One year and one month ago.

Good call on the flowers. I know I revert to child mode, but I can't help but sniff the tulips. There are others in this bunch, but that's the only one I know. What scent? One of them looks like an orchid.

"Now, what was so urgent that you had to come over so late to tell me?" I try to put on a strict face but Dave's eyes are making me melt. It isn't that bad. Barely ten. But I do have to work tomorrow and the girls have school. "Okay," he says, "I'll make it quick and won't be here long." He inhales. I smell good and I know it. Lavender-scented bath right after putting the girls to bed.

"I needed to see you in person, and I'll be busy for the next few weeks." He explains that he has a new job.

"When do you leave?"

"Early next week. I'll be busy and they haven't promised I'll be in an area with cell service. But it's something I'd like you to consider. For later."

I try not to let this rock me. He goes on about how it is a great opportunity and he wants me to be excited for him. I know what's coming next. I try to act interested and ignore the alarm of panic in my head. Facts fly. It's with a smaller company, so there's a better chance of promotion. He tells me what a once-in-a-lifetime opportunity it is. "There are great schools in the area, and lots of housing options."

I blink at that, flashing disbelief at his optimism. "So, it's out of town?" I pull my robe tighter around me, hating that even my voice sounds vulnerable.

"Yes, in New Jersey. But here's the thing, Deids. I want you to come with me. You'd even be closer to your sister." He said it. Time stops and I wait for him to laugh and say, "Just kidding!" But he doesn't.

"What?" is all that comes out. Not exactly an answer. But what does he want from me?

"I want you and the girls to move down there with me."

"It's not that easy. I have—"

"Deirdra, we're a team. More than that, I hope. I want all of you with me. *Todos juntos.* When two people love each other—you do love me, right?" He is blabbering and I can see in his mannerisms that he is close to desperate. Breathing quickly and darting eyes. He's panicking. Not as much as me.

"It's not that simple." My words tumble ahead of my thoughts.

"It's as simple as we make it. Maybe you should ask the girls." He lays a hand on my arm and I know he means it to be reassuring, but it seems more claustrophobic. Like he's trying to hold onto me when he knows it just won't work.

My mouth has a mind of its own and spills out all my doubts. "I can't just pick up and leave everything; it would interrupt the girls' world. They have school and friends, and are now just getting to the point where they are making it. I can't just..." His face tells me I don't need to finish.

"So you're...no?" He's barely speaking at this point. Maybe it is the tears that block my speech or his anger. His voice shakes. I hate myself.

"I've got to take care of my girls," I keep saying over and over again. Broken record.

"That's not it at all, Deirdra," he says. Anger fills his voice. "You can take care of the girls just fine in Alabama. "You're just afraid to leave the comfort of what you know. You're afraid of something you're going to lose. *¡No puedo creerlo!* Well. I leave next Monday." Monday is six days away. I tell him I'd think about it.

But I don't. For the rest of that week I'm just in survival mode. He's been great and we have been amazing together. It's the first time I've gotten to share with someone as much as I have. So I am losing that much more. And now tomorrow is almost here. Monday.

Dave comes over nearly jumping out of his skin with anticipation. After all this, he's still just a kid at heart. He stands in front of me, his heart in his hands, expecting a different answer than I can give him.

"I can't." It's not even a whisper, but he's watching me so intently and he tenses, so he understands.

That silence. It's killing me.

No retort. Nothing. He turns his back, with none of the cheerful jaunt I've grown to love. He stumbles to the door and when it doesn't unlatch – I've been meaning to ask him to fix that. He's gone. He slams the door on his way out. Who wouldn't? Something must have fallen off the wall because I hear a loud crash, but I go back to see what it is. Nothing good. My tears consume me. Crying. Maybe it's the kids. It is sobbing. Like someone...

He doesn't turn around. I've decided. I pick up the phone and my finger hovers. I can't. He gave me this chance and I blew it.

PENNY

Present Day.

The classroom looks like war. So much stuff. It's the size of Mommy's room, but with little chairs everywhere and kids—right here. "Hi!" he says, but the teacher tells him to go finish his words on the board. The desks are not set the same way like normal. They usually come in rows where I can see everyone. But today they are in little groups, with the desks bunched together, secret monsters waiting until Teacher can't see.

Wait, we have to work with everyone? I don't get to stay with Lydia? She has been with me for as long as I've been coming to this school. She doesn't need me to write questions on a paper. I can work without talking and she doesn't ask me stuff.

Teacher sees me and she is going to say something. I'm frozen and I can't spot where my desk is. Where is it? No name. All my thoughts are coming out jumbled. I can't think. I can't breathe. Don't make me do this, I want to say. My head is dizzy feeling. My space is not mine anymore. It changed. Can someone tell me—

"Penny, you are going to be over here. You're with the first group; come with me," Teacher tells me.

Oh, good. That means that Teacher can tell me what to do. That will help. But then Lydia is sitting somewhere else. Not by me. This group doesn't start with creature building, which is fine with me because the reading is fun. I like the poems section because it just has some words on each page, not long sentences like others. It's still hard for me to read because I don't understand the extras, what Teacher calls "except-tons to the rule." I don't understand. But I do know it doesn't make sense when I try to figure it out. I want to hit myself or cry. Or scream. Or all of them. But then they would look at me or say something is wrong. And Mom would be sad. And if I don't do good she might never come back. I try to listen to the other kids around me for help but Teacher says, "This is what I want you to do." Teacher—her name is Miss Maco but all of us call her Teacher—gives a sheet of paper with lines and a square at the top, like when I was first learning to write. I like the empty pages better. Better for dreaming. The happy dreams, of course.

Kids yell out, "Look at this! These pencils here make me a walrus! Miss Maco, look at this!"

"Kennedy, clean the pencils with our class hand sanitizer and then put them in the case. Only use them on the paper, not in your nose!" Then she turns back to me but whispers to the desk, loud enough for me to hear, "You'd think they'd be old enough..."

We do reading, but I only read three pages. Martin reads five. And I think Bonnie finishes all the chapters. Teacher tells her to re-read it so that she can learn more. I guess re-reading it means it's like watching a movie again and she won't be surprised by the ending. I like watching movies again and I want to try it with the book, too, but I can't even finish this chapter. Next day Bonnie might move groups. Another friend gone. Miss Maco tells us in the next group we're going to practice cursive. She gives everyone a journal, but I like mine best because she says we get to decorate it however we want to. Mine is red, like hearts. But we have to do this at home. And I don't have a way to decorate at home, I don't think. Does Aunt Alexia have markers?

"Teacher! This computer is flashing black and blue!"

Teacher helps her with bow and pigtails and another student says, "What's black and blue and red all over?"

"A zebra with a suntan?" Bonnie says.

"No, that's black and white and red all over!"

"Guys, get back to your work. We only have twenty minutes." Teacher says this a lot.

I try to make something with my markers here and I still see the red journal paper under it. Mom isn't with me. I make the little black marks into more black marks. Mom is gone. Mark. Mark. Scribble. I am by myself. I fill up the whole front of the journal with just two empty spaces: one for my name and one for the other. Both red. My hand hurts.

"There's something squishy under this table!"

"Ew, it's a booger!" Dory holds her hand out, shaking it in the air. A girl screams. Maybe Dory will start crying. But she doesn't. Teacher puts her in a different desk. When the cleaning person comes in, she has a T-shirt that says, "Kids are my happy place!" I like that. And she smiles at me.

I draw an outside line, oh-so-careful on my hummingbird, and then put some marks for red feathers. I finish my name at the bottom. In purple because it's my favorite. I've made the very best because I've had so many years to get it exactly right. First in our old house, then with Aunt Alexia and Uncle Edmond. I imagine it flies to Mom with messages. Even Lydia really likes it, but her journal has bright stickers and some fancy tape on the edge.

Tomorrow we get to do computers. There are computers in the classroom, but we haven't used them a lot. Teacher says with our new stations we can use computers to play games or listen to books. On the computer! I didn't know we could do that!

"Teacher! My hair is caught in the chair!" A girl with long, blond hair waves from her seat. I think she's Sarah? Not sure.

"Hey, you made a rhyme! Okay, class, that's it for centers today. Sadie, don't move!"

When I turn the page to the middle of my book, it rips the side. I hit my head on the desk. There is no thinking except: *You're so dumb! You can't even get that right. Why. Does. It. Always—*

"You did great, Penny." Teacher bends down by me, talking in my ear, just her normal voice. She puts a piece of tape on the edge of the table, and I try to put the page back together. Not even a stop, or a hand on my shoulder, like most teachers. She says something else, but I miss it because a song comes on the CD, with a little skip at the beginning. It's Mom's! The one she sang for the Bigwigs! We always dance to this.

You must run, you must fly. And then twirl all around the place
    WHIR-WOP
So get out there and give everything you've got because
    TAP-TOCK-TAP
Others need you DEE-a-DOO to bring them DIR-a-DUM
Your best self BUM BUM. Yes, it's true! You're not just a reserve sitting on the shelf
    DIR-a-THWACK
Give the best you can, full of life, wonder, and awe
    WHIR-WHOP
Use your brains, passion, and yes your very own love
    TAP-TOCK-TAP

They will drop their jaw if you bring it all

...

Smell the scent of rain SWISHHHH

"Scent of rain." I don't know what that means, but my finger bounces along when the guitar does some whipply-whoo with the music. Then it goes back to " ʷʰⁱʳ -whoop!" and "tap tock tap!" Something about the person singing, looking at others and jumping and the rain outside. I like the rain falling. When we line up at the end of the day, Teacher plays it again. It must be her favorite, too. I listen harder this time. Songs are like talking, but not. The rain is something pretty. But in the song the rain seems sad.

"Soar! Look, I'm superman!" The boy almost steps on my toe. But I want to jump like that. Just with nobody seeing. I knock a pencil cup from that other desk and they all go everywhere. Teacher says it's okay, and she picks it up. Teacher says to get in line and I do. It's time to go to another room now.

"Can I show you something?" the kid behind me asks. I pretend like she wants to talk to someone else, not me. I won't say anything. I can't break anything again.

ALEXIA

Present Day.

There she is. Penny sitting in that same chair. She always seems to just sit there, as if the chair will float away if she doesn't. I remember the balloon that Penny drew. Miss Maco is always prompting me to encourage her in any artistic endeavors. The counselor also visits the class a couple times each week now, given Penny's lack of speech. I've tried to tell her that she can talk; she just doesn't, though she responds a little more with us now. The counselor once said about Penny's art, "It's a part of her personal expression and she will be able to communicate in that way."

I watch Penny as she pretends to read her book. After a few minutes, the page will turn and her eyes float over the illustrations. According to the cover, the book is about elephants. Is that what she likes to read? Books on nature? There is music playing softly in the background, something Ed turned on, but Penny just sits still, as if she does not hear anything. I decided yesterday that I was going to try something.

I called her and got no response. "Penny," I tried a little louder. Nothing. Then, "Penny, I'm going to make pancakes for dinner. Did you want to help me?"

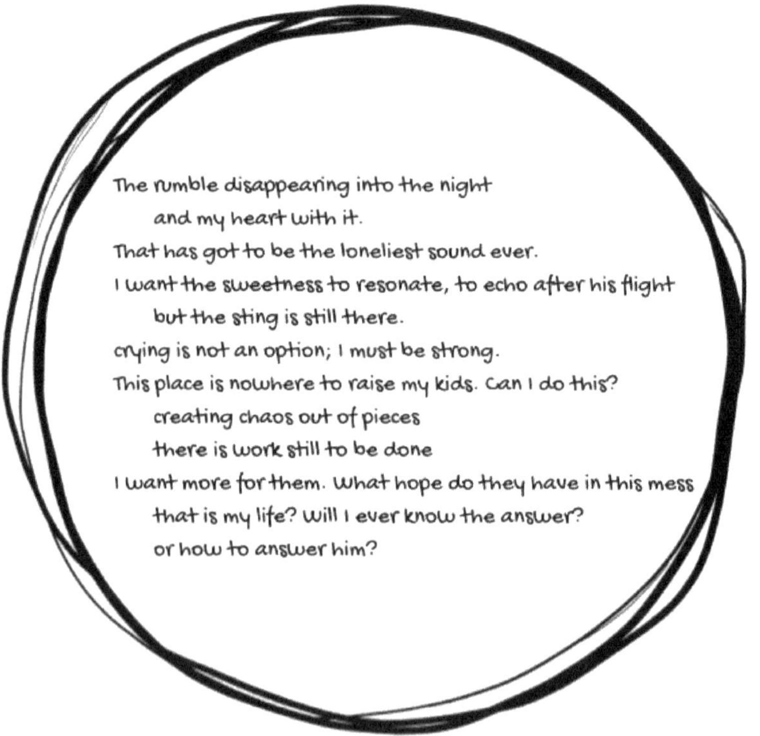

She looked up at me, but didn't nod or shake her head.

I slowly got up to walk toward the kitchen. My knees screamed at me from the previous day's gardening. Once I entered the kitchen and pulled some bowls down, I was surprised and pleased to find Penny trailing in behind me. My voice came out squeaky, "Well, hello there!" I tried to act normal, but I don't think it turned out so well. Penny didn't seem to notice. "I'm so glad I'm going to have a helper! Here's a bowl. Oops. I mean...here! Not very smooth today. I'm going to give you a small spoon and you can help me pour the ingredients in the bowl. That's all the stuff that we mix together to put in our pancakes." One of her new teachers had emphasized at our first parent/guardian/teacher conference the importance of explaining things to kids, even if I use unfamiliar words. She'll pick up on vocabulary that way.

DEIRDRA

One year and two months ago.

"My life is just too complicated for dating right now."

"What? Where did this come from? I thought we were having a great time!" I don't give him a chance to say anything as I turn to walk back inside. He says something like, "Ung—" before I slam the door in his face. I can imagine his comeback, "No way, José, woman! We just had an amazing night and you showed me some beautiful dance moves! Now get over here and kiss me!"

But instead I leave him standing six feet from his car with empty air between the shut door and him.

Blocking out everyone, like I always do. I always have to. I can't let him hurt these girls. Ignore the nagging voice in my head that whispers, "Or is it really you?"

He is sitting in his car when I come out of the house again. He must be watching me through the rain-blurred window. Insight into my soul.

Right?

I knock once. I know he won't open it. The lever on the window must be stuck again. He slowly cracks the door open. "Dave, listen," I start and put my hand on the door so he doesn't slam it. "I didn't mean what I said. Or the way I said it. I...it's just so hard for me to figure things out. My life. You. Where you fit."

"You don't have to dump me a second time."

"It's just that I want to try to help myself for once. I appreciate you being here for me and the girls, and I know you want the best for me. I know you could take care of us. But I need to find out if I can do this myself. I need...I need to feel like a good parent."

"Um, okay. Hey, hey, stop crying! C'mere," Dave says and it sounds like he's making an effort to speak softly. I get into the car. Silence wraps around me. I sniff, then start giggling when snot runs down my face. Always graceful.

"I'm dripping all over your seat!"

"Maybe I should take a step back, is that it?"
He actually said it. He didn't accept my halfhearted invitation to finish eating, but I wasn't going to do a guilt dinner.

"I love you."

"What?" I honestly thought I heard wrong. This couldn't be right.

"You're going to make me repeat it?"

"But really? We've only known each other for a few weeks."

"We've only been *dating* for a few weeks. We've known each other for like, six months."

I don't say anything. My heartbeat speeds up. This is what I've been waiting for, right? What I've wanted since I was fourteen years old and had my first kiss? Well, almost kiss. It was a kiss attempt and he ended up smacking my ear. But this is different. He is different.

"I know it's complicated. But I wanted you to know where I'm at."

The only question is, where am I?

PENNY

Present Day.

Kelly watches me draw a circle on one corner of the page. Then over and over again I trace the line. We have been doing some art in school, but I don't like to do much. Kelly told me to "interact" with those kids. Which is going up and finding a group. But for that I have to talk. She watches me, no voice, while I crumble up a paper. We're not at school, so I don't have to try using the other side. And talking makes that funny feeling in my stomach. I've done lots of crying since starting school. Kelly got to be there last time with Aunt Alexia when they picked me up. Kelly said that I have a cool classroom! It does have jungle vines hanging from the ceiling and a waterfall to walk through in the doorway. It itches. It is all made of paper and I guess it's impressive if I want it to be. Teacher says it. Every day. "Isn't that impressive?"

"There is nothing wrong with that first drawing, Penny—" Kelly grabs my hand. "I know, I know. Penny, I can help you draw something. Do you want to make a hummingbird? Or maybe just a pretty flower?" She grabs one of my school books off the desk, turns to a page, then shows me. She doesn't draw either of those. It's a little girl smiling at the picture person. "It has been a long time since I saw you smile," she whispers and puts her arm on my shoulder. She feels warm and I don't mind. "And really knowing people is hard. But we're going to try. Together."

DIERDRA

One year and three months ago.

I enter the place, blindfolded and dizzy, unsure of my next step. I'm not given the chance, just shoved from behind. One of my unseen captors. This does not help my dizziness and I stumble over a small ledge. Surely this is a joke. One of my friends has kidnapped me and is about to throw me a surprise party. For my birthday. I had determined not to celebrate this year and someone has thought better of it. My mind tries to be positive but something in my gut tells me otherwise. This is not a situation I want to be in. The thing that throws me off the most is the smell. This doesn't smell like someone's house. And the sounds here echo more than if there were walls just a few feet away. It must be some sort of warehouse. Noises of things being dropped or banged against one another meet my ears, but no human sounds. It's like the whole world has stopped.

"What—what do you want?"

My voice sounds thin and shaky, so I clear my throat and try again.

"What do you want?" This time my question echoes and it doesn't seem like the building is infinite as I thought it was. There is silence. Apparently no one is going to answer me. Is anyone there? Instead I get another shove behind the knee and I continue walking. I am shaking, and I don't think it's only from fright. They must've given me something. I feel too excited and sluggish at the same time.

"You've fallen behind, Deirdra, and we can't stand for that."

Even though I can't see him, I can imagine him shaking his head. I seal my lips, knowing that anything that I say is going to incriminate me. Yes, I have ignored them for the last few weeks. Dave has been a distraction. Before I can think, my head slams to the side, against what I can only assume is a wall. It feels like my head is crushed, but I'm still alive and thinking, so it can't be as bad as that. I tell myself that I have experienced this before, but in this moment, it seems like this is worse than anything I've felt before. I try to think back to what I could've done to cause this anger.

"You didn't follow up on your end."

What in the world is he talking about? "What—" The words are barely out of my mouth when he slams my jaw again. Definitely a fist.

The silence. Is the world watching, or is it just me in here? My desperation almost makes me cry, but I shut my lips again, tasting blood.

Darkness. Noise all around me. Silence in my head.

ALEXIA

Present Day.

"Who could be ringing the doorbell right before dinner?" I shoot Kelly a crazy smile as she sits at the kitchen table finishing homework. The man on the other side of the door is tall. Shaggy. Giant smile. Maybe too big. "Yes?" I'm internally debating how much kung fu I've learned from the movies. Then he reverts to a serious face, like he realized he might need to tone it down. He stammers for a minute, but his eyes focus behind me.

Kelly squeals, "Dave!" I wave her away, wanting a private moment with this man before he enters my home.

He holds out a peace offering: a bright red, king-sized Kit Kat bar. "Hi, um..." he starts, stumbling over his own name. Not a great start, but I'm willing to give him a chance. For the girls. He doesn't resemble any of Deids's dealers. But I'm sure that's what they would want her to think. "My name is Dave Abundis." His accent comes out in the name and he purses his lips after speaking, looking at our giant house. Now is when it counts most to make a good first impression. "I'm Deirdra's boyfriend. Or at least…" It's like he can't get the words out. Probably dumped now, after that fight Kelly spilled about. I smile and can't say that the visit isn't completely unexpected. "I, um, just wanted to pop in and maybe—"

"Oh, Dave! Yes, Deirdra has told us a few things about you. I haven't heard from her all this week! I'm Alexia. Come on in."

"And the girls? I promised Deirdra." He almost says something else but stops, just darting his prodding eyes into every nook and cranny of my house. "No, I haven't come to carry away all your possessions." He must notice my expression and put his hands in his pockets as if to prove his point.

I'm not sure I believe this stranger, and squint at him, trying to size him up. Instead, after excruciating silence, I say, "I'll go get the girls in a second. First, though, I'm just wondering. How did you get my address? Has Deirdra been in contact with you?"

"I am, well, I've seen her a few times at her work, but she hasn't been there much. We're…trying to make this work. It…well, anyway…then, yesterday—"

"You saw her yesterday?"

"Yes, I—"

"How did she look?"

"Similar to you, really. It's pretty *loco*. You have some same features, especially the eyes. *Ojos bonitos*. But she doesn't eat enough,

He's probably relieved; my life is so full of chaos
The voices are still there, replaying over again in my head
Doubts are here, in this house, in each act, in my mess
    My mess will always be here, calling to me, calling to me.

"Mom, help me please. This book is hard. Will you read?"
How will I ever be able to figure out what they need?
Despite the chaos of the day we sit on the couch with snuggles and hugs
Push away my demons for this moment.
    Still, still.

He is gone, leaving us here; he is on the outside
He doesn't understand this life, he's just along for the ride.
And he never will.

Now snuggles and hugs are all I need
Sitting with my girls and a story to read
    My chaos is here...
    ...still...
    ...calling to me.

even when I'm paying. The last time I talked to her I tried to be helpful, but I don't have a lot. It seemed like she was busy working. Nothing but texts." He stops, as if expecting me to add that I don't believe him for a minute. "Deirdra seemed, um, distant. But I cannot figure it out. She's hiding...um, and we are supposed to talk tonight, but I wanted to drop by first and see the little *chicas* so I'd have something to tell her."

"Of course. Penny! Kelly! Someone is here to see you!" The girls come trampling down and even Penny gives him a stiff hug.

"I missed your *abrazos*!"

"Wow! I am not used to seeing the girls react like that! I mean, uh, they obviously like you a lot, and that's not true of most people with them." There was more admiration in my tone than I meant to convey to this complete stranger. "Settle down, girls." Someone has to stay practical.

"Good afternoon!" Ed's voice is loud and cheerful. "And who might this be?" He offers his hand.

"Dave Abundis. I just dropped by to see the girls and to bring some treats!"

"Yessssss!" pipes Kelly.

Dave laughs. Such a great reaction for a little chocolate. Their eyes are as round as saucers.

"Hey, Dave—" I start.

My questions are drowned in excited squeals. Edmond joins us and almost immediately golf and the great outdoors are brought up, so Kelly asks about the park. "Sure!" Ed answers. "Let's get everything and go." I decide watching from the window is best.

The afternoon goes by in a flash. They are all red and sweaty. Ed puts the stuff away, and I can't help but make a funny face when Kelly hugs me. Maybe it is the sweaty kid smell, something I still need to get used to after all these months.

DEIRDRA

One year and seven months ago.

When I see him, I look around for any means of escape. I don't expect it, not at all. I shove a twenty in his hand. "Woah! No way, no how! It was just a sack of groceries. And that was weeks ago!" He tries to give it back to me. "That's probably more in tips than—"

"I don't want to hear it." I counter. He sighs and rubs his hand through his hair.

"Prideful woman!" Then he gets red. This man is embarrassed! He ruffles me a little, maybe, but he hasn't offended me.

"I can't take charity."

"Can't I treat you to breakfast? You can't even call that charity, or whatever you think it is. I just think it's a good deed. Part of my personality." He wiggles his eyebrows and I can't help but laugh.

I suck in my cheeks. Enough said.

"Well, you'll have to get over that!" He tries to shove the bill in my purse. "Really? Let an *hombre* treat you, okay? And then maybe on another date? All you do is work, and even when you're not working, I can't reach you. Please. I owe you." He waves the bill between us.

"Are you bribing me?"

"Yes, of course *estoy chistando.* I'm joking! But really? Food? Can we at at least get a burger?"

Present Day.

Tea and calm.

"Lord," right now my mind is anything but calm. It's been forever since I took time out to do more than a "Help me!" prayer. It's easier to gather my thoughts here in writing. Or typing. "I don't know what to do about this. But I know that You hold these two little ones."

Penny spoke tonight. Not once, but twice! Dave's presence must be a factor. Was that what made Penny comfortable enough to speak out loud? Most of the time, when asked a direct question, Penny just goes wide-eyed and looks terrified. They hug him like family, so he can't be all bad. Ed sure warmed up to him. We'll have to get him back here for another game of tag with the girls. And maybe some dinner.

Okay, so this *was* a help me prayer after all. But also one of thankfulness.

PENNY

Present Day.

During what Miss Maco calls "nurse visits," a blue flower lady comes to the classroom. She has blue flowers all over and has blue pants and a blue flower necklace. Does she have blue eye makeup on, too? I watch from the table as she asks some of the kids stuff and writes things on her paper. Then it is my turn. I can't get out of it.

"What is your name?" The blue thing around her neck swings back and forth and the silver thing on the end looks like a bell. I am not going to answer my way.

"Okay, Penny. And how old are you?" She stops like she wants me to answer.

"Do you know when your birthday is?" And then waits.

"What month?"

When I still don't say anything, Miss Maco answers. Like I'm not even standing here. "She doesn't speak, hardly at all, and she's only just now started playing with the other kids, which is great! She has a tendency to hit if something upsets her, and it's really hard to get her to complete tasks in class, unless I work with her one-on-one and take extra time."

The Blue Lady nurse writes down stuff and when she leaves, she smiles. This is not the last time. It never is. What about when she comes back? I try to breathe. She's going to find out all about my family and my mom will get in trouble and I'll never go back home. Happy noise floats from the playground and I am glad to go. Still not going to play but the other kids...I don't know. I close my eyes and sunshine hits me. Just like the noise. The voices come close to my ears again and again. The sun beats on my eyes, hair, hands, nose. I don't mind that so much. They are happy. I like that.

Today is probably one of the last times that we will get to play outside because Miss Maco told us it'll be super cold next week. They said it in announcements. Tim told Teacher that is how he gets stuck inside with his two little brothers. He says they like putting peanut butter in his hair while he is sleeping. Well, except one time. That other time, he did it himself. Really! He told me it feels good when his foster mom washes his hair. I didn't know what foster mom means and he said that means he is just staying at that house for a little bit, but right now she does all the things a mom does. Like Aunt Alexia? Miss Maco tells Tim that she will be sure to get him toothpaste to get out any peanut butter from his hair. And she is our mom here at school.

From the swing set comes SQUEAK! SQUAWK! SQUEAK! SQUAWK! Then big SQUEEEEEK! SQUAAAAWK! when Carla zooms into the air and back. Back and forth, back and forth. My eyes open and try to follow my friend, but I'm staying right here. Carla's feet fly closer and then back. Not me. I'll stay right here. Already too much leaving. When she lets go, Carla flies forward. I yell as she lands with a THUNK on the ground. Then she jumps up. She isn't hurt. Carla has a giant smile and she skips up to me, ignoring Miss Maco's yelling to not jump off the swings. The girl looks over at Teacher but talks to me.

"Were you watching me?" Carla asks. She grabs a big breath with her mouth. "Did you see me jump?" I study my shoes again. We're not supposed to, but it looks fun. My feet are little, hidden turtles in the dirt. I'm still here and now so is Carla. Even though she was flying. I make sure by wiggling my toes. I lean back a little bit when Carla goes closer. Maybe she's trying to read my thoughts.

"Do you want to come with me? We could have a contest! It'd be fun!" She starts to pull at my hand. "C'mon! Let's go!"

I pull my hand away and look back at Carla's eyes. I try to tell her. Maybe she really can read my mind.

I can't, I've got to keep my feet here.

I'm scared.

I don't want to fall. And I definitely don't want to jump off! No words come from my mouth. My head moves side to side. I don't want to do anything.

"Carla, what is the rule about the swings?" Miss Maco is here now. I am watching Carla so much that I didn't see her move. She is always remembering Carla what the rules are when we're outside. And Carla doesn't listen.

"Stay on the swings and don't jump off," Carla says really soft. Then she looks at Miss Maco. "But it's just so fun to jump off the swings. And I do it at home all the time! I'm really good and I won't get hurt and I wanted to show Penny how to do it."

I don't look at her when Miss Maco says, "I know that you like to do this, but see all these kids out here?" She moves her hand to all the kids on the playground. "Do most of them know how to do this? What if they try to jump without all that practice that you've had? What would happen?"

"They'd probably fall." She picks up a rock from the ground. "So I just need to jump off the swings whenever I'm at home?"

"That's right! Now, you can go back to swinging, but I need you to swing normally, without all the fancy tricks. Other kiddos are watching you." Carla says yes with her head and turns to me. "Well, since Miss Maco says that we can't jump, do you want to play freeze tag?" She shoots her hand out and hits me on the shoulder. I don't have time to move. "You're it!" she screams and runs across the playground before I see what she's doing.

"She's one of those wild horses with no fence." I look up at her and nod. I don't really know what she's talking about. Then she bends down toward me. Are you going to go after her?" Miss Maco asks from a few feet away. "Go run!" Miss Maco runs, not fast, to the end of the slide and turns to me. She points at Carla, at the other end of the playground. "Go get her! See if you can catch her!" She pushes my elbow, just two fingers. Carla turns in circles so fast that I don't even notice. "Look. I'm. On. A. Space. Ship. Um. Um. Um. Oooh!" She loses her balance and walks like a penguin for a few steps then falls down. She sticks her hand up. "Penny, we've got to do that again!" I wait where I am, but very soon Carla touches my hand again. "You're it! That means that you have to run after me. C'mon!" She runs a little bit like Miss Maco had and then stops. "You run after me and then you have to touch me."

I look at my feet and I take a few steps over to Carla. I put my hand out and say a word that comes out like "Yaow!" I miss Carla's arm. Tears are big lakes in my eyes. This is why I don't want to play. Not fun at all. Just then Miss Maco is beside me.

She whispers, "Well, go try to get her! Run after her and catch her!" She smiles even when I don't move. "She's waiting for you." Carla has stopped, her always-sunny smile on her face. She spins around again.

She says a joke about a dog and a mud puddle. I keep thinking about it, even when it's time to go back in for writing. Maybe I can make a joke? She left her rock animal on my desk today. She just said, "Look closely."

We can use it in our play world tomorrow.

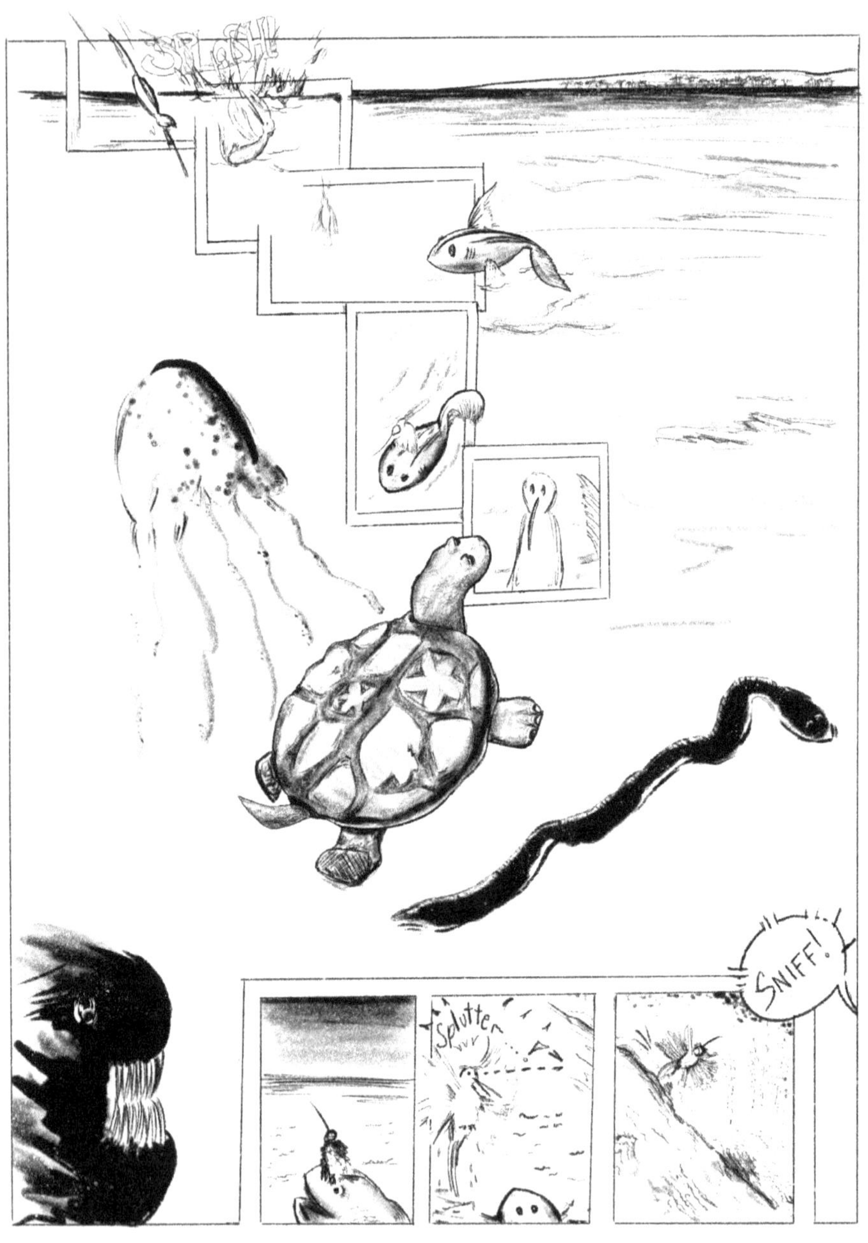
SPLASH!
SNIFF!
Splutter

ALEXIA

Present day.

Ugh, I'm crying again! Whew. Okay, at least now my heart doesn't feel like it's going to beat out of my chest. This heart is a funny thing. I feel so many things for my sister. She makes me mad, sad, excited, loving, concerned, anxious, curious—all at the same time. Sometimes, in my mind, she's still the little kid who kissed a frog on a dare. The girls whiz around the tree, laughing at invisible spiders that are attempting to land on their heads. If only life was that simple.

It used to be that way for D and me. She was my best friend, at one point. Now, we hardly speak. And when we do, it's to yell at each other. I once blamed it on the fact that I was too young to be raising a child when I was just a teen myself and Deids retorted that I must have been the one that set such a good example for her. Ouch. I did my best, but she was seventeen when she ran away and by the time she was eighteen, she was pregnant. Not a lot I could do about that and she didn't want me in Kelly's life. Now on the verge of raising her kids. It's been months. Hope is...well, it's somewhere. I just don't see it.

"Nuh-uh! It was my turn to seek you! Go run! *Run!* No, I still see you! Ugh, you're doing this all wrong." Kelly giggles at my insistence and runs off again. We're playing hide-and-seek tag in the yard.

Deids herself told me once, "Nothing will ever reach your high standards, will it?" Then she went off on me judging her and that we never had anything in common anyway. With these girls though, decision-making is now more of a day-to-day process. I'm better at that. Squeals of laughter flitter from behind one of the bushes.

Is this how my sister feels all the time? Constant worry that I am not doing enough and distraction that they are going to stick something dangerous up their noses? She is so dedicated to these children, even now when she can barely hold down a job. That's Deids, always wanting to do what she can't.

"Hey, Grandma, come look over here." I stifle a sigh as I walk over to Kelly, sprawled out on the grass on this unusually lovely day. She points up to the sky and I see the fluffy clouds. As a child I used to imagine that they were all blowing to some gathering, like the gods that I would read about in Greek mythology.

"I'm your Aunt Alexia, Kelly."

She nods absently, but only time will tell if she actually catches the information. She pats the ground.

"Um—"

"Please?" That grin could make me crawl into a hole full of spiders. And I hate spiders.

"Why can't you be my grandma? Stacie has a grandma that lives with her. But her mom also lives with her. Why isn't Mom here?" That question comes quicker than I imagined, but still not completely unexpected. "Why does she love the drugs more than she loves us? I—" She plays with her fingers for a few moments. "I don't want to stay here. I don't want to be stuck here forever."

"Oh, hon," I roll onto my side, propping my head up on my elbow. "You're not here forever. You just need to stay with a grownup for now. I know it's hard. Your mom is trying, but she doesn't quite know what she's doing. She is trying to find her own way."

"Isn't that with us?"

Such wisdom for a young girl. She must have thought about this a lot. I do not really know how to answer. Do I share honestly or in an easier way for a child's heart to hear, though not exactly the truth? I am saved from the tough question by the sudden snap and subsequent spray of water that come from the sprinkler system as it is turned on. It's more violent from a foot off the ground than it appears from my front window. I jump up and immediately start yelling for Ed, who says that he programmed the new sprinklers for six in the morning, not evening. The fact that both myself and Kelly are soaking from head to toe is an indication he did the former, but Kelly starts to laugh and dance around in the sprinklers.

We meet to eat, with laughter and food taking up most of our time.
My cooking skills are not great, but Dave thinks they are sublime.
We set a date for him to make me pizza and then tempers start to rise.
Dave is upset about how much I am working, how my time is decided.
He doesn't understand that my work needs me now, and I can't take his side.

Money is food and food is love. My girls need these more than they need a hug.
Dave turns away, unsure what to say. He walks; I can't let him get away. Hey!
I am solid now, even if it takes time. I am doing what it takes to keep all of mine.
He has no right to judge me for my time that I spend! In the end
I don't need him. Why is every conversation something that I have to defend?
My life is my own, and Kelly and Penny. He doesn't know
The second he doubts me I feel trapped, like my whole world is about to collapse.

"It's like home! Weeee!!" She twirls again and again and I see Penny's shadow observing from inside the house. I let Kelly romp around for a little bit. After all, we're raising two kids, aren't we? Raising. Maybe Kelly's right. Who knows how long we will have them. Maybe this is just the wake-up call that Deirdra needs. I turn for the house and imagine the dry clothes that I will be replacing my maxi dress with. Not the greatest time to be in my Sunday best, I muse.

I wipe my feet right before entering and nearly break a gasket when I see that Penny has been drawing on the kitchen table. Some of the pages have fallen to the floor and crayons are everywhere.

PENNY

Present Day.

Aunt Alexia and Kelly jump around in the sprinklers, but then Aunt Alexia comes back toward me. There's a thump outside the door and my body jumps. Stay outside until we're dry is the rule. My arm bumps the table and crayons slide across the surface like ice. Not again. They all fall to the ground, but I try to pick them up and Aunt Alexia is there. She is mad because her eyebrows do that scrunchy thing, but she doesn't yell. She says that I need to pick up every last one of the crayons, and I do try, but my finger almost gets stuck trying to find the yellow one under the stove. All the others are back in the box when Aunt Alexia comes back and she doesn't look as mad. I am in trouble. It always happens and I didn't do it right.

She opens the door and the phone rings at the same time. "Hello?" Aunt Alexia answers. "Oh! Deirdra. Finally!"

We're going back home!

PENNY

Present Day.

Mom's closet is my favorite because of all the pretty outfits. Mom sleeps and her snores come from her bed, but I'm quiet, with my crayons next to me. Purple is my favorite. Like unicorn hair. A buzz from her phone. I freeze like ice. Mommy stops snoring. She takes the phone but doesn't say hello and throws it across the room. It goes right next to where I'm hiding. I don't move. She walks out and calls Kelly. I can hear her voice but not see. KNOCK! KNOCK! comes from the front door. Kelly runs from her room so both Mommy and Kelly are looking at me. She does see me and stops, but even though I hear a voice, she doesn't answer it. KNOCK! KNOCK! again. And this time, RING!

"Deirdra, it's been nearly a week. Where are you?" The voice on the other side of the door.

"It's Dave!" Kelly loud-whispers from the window. She is down so low, only her eyes show.

"Don't you dare open that door! We're not having any company today." It's not a happy day for Mommy. She sits close to me, on the step where we can watch the door. Then she says, "Go on," and I know she is talking to me, but her eyes are not looking at me. I use my super fast legs and stop by Kelly. She bounces on one foot then the other foot, like she does every time we see Dave. We don't say anything because Mom says no. Even though it's Dave. And Dave's not a stranger. We know him. Mom is not in a listening mood.

I can hear him on the back side of the door. "Deirdra! Are you there? You can't stay in there forever." More knocking. Lots. He leaves after lots more knocks, even some on the window. Mommy sits and sits. We start coloring pictures of her, doodles on song pages, and then go to bed. I don't dream.

Mom comes in when sun shines in my window. "I have to work this morning, girls." She puts lots of makeup on her eyes and does her hair really tall, all up on her head. "It'll only be a couple hours. Here." She gives Kelly one of my school papers. "You can practice so she'll be ready for school tomorrow." I'm happy about this but Kelly is not. Her face looks like she smells something bad.

Mommy does come back. Just getting dark. She is on the phone. I sit still. Kelly watches with no talking. Then someone else says something loud. Mom spills a little bag on the kitchen table and does something that I can't see. She takes the sink trash can and holds it in her front, like I do when I'm sick.

"I...you...to come here. Focus! Now!" She yells at the kitchen floor. Mommy breathes funny, like she just got done running. She sits in the middle of the kitchen and the other person keeps talking. BUZZ, BUZZ, BUZZ is all I hear. But Mommy doesn't answer. She stares at the wall. Kelly is yelling. "Mommy! Mommy!" BUZZ! Stare. "Mommy! Mommy! MOMMY!" BUZZ. Stare. Kelly runs past me but I'm staring at Mommy.

What's wrong with her?

I cry as Mom moves back and forward, back and forward. Back and—

Mommy falls. There is a long needle next to her. I scream, too, and cry with Kelly.

Someone crashes in the door and I move back against the wall. It's big and solid. The person is Dave. Kelly is yelling at him. He bends close to Mommy and says something to Kelly really soft. He points at me and Kelly gives me a big bear hug. She tells me, "It will be okay. It will be okay. It will be okay." I stop screaming because she's here, but one of her tears lands on my hand. She's scared, too. Something inside me feels better. It's not just me with these feelings. The inside hurts.

"What do you think you're doing, anyway?" Mommy tries to stand and falls again. Dave takes her with one hand on her arm and the other on her back to the other room. The grownups don't close the door so I listen. Nobody told us to move. Kelly squeezes my hand.

"Your daughter let me in, Deirdra. Alexia called me after you called her and since I just came over, she told me to check on you.

And the girls." I hear the high WHEEE-  sound of sirens.

"Did you call the police?" Mom screams.

"I had to, Deirdra. Look at the state of your house. And you! I couldn't even get you up when I came in. How can you leave those two children alone to fend for themselves?"

Mommy cries. "I...I put my own kids in danger."

"They're good kids, Deids. This is not how you handle life! They don't deserve this! They don't deserve this treatment." Dave is mad. I've never heard that voice before.

"I know they don't! How dare you!" She points to Dave, who steps back into the kitchen. "How dare you come in here to tell me how to run my life! How to raise my own kids. Well *sor-ry* if my lifestyle doesn't live up to your standards. Get out! Get out of here!"

The wind, bone-chilling
like a slap.
Blink and rush past.
Leaning into the icy wind,
white paper flaps on the step.
Watching her?
Paranoia.

Fear vanishing with one peek:
"Deirdra, enjoy! I'll see you soon."
Dave.
Uncertainty becomes expectation.
a gift? Focus.
Don't blow away.
Unexpected gifts of possibilities.

Slam of the door.
heat rushes.
a cracked window.
Small blast of reality.
No words inside the heart
but squeals of hope.
Supplies enough for pancakes,
mounds of a golden haven.
sweet in the dark.
Disturbed by the heaviness of unpaid bills.

Stay strong.
Don't crack.
Too late?

PENNY
Present Day.

Most mommies or daddies see something that needs to be fixed and they try to fix it. Even if they don't know how, they try their best, by kissing a boo-boo or holding a hand or giving a hug. Others have more, so they give gifts, like coats or trips or their own room. My mommy can't do any of this. She doesn't know what to do with broken. Broken things aren't something she wants to fix. Broken things hurt Mommy. So that's how I know, I have to get rid of it. This is a thing that can't help Mommy. There's one that's super tall, above the toilet, and I can't quite reach, but I take the front thing and let it hit the bathtub. It makes lots of noise, but Kelly is listening to music now, so she won't check. Then I find what she keeps, right next to her bedside. This is her favorite. She comes here all the time. I reach under and it doesn't look like something important. Just a couple things from the kitchen and some powder stuff. I don't know how I'm going to break all this, so I think of a better idea. I put it in the toilet. It stays on top and wiggles, then sinks to the bottom, sliding down to the hole. She will find that these are gone, and I can't flush it—that would choke it. So I just close the toilet lid. BANG. That's it.

Mommy might be upset for a little bit, but she will see this is better. I'm trying to help where Mommy can't.

When Mommy comes from work, she explodes. Really. Like a volcano. Her hair flies everywhere and her arms are motions all around. Mom is red. "How dare you touch my stuff! That stuff can be dangerous for little kids! You are forbidden to ever go into my room again! Do you understand? Never!" I messed up. After yelling words we can't say, she cries. Then yells again. "You're trying to kill me by taking away my medicine." Okay. I guess maybe I found the wrong stuff. I don't see Mom for days after that.

She stays in her room and Kelly and me eat cereal. She's recovering 'cause she's sick, she tells us. The monster is still here.

PENNY

Present Day.

CLICK-TAP, FUZZZZZ! Kelly turns on the radio. Some people use their phones to listen to music on apps, but we use the radio that plugs into the wall. We listen to a lot of jazz, which is soft and happy. A little fast. "Upbeat," Mommy calls it, and it "calms her soul." I like listening because music says a story. I close my eyes and it's like I create a picture in my head even better than morning cartoons. About fairies, mountains, and sunshine in the daytime. But at night sometimes there are dreams about lightning and scary monsters trying to get Mommy. She can't save us. That's when I wake up wet and climb in with Kelly. She mostly lets me.

But when Kelly and me are by ourselves, she doesn't even want to play with me because she's got homework and stuff. But sometimes, the best times, we sit together under a pile of blankets on the living room floor. She writes and I draw. And we don't wonder about the house without Mommy.

Right now it's just me, which is sometimes okay, too. If I don't think about the bad dreams. I dreamed last night I was stuck under something, like a tent or a blanket, and no matter how hard I tugged, I couldn't break out. I needed to scream, but I couldn't make a sound! I woke up and my throat hurt. Maybe I was screaming, not knowing. I didn't dream about the lightning, so... The last time I dreamed the bad dream was after school started. That was a crying week, full of horrible, awful, terrible, very bad days, or whatever that book says. My teacher likes that book and I don't know why. It makes my head hurt.

My teacher, Miss Anderson, she smiles too much, and is always asking us to do things with everyone, like singing songs, dancing around, and shaking other kids' hands. I don't know these kids, and I only dance with Mommy. She is a very good dancer! Miss Anderson looks funny when she tries to dance to the music. She jigs. Not jiggles, she tells us, but jigs. She says, "Hip-hop with lots of hop." I want to dance like Mommy does, without seeing everyone and doing whatever, but what will they all think?

Sometimes it's like I'm having a nightmare dream when I'm at school. The kids all whisper about me when I'm not looking. I don't want Miss Anderson to ask me something and I give the wrong answer and everybody laugh! She hasn't asked yet, which is good because I'm not saying anything at all. I won't because it could be wrong. Then everyone would laugh and I would cry and my teacher would wonder why she asked.

The really, really, bad nightmare was the lightning. Right before bed Mom called us out in the front yard to watch the bright lightning rip open the sky. Lots of thunder, too. That was the scariest. I was shaking all over with another and another, and even closing my eyes, I still saw big flashes inside my eyes. Even when we went back inside it was there, inside my ears and my eyes.

Kelly didn't think the storm was scary at all. She just said, "Wow!" every time there was a flash and then thunder that sounded like a CRACK! I did like the rain. I like getting wet. Sometimes with a bath, I put my head under the water while it's going and pretend I'm sitting under a waterfall. I've seen pictures but I'll go see a real one someday. Lots of things are scary, but not water. No way.

But the times I sit by my favorite window, and the rain goes down down the glass, I don't like that. It is like someone crying. Then there's thunder and during storms, or when Mom's gone from home, I crawl under my bed covers, even when it's not nighttime. Mommy says I don't need to be afraid of the big things like weather or someone coming, but how does she know what's gonna happen? There are kids at school who practice kicks and stuff, like what they learn at their classes. I want to learn to fight like that, to get rid of the big rock in my chest when I have that afraid feeling.

* * *

Mommy has two jobs now and she works, works, works. Tonight we're staying with neighbors, the Komdars. Their house is real fun. My favorite is the corner of their basement, near the washer machine. It's noisy down there sometimes and the air is hot, but the sound of the dryer makes me fall asleep. One time Mrs. Komdar saw me there, but she didn't give a spanking, she just gave me a POP-Tart. She sat down with me after that. I found two pennies on the floor, like my name, and she let me keep them. I put them in my treasure box, the one under my bed. When there are storms, or loud music, or scary places, I think of my box of treasures and I remember these times.

Alexia

Present Day.

"Alexia. I need you!"

Who is this?

At first I think it's a wrong number and keep expecting to hear Ed's WHACK on my shoulder to jerk me back to reality.

"It's me. Deirdra."

"Oh! Deids! Are you okay? Are the girls okay? What is it?"

I haven't heard from her for weeks, ever since the girls went back. The six days they'd spent with me and Ed had been good for us and Deirdra had promised us things would change. I want to believe her, but maybe I've been overly optimistic.

"Everyone's okay," Deirdra said. "It's just that I—"

A long pause. "Hello? Deirdra! Are you still there?"

"I just need you...to come get the girls." Oh, great. "Just for the day. You've got to protect—" She is getting to something, I'm sure of it. I don't hear voices for a long time, just a rattling static, then nothing but silence. I nearly hang up. "I'm trying to tell you, um...I'm so trying hard not to fail these kids. My kids, I mean. I really just need you to take them to school. Just today. Afterwards, we'll talk." That bombshell is bound to drop!

This time, Deids does hang up. I want to help, but I know she is hiding something. It's not just work. She's not telling the whole story and I can't figure out how to get it out of her. Until I can gather more information—

I already sound like a detective in one of those mystery novels! But I have to think the worst right now.

Of course, I leave right then, early morning and all. I barely have time to get my coat and Knight Edmond pulls around to get me. He knows me well enough not to ask questions, but I fill him in as we zoom down the highway. Within an hour, we make it to their house. Maybe a little fast, but still, we survive the trip. Will D?

At first, nothing looks out of the ordinary. The flowers that Deirdra loves to tend to are healthy and colorful. They actually look perkier than our last visit. Maybe they've been taken care of? What does it say for the rest of the family? This is a good omen. She has something to occupy her mind and not fall into...wherever she goes when she starts using. At first glance, it doesn't look like anything had been broken into and no tell-tale alarms. She is seeing someone, right? The shutters in the front are closed and the side gate I notice has a new lock on it. This seems promising.

I'm going in. "Go around that side and check things out!"

Penny peeks out from behind the screen door and clumsily works the lock. She has to stand on tiptoe. "Hey, sweetie! How are you? Did you know Mommy called me to come over and help out today?" I try to keep it light. Kelly, at least, is buying it and she bounds in from the kitchen.

"Yeah." She tells me that she had heard Deirdra call me. She holds a box of breakfast tarts and both girls are watching, their backpacks stuffed to the brim. "Mommy said we should pack our stuff and stay the night with you after school is over."

I urge the shock not to show on my face.

"Right. Okay, well, that sounds fun! Why don't you make sure you have everything while I go and check on Mom?"

But Kelly won't let me. She tells me with a shake of her head, "She locked her door. She doesn't ever do that, but she said she has to today. It's time to be extra quiet." I ask how long she had been up there and she only shrugs, not giving details.

"Here's what we'll do. You go outside and find Uncle Edmond and I'll be out in a few minutes. Deal?"

They seem to get it, or at least they are distracted by the hunt. They both dart out the door to find him.

It takes begging and pleading, along with some sweet-talking, to get Deids to respond. This is the most bizarre conversation.

"Honey? Are you okay?"

From the other side, so close it sounds like she might be leaning against the door, she yells, "You've got to get out!" Something thumps against that side that makes me jump.

"Is someone in there with you, Deirdra? I'm calling the police!"

"No!" she screams. Then quieter. "No...it's not." What? She gets quieter as she talks. "Please. You can't call anyone. They don't need...to know."

Know what?

"I've got to keep my girls..." she continues initially, but then nothing, like she's lost her train of thought. She's lost something, alright.

I put my head back against the door and remind myself to be gentle.

"This is serious, Deids. Tell me how to help. Who to call."

I try the door again, knowing it still won't open.

"No, Alexia...don't call anybody. I just need a day. Then I'll be...I'll be fine."

Just a day. How many times have I heard that? What makes her think she can pull something like this on me again? Yet here I am, buying. I'm sick of her empty promises.

I don't stay long. Ed's expression is a question mark, but I have no answers. I feel like I have been punched in the gut. Same old story. The saddest part? "Is Mommy okay?"

I force a smile, wanting to believe it.

"Sure she is, Kels. She just needs some rest."

And of course, she doesn't call the next morning, and she quits answering her phone. Not turned off, just abandoned. I ask Ed if we should tell the girls.

"What would we say to them?" Like always, he is right, though I won't admit it. What would we tell them? That their mom has forgotten about them? That she is too busy with her own affairs to worry about her children? Or that she really is too sick to take care of them? "Nothing. That's what we'll tell them. For now."

DEIRDRA

Two years ago.

"Refill on bread?" The waiter slides a tong with a piping hot garlic breadstick in front of my nose and I grin, noticing that Dave follows suit. At first I protest, trying to keep up with my latest diet. This one doesn't seem to be working, but maybe it's nights like this that kill it for me. I have definitely put down at least three breadsticks. The waiter laughs. "Everyone does!" These practically melt in my mouth.

Dave says, "You're cute," and I can't help but smile. Such boyish charm. "You could definitely stand to gain a few pounds." Yep, he's not aware of what real women need nowadays. I consciously rub my cheek, reminding myself that I've only had half meals once this week. Gotta cut back. Besides, meals are so expensive, and it's better to give money for my kids. Dave doesn't have kids. He can't possibly know. I've taken care of my daughters just fine up to this point! I toss back one wine and motion for another.

"Ah, it's so great to have finer things in life! I'm so glad you kept these reservations, even though I was thirty minutes late."

"You sure you're okay? You seem unusually tense."

"A few more of these and I won't be," I retort. Another swig of wine and a grin. Remorse has never been my strong suit. He looks down once. My comment strikes a nerve, surely, but it's not a jab. Not really. Even though he's silent enough not to say anything when I order another wine, he might flinch at the dessert prices. The molten cake is the best I've ever had. Each is huge enough that we save some for home. Maybe we should have split it? Imagine the grin on the girls' faces!

* * *

I invite him for brunch that Saturday and the girls pull out their favorite food: a box of Pop-Tarts. He stares at the girls' faces, a carton of eggs in his hands. He's speechless. "That's a new look for you," I comment as I grab the eggs from him.

"Oh, so you're domestic now?"

"Sure, when I need to be."

"*Vaya!*" Go on!

A thump from upstairs and I hop towards the stairs immediately. "Mom!" Kelly's quick call is insistent.

"Probably Penny!" I offer as an explanation. I smell it before I see it. The mess of child vomit and my youngest bent over the toilet. I almost hurl, but shift into mom-mode. "Dave, can you bring some rags? I have some in my bathroom." I hear more thumping from the other side of the wall. How hard is it to find some towels? Then silence.

It takes him several more minutes and I am on the verge of yelling down the hall myself. He looks distracted when he comes in, but when I ask he replies, "We can talk later." Penny is enough of a distraction that I don't have time to worry about it right now.

When I come downstairs, I plop next to Dave on the couch. He holds up a bowl of something that smells like chocolate and looks like soup. "Our leftovers from tonight," he offers. His eyes don't leave mine. He leans over for a quick kiss right on the lips. I am startled. Our first kiss and that's it? "Mm-m-m. You think it's worth it?"

I lean closer and I'm lost in his gaze; intense, but gentle. My clever comeback disappears and I hold my breath, my heart speeding up and time slowing down. How can this still affect me so much? His eyes move down my face.

"Mom?" Kelly's voice is unbearably close and we scoot apart. I nearly drop my molten mush. Dave's hand snatches it as my daughter's insistence pulls me upstairs. I lock eyes with him and smile, which I hope comes off as apologetic.

A quick goodnight to the girls, but I still melt with their arms holding tight around my neck. Tonight, Penny leans into my shoulder for longer than normal, a sure sign that she's not feeling quite herself. Another kiss on both of their foreheads and I smell their hair. Still my favorite part of the evening. I finish up and head back downstairs to Dave.

I ask, "Now where were we?"

He hands me the bowl with a smile. "It was a little hot," he says, but does not lean in.

"So you've tried it?" I stick my feet beside his on the ottoman and take a bite. "Oh, this is better than it was at the restaurant!" He nods with a grin, again not looking away.

"Much better."

"Much, much better." I laugh, using my favorite Christmas movie quote. We make plans to watch a movie the next time he comes over.

"That's right, next time," he says. "As often as you'd like."

I look into his eyes and I know what he's really saying: He wants to help. I try to fend him off at first. "Uh, that's sweet of you, but I can't ask you to do that."

"*Por qué no?*"

I stare back blankly.

"I thought you knew Spanish!" he laughs.

"I *do* know, but more like *hola* and *baño* for the basics and that is it. You've always got to know how to say hello and get to the bathroom! But then with 

your accent...it throws me off and, well..." My confidence is melting like this cake. Dave moves closer and I inch back. "Wait. Can I talk to you?" The words are out of my mouth before I can stop them.

"Listen. We can't keep going. I can't make this serious." I take a deep breath. Nothing can make this easier. "I have been managing things on my own for quite a while now. I know, I know I work a lot, but it's in order to give my girls everything. Everything that you see here, it's because I worked for it. And I can't have you coming here and sweeping me off my feet, saving the day with all your treats. Yes, there are times that we do have to scrimp, and I can't always buy them Kit Kat bars and things..." He shifts his weight, saying nothing.

"If you're trying to make me feel like a heel, well, it's working." I expect him to come up with other accusations, but I get nothing. He just sits there with his mouth hanging open. I stop him with my hand when he opens his mouth. I don't want to hear it. I can't. I might melt.

"Wow," He continues, shaking his head. "I really want to crawl into a hole right now. I thought we were doing well." I think he is going to turn but he doesn't.

"I want you to let me do this," he finally replies. "I am not about to miss out on any fried chicken and I think it's a good idea to meet up, maybe next Saturday night?"

I laugh, harder than I have in a long time. He's as stubborn as my sister, and I haven't talked to her in years. Who can resist this charm anyways? "Chicken for the girls sounds great. But are you going to bring some wine instead of hot chocolate stuff?"

"Well, I can't because I'm a recovering alcoholic. Didn't mean to get this personal this quick." He rushes on, "It got really bad after I divorced my first wife two years ago." So maybe not as perfect after all.

I don't tell him my little secret. Just a shrug. "That's fine." I put my hand on his shoulder and he sighs. Must've been worried about how I would take it. "Saturday night." It's just dinner, right? And with the girls it's not a real date.

* * *

Traffic is awful that night and it takes Dave twice as long as usual to reach our house. We have so much food! Then when he comments that there is enough for leftovers, and tries to give me some ideas other than nachos, such as chicken salad or chicken sandwiches, Kelly chimes in with a suggestion of "chicken pancakes." That's my girl!

I think we shock Dave. I get more chicken for Kelly and tell them I am running upstairs for a minute to check on Penny, who is taking a bath. She is happily silent, but I always have in the back of my mind the scenario that she might drown. Instead, she's busy sinking imaginary ships with her duck squirting water out of its butt towards her LEGO pieces. She's fine, I assure myself.

"Pretty nails." Dave is attempting conversation with my oldest and failing.

She states, "I'm going to be a beautician," even though she chose one of the ugliest colors in the box. But who could resist that girl's gap-toothed smile? "Mom didn't paint them. I painted Mom's!" Thanks to her, my nails are a bright green color, like a lizard.

"Whoa! Talk about a little artist. You're like, what, eight? Well, that answers the twinsie question." He looks at me when I walk in. "Color me impressed."

"That's not a color," Kelly points out.

I push my hair back under my headband. Too rushed from work to put it up properly. "Sorry I'm such a mess," I murmur. I almost miss Dave's reply — "You're beautiful" — as my little one holds up her hand and grabs mine for a closer look.

"Beautiful," he repeats and Kelly shines. When I let my eyes travel back to him, he's still looking.

We do watch a movie, all of us with our chicken in the living room, and spend the first ten minutes comparing the patterns on our socks. Penny loves the hearts. I get them to focus and we rewind it just so that we can sing the intro part. My favorite because of the upbeat music. They are not as enthusiastic, but even Dave joins in. When I break out into a little dance he says, "You are one awesome *chica!*" He laughs and it looks like he's impressed. I sway my hips one more time before sitting down.

PENNY

Present Day.

This night and last night and the other last night, Mommy screams when she's supposed to be sleeping. She sounds like she's fighting with someone because she yells but is asleep. Maybe she has dreams like me. I crawl out of bed and go all the way down the hall to see, even though it's dark. Her door is open and a lamp is on, next to her bed. I see Mommy's back, so she doesn't see me. She bends over, like her arm is hurt. It really does look like she puts a Band-Aid on herself. Kind of. A clear tube thing is in her hand and she brings it up to the light and I see the thing. My heart jumps. It's a needle! Why would she poke a needle? I get shots but that's at the doctor's. My mouth goes closed. She would be super mad if she saw me. I don't know what this is but it looks like she's all secret like. I almost fall trying to get back to my room fast fast, "lickity split." I hold my breath, but Mommy isn't following.

When Aunt Alexia comes over I know that I'm going to be in trouble. But Mom doesn't even look. She tries to learn how to cook

When the door slams I am alone
Oblivious to the giggles that surround me
In my ears, they are laughter that reveal where I've fallen
Desperation
To survive in this swim upstream
I can't do this
Everyone has left me here
Abandoned.

I have to do this: Earn that proud look on her face
I'm lost in my haze, this hateful happiness!
Lost in a shadow they don't see
I can't find my way
Follow the pain
Must ignore
The laughter that haunts, belittling this battle within
I can't ignore what my kids need
They need...
...
The needle.
My true friends are at the end of this needle.

like Aunt Alexia, but since Aunt Alexia came over, all they're doing is talking. They're arguing. Kelly used that word the other day, and it sounds much smarter. I want to be smart because that makes Mom proud. It sounds like those dogs in the alley barking back and forth. One barks, the other one barks. The first one answers so the second one barks. Most of the time, their tails are wagging, too. My teacher says that Tail Wag means the dog is happy. Then why do they bark like they're mad?

The monster is in our house! Whatever makes Mom put that needle in her. The sickness is here. It's just hiding. I know it.

PENNY

Present Day.

I walk in from lunch and some kids are already sitting. I usually don't see these kids, but in the last couple weeks, we've been coming into class for the last subjects. Probably that huge test we'll be taking in a month or something. I ignore their looking, just glad they are not talking to me. It doesn't stay. One sees me and turns around, not facing me. I think they're whispering. Then another waves at me.

"She doesn't speak," one says. "She just sits there."

"Like something's...wrong with her tongue?" asks a girl in a purple sweatshirt. My favorite color.

"Did something happen to her?"

"Does she not like us?"

When they all stare at me, I want to crawl under my desk to disappear. Why do kids think that because I don't want to talk, something has to be wrong?

"Come on, Penny." A girl they say is Pat points to a desk close to her and her friends. "Hurry, before Miss Anderson comes in."

I don't see many other desks with empty seats, so I walk over and sit next to her. One person plays on her phone, another is trying to finish the homework for this class. Someone has a wrap of Smarties and acts like he wants to give one to me.

I look at him and take it. I don't remember his name, but he is always smiling. A good thing. I don't eat it, just roll it around in my hand. It's the color of a daffodil. I almost POP it in my mouth before he stops me. "Woah. Hold it! That's not what you do with that." He waves one. He crushes the piece with his thumb. Then he rolls it into a part of his paper he tore off. It goes to his lips and he pretends to suck it in and blow out. A little puff of powder floats in the air. Like he's smoking! What?

I figured out that sometimes people do stuff that is against the law, but most of those people are adults, not kids like us. At least I thought that. Maybe the kid's home is the same as mine. Mostly taking care of himself. I want to ask if someone does drugs like my mom, but don't have the right words. We're not supposed to talk about that at school. Plus, it might make him mad. I sit there in the middle of everyone, not moving and wanting to cry. Almost.

A boy leans over to another kid and says, "Hey, you have something on your new shoes." She looks down at her black shoes. I wonder if they ever get dirty or if her mom gets mad if she runs in mud puddles. We've had lots of rain. The boy's finger snaps in front of her and he twists away when he laughs. "Ha! Made you look!" He tries this again and again. All three times, that girl still looks down. By then, she is laughing, too, and does it again with her friend, the one who is on her phone. We're supposed to put it up when we come to class. At least sitting with these kids I have a place like I'm part of a group. Not such a bad thing.

"Alright, everyone, are we ready for our spelling practice?" Another one of my favorite things. Not!

PENNY

Present Day.

"Here you go, Hon!" Mom turns up the radio with the familiar notes of the song. "What do you think?"

I tilt my head for better listening, like I've seen my sister do when she is thinking hard on a tough math problem. I try to figure out what are the differences in the notes, but to me it's just a string of music. I guess that is maybe guitar, piano, drums, and—what else? What other instruments do you need in a band? Kelly and me play air guitars all the time, but none of the songs we play in our heads are like this. Then there is a beat without music, right before the words start. I only catch some of them. "He's forgotten...you there! Feel like...of society...rain just keeps coming."

"*Boom!* Boom!" Kelly and Mom do this part together, pounding on the seats. "Okay, here's the best part!" I don't remember the words. So I stare at my hands. At one verse, Mom forgets the words I guess and starts mumbling, then blurts out the last line really loud, "...WANT to be. But you're getting there! You are sent of rain!" Then she laughs. I like to hear her laugh.

Mom turns to me and her smile goes away. "Hey, lighten up!" She pats her hand, touching my shoulder. "It's fun to sing." Her smile comes again on her face. I like to see Mommy smile. Like when I was a very little girl and running in the park. That was before "life happened," as Mom says.

"Singing brings out the joy in your soul," Mom says to us, but her eyes stay on the road. Big breath. It doesn't seem that Mom has lots of joy, even after singing. "It's really hard sometimes..." She doesn't finish. Maybe she's crying. No, her face is not sparkling. "That's why we remember the good stuff, girls. Because sometimes it's easy to forget."

PENNY

Present Day.

I make a spot, almost like a nest, next to Mommy, who has passed out again and is laying on the floor of the hallway. I'll be the mama bird this time. I sit near her legs, my back to her and my face toward the front door, the downstairs. This is like that story that Teacher read to us about the knight taking care of the princess while they were on a journey and she needed to sleep. The knight knew that the princess needed sleep because they had been walking for a long time, but that it was not safe for her to stay. I look at Mom's face again, but she doesn't see me. It looks like she's sleeping. Like an enchanted sleep in a story. And it's not safe for her to stay here by herself because she needs protection. She always says that to me and now it's my turn. This means right now I am the only one who can protect her. I look around for something, a sword or something, but nothing I can find here on the floor. Staying by Mommy is best.

PENNY

Present Day.

I don't answer the screaming doorbell. Neither does Kelly. Mommy has the porch light on, like a flashlight in the dark, but we sit still in our room. Like she told us. The house smells like outside because Mommy started the oven on to make dinner. She hasn't turned it off yet. Someone outside wiggles the doorknob and I squeeze Kelly's hand. The person steps past the door, over the barrier, and into our kitchen. Kelly squeezes tighter. I can't see a face, only brown shoes and jeans from where we are sitting. Mom would be able to see him. If she were awake. I peek up. It is a man, wide-eyed and breathing hard. He looks at me. I want him to stop looking. Then he sees Mommy.

On the floor. In the hallway upstairs. She doesn't move. And I don't know what to do.

The man says Mommy's name and I know who it is. I've heard it before. Kelly and me squeak at the same time, "Dave!" But he isn't looking at us. He didn't come for us. Nobody ever does. He runs upstairs and bends close to Mom. Even right next to us, he doesn't look at us, just starts talking. I think he's talking to Kelly. She jumps up and hugs him. "Dave! It's Mom. She isn't getting up. I tried to tell her that the oven is still on and I don't know which button to push, but she isn't opening her eyes!"

"Okay, okay," Dave says. "We'll figure it all out and wake Mommy up soon. For now, do you know how to tell time? How long has she been here?" Kelly is really good at time, so she should get it quick! The clock on the wall says 8:07, so Mommy has been here, not moving, dinner not getting cooked, for thirty-four minutes. But Kelly doesn't say this. Her mouth is open and she looks like she's about to cry. I punch her arm. Maybe she needs a jolt to remember, but Dave puts a hand on my arm and I swing at him. He moves away like lightning, and he almost tells me something. His mouth opens, but he turns to look at Kelly. "Go back to your room. I'll check on Mommy and let you know when I find something."

"Find what?" I want to know, but my voice stays in my head.

Dave goes down to the kitchen for the oven and uses his phone. If only Mommy would have let us use her phone. Whoever he talks to says a lot of things, with Dave just listening. He says that she is "under-sponsive" and then a lot of "uh-huh," "okay." He walks back over to us and gets beside Mommy. He leans over close without touching her and stares at the wall. I have done that. He's listening for something only he can hear.

"Yes, but not very much." He says this in the button to the person sitting on the other place where the phone goes to, but it looks like he's talking to his imaginary friend. I smile. Like mine!

Then the cloud comes back. This is a serious time. "Okay, yes." He hits a button and puts it next to Mommy. She doesn't answer it, but I can hear clicks on the inside. He touches Mommy this time, up and down her arm, stopping moving to hold her hand. When he puts it down, he says something really soft to himself. His world. Then he speaks to the phone again. "She is fine. Unresponsive, but breathing...It doesn't look like she broke anything. Her eyes are dilated, but I can't find any lumps on her head...Yes. Yes. Okay. I need to call her sister...No, but she can be here...Okay."

He calls another number. His eyes go to me and I pretend to look close at my hands. Looking right at adults makes me uncomfortable. He looks back at the phone as it talks to him. "Yeah, Alexia? Hi, it's Dave. Um, something happened with Deirdra. Yes, she's at home. I called 9-1-1...The girls are fine...Yes. Yes, they're coming... Okay. See you soon...Got them...Yeah." Dave goes down the hallway and back to us. Down and back. His watch might be broken because he keeps looking at his watch. He doesn't say words to us, but whistles one of our favorite songs. He doesn't dance. Mommy would. But she can't. Mommy is on the floor. I'm supposed to laugh when he adds a wahoo whistle at the end, but I just feel the crying coming up through my throat.

Is Dave going to save her? My mouth doesn't ask this. Kelly sits by Mommy and starts yelling when Dave tries to move her. He picks her up once and she kicks him, then runs back to sit with Mommy. He kinda crouch-sits next to her and whispers something. This time Kelly doesn't yell. She reaches up and he lifts her into his arms and she sticks her face in his shoulder. Like she does with Mommy for a hug.

"It's all going to be fine, Kels. Promise."

Then the ambulance siren sounds really loud. Right outside the window. The house blinks blue and red. Strange voices come. Dave tells Kelly to move over by me. We can still see Mommy from there. The people in uniforms bring a long thing, taller than Mommy but on the floor, and put her on it. She still doesn't move or speak.

"Alexia, you can..." Dave talks to the phone again but he turns the other way for a while. He puts the phone in his pocket and looks back at us. "Let's go downstairs." Want to play a game? Your Aunt Alexia is going to watch Mommy at the hospital." He stands with us and I lean toward him. It's my thank you because I know he's helping Mom.

Kelly squeezes him hard. "I'll never let go."

Don't let go. Don't go, Dave, whatever you do!

"Girls, how about I fix some spaghetti to go with our game?"

"Alright! Spaghetti!" He looks happy, but he doesn't look at me. I'm okay with that, but Kelly frowns.

"That's not how we do it. Mommy puts the meatballs on the side."

Where is Mommy? I tug Kelly's sleeve and she asks Dave, "Can you give Penny a meatball?" Wrong question.

Dave moves where I can't see, but I hear his voice, hiding behind the wall. I know he's talking about money, but I don't understand. Then Aunt Alexia comes. I cry again. I don't know why, but what happened to Mom is bad and I am mad and sad and want a hug, but not.

He says, "I found a needle, too. Plastic bag. Okay. No. Right. Got it." Talking to himself. "I couldn't just carry it downstairs in full view, so I stashed it at the very top of one of the bookshelves in the hallway." Dave taking down books. He's messing up our house!

We eat dinner really fast and ask to watch a movie after. He'll say yes to anything, right? There are so many princess movies! We choose one and are comfy enough on the couch, the show getting all our attention. This is the only bad thing, right?

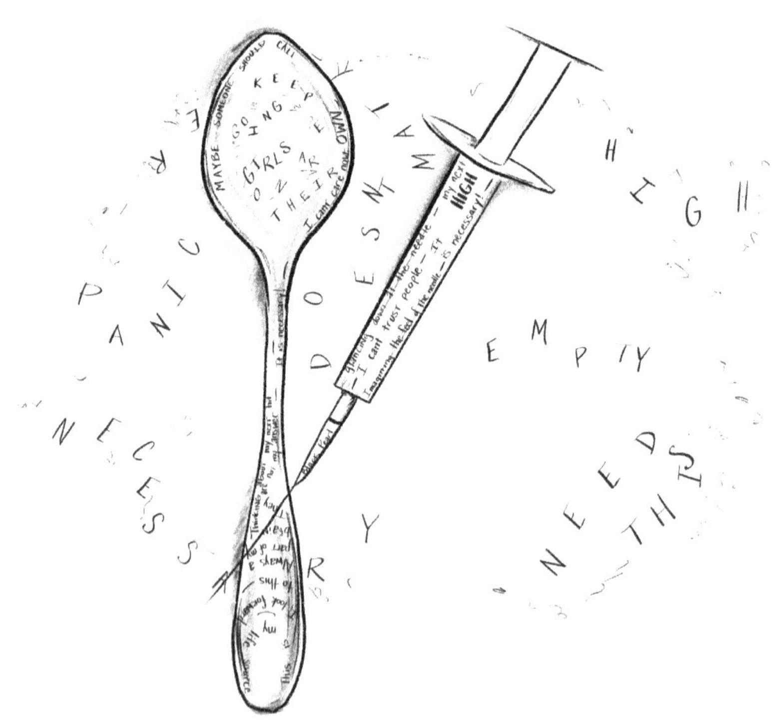
PANIC
NECESSARY
KEEP GOING
GIRLS ON THEIR OWN
MAYBE SOMEONE SHOULD CALL
DOESN'T MATTER
HIGH
EMPTY
NEED THIS

ALEXIA

Present Day.

That was the longest drive of my life. The sky at dusk was brilliant and breath-taking. I'm not sure if I was more worried about the girls or Deids. I told her I loved her, and even called her our pet name from our high school days. I'm not sure if I'm just fooling myself. It seems like it's just me holding the hope that she will ever change. I even wonder if Deids told them how long, or if she expects...something. I have more questions than answers, really. She was responsive, but not making a lot of sense as we watched her wheeled into the ambulance.

The kids scramble along in front of me. Back to the now, something that I can focus on. I love the "before bed" time. I try to act like everything's normal, though I know their thoughts are back home.

"Wow, that's amazing! So many colors."

What has surprised me most is Penny. She's turning into quite an artist. Kelly explained her little drawing. "It's a hummingbird. This is how it gets nectar from the flowers. Did you know that a hummingbird can beat its wings more than fifty times a second? Penny has a little hummingbird friend. Imaginary, of course." She rolls her eyes like the pre-teen she is now. What a character! She gets so excited by her own recitation, she jumps off the bed and bounces around like a little monkey, her hair twirling around her face. We enjoy a laugh, then I have to let them know. Might as well get it over with.

"Listen, girls. I need to tell you both something. Did your mom tell you anything about having to go away for a while?" This is the second time in less than six months, and I can't see the cycle changing.

Kelly tells me, "She said that we needed to stay here with you for a while. In your house. I brought my favorite animal I like to sleep with, in case we stay here for more time. Mom said we'll be together soon, but I don't know what soon is, exactly. How many days is soon?"

How to tell them?

"Hon," I start, not really knowing how to phrase it, "I'm not quite sure yet, but it will be a little while." I try to come up with some comforting words. Where is Edmond in this sort of situation?

He is so much better at this than I am! "Your mom has some things to figure out. But she wanted me to remind you how much she loves you, and that everything she does is for the two of you."

The girls nod, but I can tell from their blank expressions they most likely have heard this spiel before. How much do they believe? How much do they really understand? I distract them with the connect blocks that Edmond and I pulled from the attic. It's amazing how kids can move from one subject to another, one mood to another, so quickly! School will be starting up again tomorrow, so they can be with their old friends again. It's not going to be a quick stay in any case, not if she had me enroll them in school. Even the somewhat familiar environment could seem hostile in the light of what they've been through in the past several years. Half their elementary school years are gone. Do I remember how to do this? Deids and I used to have it down to an art! I would always remind her of what we needed to carry and what she needed to notice. By the time we were teens she would just roll her eyes, like her daughter, but I kept at it. One day it would sink in. Then one day, she was gone. With Kelly's birth it didn't get better and she just built a wall. Until she needed me, of course.

What about Penny? She is not like other kids. Will she ever feel comfortable at school? I can't believe that in all these visits I haven't asked Deirdra how she handles Penny's outbursts in class. If she even knows about them, which the more I find out about their little family, the more I doubt it.

When the girls are comfortably curled in their beds, I sit at my computer, looking for the webpage I pulled up the other day. I dial the number. At first it's busy, so I go into the next room where Ed sits on the couch watching a game show. I need the extra support, so I sit next to him silently and slip my hand in his. He doesn't say anything, which is a relief because my mind is whirling. Is this right? Should I wait? After a few minutes I dial the number again and the call goes through.

"Hello?"

"My name is Alexia Sikes and I need to make a report about a member of my family." *My* family. Who knew it'd come to this. Ed squeezes my hand.

My brain tries to link
together: I need to think,
but my heart starts to sink
into the abyss of reality
but I should keep going, though
tears stubbornly
streak
down
I have lost everything, what
is the cost?

Dave hasn't called
in the longest
and my kids are tossed
to the home of my sister
who has accosted
my nights
to
visit

It is winding,
never quite finding
time, my NarcAnon classes
keep reminding
that I must keep trying
and trying.
I'm trying,

they're lying,
I'm lying
to
her

And waiting
for my life to change, the pain
is intense and immense and the strain
of maintaining
my daily life, gaining

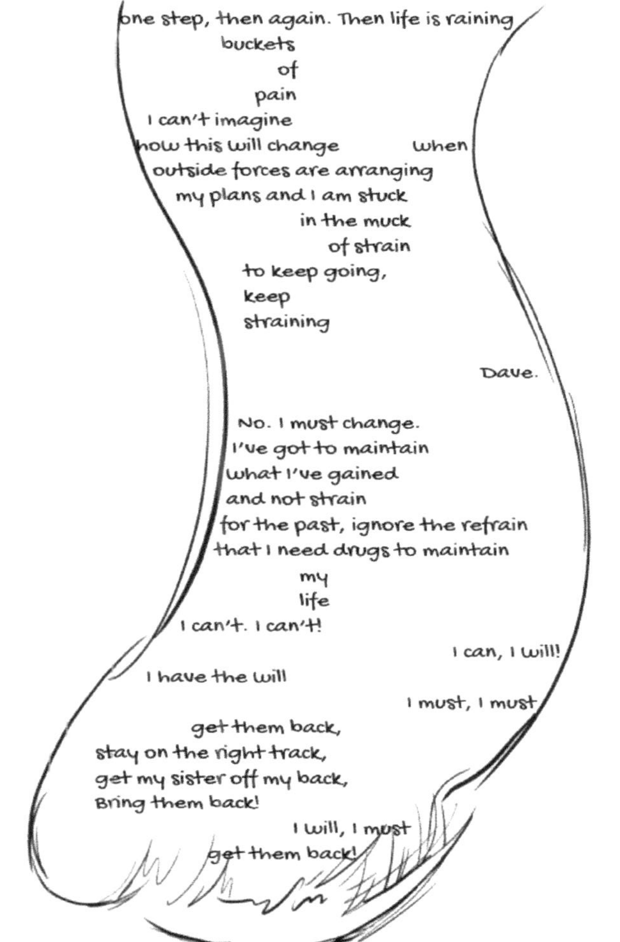
one step, then again. Then life is raining
buckets
of
pain
I can't imagine
how this will change   when
outside forces are arranging
my plans and I am stuck
in the muck
of strain
to keep going,
keep
straining

Dave.

No. I must change.
I've got to maintain
what I've gained
and not strain
for the past, ignore the refrain
that I need drugs to maintain
my
life
I can't. I can't!
I can, I will!
I have the will
I must, I must
get them back,
stay on the right track,
get my sister off my back,
Bring them back!
I will, I must
get them back!

DEIRDRA

Two years ago.

There's no time. A knock. That must be Al. Bring on Judgement Day! It's just temporary, after all. I can hold it in and everything will go back to normal. The second Alexia walks into my place, I know I shouldn't have called. She won't do anything but bring her judgmental measuring rod. Like an evil Mary Poppins. In the minutes before, I shouted at my girls. All their junk, their whole life in garbage sacks, locked temporarily in Kelly's bathroom. Penny even put her favorite unicorn animal in at the end. "Good," I tell her as weak reassurance. "To keep it safe. They aren't afraid of the dark."

Where have I gone wrong?

PENNY

Present Day.

Kelly's talking slowly, like Mom does when it's time to move places. This means it's not good, whatever it is. "How much do you know about Mom?" Then she says other stuff. It's hard to understand her at first because she says all the things in a whisper. Like nobody should hear. She talks about us being with Uncle Edmond and Aunt Alexia. Bringing our stuff with that lady. Mom not helping us with school. Mom staying out during the night. Too busy to take care of us. She's distracted by the drugs. The hospital is trying to help. And I don't understand.

"Can you try to talk to me, please, Penny?

But when I open my mouth, nothing. Silence is winning. But it's important. Kelly won't get mad. She won't.

"Mom is sick." My voice is small, like a mouse.

"Right. Today, Mom was really sick. And Dave found her. He said that Mom cannot take care of us right now because she has to take care of herself. What about Mom's, um, stuff? The drugs she takes. What do you know about that?"

That one is hard. I'm not supposed to. My eyes are on a picture from the fridge. My unicorn. The one that flies over the mountain. But not away from Kelly. Not my family. Mommy. "Drugs?" They talk about that sometimes at school. But what I've seen is different. I try to tell her better and point my finger inside my arm. That's where.

"Right. She puts the drugs there. And it hurts her. Dave was just telling me. Um, let me see if I can remember it all. He made me say it again and again." Kelly moves her head up to the ceiling. Her eyes squeeze shut. Then she looks at me. "Sometimes it's hard for her to make money or even get us food. She gets really worried and only sees some problems as big problems. She doesn't know how to help us. What else?

"She has been using drugs to help her try to feel happy, even though drugs are really just tricking her happiness. Aunt Alexia says drugs only make you happy for a little while, and then they make you feel really sad or sick after, like Mommy, and then that makes Mommy's brain think she has to get more drugs." I know this already because Mom had told me something like that. When I broke her stuff. "Dave told me drugs are super expensive, so it means she has to get money and she has to work more and more but sometimes she doesn't have it. When she gets more and more drugs, she sometimes works so hard her mind forgets about us. Um, that's what Dave says."

She hugs me. "Dave also said that Mommy wants to do her best, for both of us. It was a really long speech. Do you hear that? She's sick now, but when she gets better she'll be back to Mommy again. In just a little while!"

I give a HUFF. The air leaves my mouth and I feel mad. My chest hurts. Why isn't Mom here? Why does she love the drugs more? I don't want to stay here. And that plant in the corner makes me sneeze. Aunt Alexia calls the plant honeysuckle, but it doesn't really smell like honey on biscuits. I don't want to be stuck here forever.

PENNY

Present Day.

I can get that puppy! I'm fast! When I run around the corner, I stop. Almost trip over him. Or her. He'll be gone soon, Aunt Alexia said, to a new home. A lot of the animals are going away because they're "too much." I like having them around, but the bags of food are super heavy! He runs and runs and runs, then gets really tired. Then through my legs and I fall over! Then Little Pup is next to me and I can't even get up. He slobbers on my face. Then he runs a little bit and stops, the tail going THUMP! THUMP! I like that sound. A happy sound. He likes playing chase, too, and never gets tired. Okay! Let's go! The light gets dark, but he does his puppy voice and I follow that.

"Time for bed, Penny!" Aunt Alexia is there and she points her hand upstairs. She tells me to go brush my teeth and I want to say that the puppy ran by the house. She shows me her "obey now" look, so I do what she says. I can find the puppy later. Aunt Alexia grabs my arm when I get on the stairs, and I hit her. Her nose bleeds and she runs to the sink, making a weird noise.

My feet are frozen on that step. I stare at her back. I'll get in trouble and I won't have anywhere to go! She bends over in the sink pouring two little rivers, one water and one blood. I want to get closer, but I don't. Then she starts laughing. Aunt Alexia says, "I should have known. I remember that you don't like me to touch you. I remember that, Penny. I'll try better." She is holding a lot of paper towels under her nose when she looks at me. "Your mom—"

Aunt Alexia comes over to me. "Your mom loves you so much. She is trying. Something in her brain won't help her heal. It keeps telling her lies. She's believed them since she was a teenager. Since before you." She's probably with those friends right now. Not us.

"Why?" I sit down against the wall and move my legs over.

Aunt Alexia sits. She shrugs, that move with her shoulders that I like using. "She has been so gifted. You've seen it. She loves to sing and she loves to figure things out. Only one day, her brain decided that it was smarter than her. It started trying to trick her, like a fox. It said that she couldn't get along with what she had. It told her that she needed to find something that wasn't there. So she started to look for other things. Not her family, but friends. Not her house, but drugs. So she can't find her way back."

Mommy is lost.

Kelly joins us along the wall. "Ooh, are we having a secret club? Let's make a tent for our secret club! I'll go get the blanket!"

"That will be fun! You know what, Penny?"

My brain is still thinking, but I look at her.

"Your mom won't be gone from us forever. We're gonna find her," she whispers. "You'll see. Just know that when she is not here, she is looking for you! She is just sometimes looking in the wrong place. Now," she gets on her knees, "do you want crackers for our clubhouse? Then we've really got to get to bed!"

Aunt Alexia 'minds us to brush our teeth. I brush mine two times because my teeth taste good. I smile at myself in the mirror like Kelly does. I try turning upside down. My face still doesn't look like a frown, just like a bunch of teeth inside my lips. I jump in bed, but not too hard because Aunt Alexia gives me her serious look. I nod and go under the blanket. My favorite place.

"Do you ever have dreams? Like those that can't be real because they're just stories, but they feel real at the time?"

Aunt Alexia's question makes me think of that one night, when I woke up with sweat. Yes I do. A huge yes. But I kind of shake my head like I don't know. Adults will stay quiet if I pretend like I am not really paying attention. Then they don't ask more questions. They only like talking to someone who will talk back. Aunt Alexia smiles and goes back to her "typing." She is done talking and my eyes go to the bookshelf, trying to know which book we read at bedtime, not tonight but the other one.

"The other night I dreamed about your Uncle Edmond. He was trying to pull me onto this roller coaster and I was screaming and yelling, throwing my hands around like I was in so much danger. My feet were on the ground, but I was scared about doing something like that, going fast and zooming through the air."

I look at her, but don't shake my head.

"And you know what, even though Uncle Edmond didn't speak in this dream, I thought something really important when I woke up. Sometimes things are very scary because it takes me away from everything I know, but it is something that I need to go through. You know why?"

I try to smile. That's what adults want, right? Only my eyebrows do.

"Even if something is scary, it is sometimes something that teaches me to try something new. Then maybe I might enjoy it, too. It means that things are not always going to happen just how I want, but it is something I can get used to, and even enjoy, you know?"

Aunt Alexia gets on the bed with me. "You know what, Penny? I know all of this change, with your mom and then moving, has been super scary, a time that neither of us chose. That is almost like getting on that roller coaster and whizzing through the air. But I want you to remember, we are going to have fun. It might be hard at times, but it is a ride that we are on together, and when the scary turns come, you can lean right on me. Okay, hon?"

I nod, slowly this time. I really listen. I think I get it. Like that TV show. We're all together in this. And we can help each other when it's scary. Aunt Alexia smiles. I know she knows what I am thinking inside me, even though my mouth does not say. Our hearts match.

DEIRDRA

Two years and two months ago.

"No, don't do that." I attempt—badly—to keep the desperation out of my voice while scribbling his demands on a pad with one hand and keep an eye on my two young girls at the same time. The ultimate multitasker, gambling for our lives. "Right. I can get it to you. Less than two hours. I know that. Sure." I hang up to the dial tone, as he wouldn't ever give the courtesy to close out a conversation. It is all business. And so is this next score. I jot down the name of the latest buyer and pray to whatever is out there that I can pull it off. I know I can't. But I've been lucky in the last couple weeks, so the string of good fortune will continue. Maybe. It has to. That's the only way. The clock screams 3:34 with bright, blinking insistence, which gives me until about 5:30 to show up on his doorstep with cash in my hands. One way to keep up this ruse and it's barely working.

His normal charge has increased. Probably smells the desperation. But this is different...I can't help it. The holidays always make that knot in my stomach grow three sizes, like the Grinch's heart, I suppose. And my heart is sunk into those two precious beauties. I have to pull this off. No time to think or second guess myself. I stuff everything in my bra and beneath my waistband and head out, leaving my kids dozing with smiles, dreaming of the movie playing for the ten zillionth time. No parental hat right now. That could get me killed.

The lock snaps behind me and I head off into the night.

ALEXIA
Present Day.

Homework. It has become a dreaded word in this house, not because it doesn't get done, but just the manner in which it is executed. Penny is trying to be more independent by doing chores and helping around the house, but it takes her forever to finish reading assignments because she's refusing to speak with me. I walk in their room and the girls actually carry on a conversation. Kelly is the only one she'll open up to right now. But Kelly doesn't want to help with her sister's homework because she has so much of her own. We are working on vocabulary words that Penny already knows from class, but she doesn't seem to recognize them. So back to the basics. Sounding out each letter individually. Then I get desperate. Penny isn't having any of it. She won't give a peep.

"Look, Penny! It's an S! SSSSS like sssssnake!" I flop my hand like a snake and wiggle it around in front of Penny. She moves away slightly, but otherwise doesn't change her serious expression. I get down on the carpet. Why am I always finding myself on the floor with these kids? I wiggle my whole body in a clumsy version of the worm. "Okay, let's do another one together." Mrs. R did say that it might take her a while to warm up. I think I got a carpet burn on my arm.

"MMMMM...like Mmmm, cookies!" No sound yet from Penny, but her mouth is closed, like she might at least be thinking about the letter sound, so I decide to celebrate. "Alright, Penny! You've got it! The next sound is U, like 'UUU gotta do this before you drive Aunt Alexia crazy!'" At this point I'm thinking that sending Ed out of the room might not have been such a great idea after all. I try a new tactic that Mrs. R uses all the time. "Look at my mouth. It's just open. Uuuh." Penny opens her mouth slightly. "Watch out! You'll let flies in there!" I tap her chin and wait for a reaction. For a moment, Penny doesn't say anything, or even move. She closes her mouth again and stares. I am so close to moving to the next letter, mentally reminding myself that we need honey to go with breakfast tomorrow. My brain sometimes—

"Flies?"

That's definitely an inquisitive face! She said something to me! I nearly jump out of my skin and in my mind I am doing an Irish jig on the coffee table. Instead, I remain composed and she asks me, "Why flies?"

"Well, it's like your mouth is a cave. My granny always told me that if I kept my mouth open, flies would get in!"

Penny almost smiles. She takes a breath, opening her mouth wide. "Uuh..." Then she does smile. "Uuuh." We both try again. "Uhhh." I break into a laugh. In the midst of a giggle, I might have imagined it, but I am pretty sure I hear her repeat, "Flies."

"Now you've got it! You remember the snake?" I motion with my hands again. "SSSS..." Penny softly imitates me. "Sss" and then "T." I make sure not to add, "tuh," which Mrs. R reprimanded me about earlier this week. She showed us some of these during parent conferences. Maybe she should make a video, if she's going to be so picky.

Penny repeats the sounds several times and I tap my finger on top of her hand, trying to help her remember the sound.

"No!"

Of course. I try not to let it show in my body language, but I am disappointed.

However, she's talking! This is progress, right? When I speak again, I remember to smile because I know that my face and hands are the things that Penny is always watching. She is not one to get caught up in a world of words and she completely ignored my face. "Is that not how it goes?" Penny shakes her head at my question so I ask how I am supposed to sound out 'T.' I'm not sure what to do with my hand whenever we do this activity, but I raise it anyway. I'm hoping any sort of motion can help us communicate. I just say it, "T. T. T," tapping the sound three times with my tongue.

Is that it? Penny doesn't do anything for the longest time and I think maybe we'd better forget it. Then she brings her two index fingers together like a sideways X and says, "T-t-t," as she shakes her hands up and down.

I act as enthusiastic as I can and attempt to do exactly what Penny had done. She smiles. "You're a good teacher, Penny!"

I don't know if she catches my words because Kelly runs in mid-sentence and they race off to play some game outside.

One more step.

PENNY

Present Day.

By myself. After so many minutes of Miss Burnett's "listening centers." She's the sub. My dream last night about Mom screaming still has me shivering cold. It sounds like she is still screaming in my brain picture. I don't want to be here. We're doing the same thing as yesterday. There are lots of people. Except at that computer station because whatever Gum Guy is doing looks interesting. I only watch him, not doing my work, I think his name is Rob and gum-chewer Rob sits at the desk in front of the computer. Even though there's a school rule about not having gum, he does anyway. One of the other kids asked Ms. Kelley another day and she told that it's something he needs to have and that he is very careful with it. She is our teacher right now. She likes to tell the whole class the most important things together. Still, I think the other girl is right. It's a rule, so it's for everyone, right? After watching for a while, I forget the gum rule as he beats one level, then another on that new computer game we got. We started these computer programs almost two weeks ago. It looks like so much fun as he sits at the desk. He has been there a long time, and I watch the mouse wiggle back and forth. That's a funny name for that weird part? It makes me squirm just thinking about it. I told Kelly I would never touch a mouse! But he clicks on little "classrooms" buttons and opens loads of games. My favorite is this

pointing game where we can make "artworks." Or I could if I used the computer.

Miss Burnett's voice makes me jump. I watch Rob for so long that I miss my teacher walking over. "Oh, I'm so sorry!" Miss Burnett smiles like she really means it. She touches my shoulder so I move my body away and I try to make myself invisible. Miss Burnett says the question again. "Do you want to work on the computer now? It's your turn."

I shake my head so much that my hair slaps into my face. That hurts. But I really really don't want to. After yesterday it will take much more than asking for me to try again. Something shiny from

Gum Guy's backpack. Cool keychain! It really looks like an important key. Maybe it opens something secret. I can try some of the doors down in the basement. Lots of secrets there! I put his key, mine now, in my pocket when he moves over to writing time.

The teacher doesn't say anything. I wonder why, but just sitting here gives me time for thoughts and my mind is full of them today. What if I do this wrong? How to explain it to Mommy? Not Mommy. I keep forgetting. Right now it's Aunt Alexia and Uncle Edmond. What do they think when I do something I'm not supposed to? What do they do? Why can't I act more like Kelly does? She has such twirly handwriting. And she makes it look so easy! If Kelly sees this ugliness she'll never help me again. That's it. I fold my arms. Not going to do it. Any of them. I can't make a mistake. Better not try.

* * *

I watch as Kelly leans on her elbows, her eyes closing. Her fingers go up and down on the pillow and I think in my head that her hand is the bear from Mom's story.

"I don't like those endings," I say to the other end of the bed. We're having a sleepover tonight and it's almost, but not quite, time for bed.

"Why? What do you mean?" Kelly says, but I move my shoulder. "You mean, like, you're not sure what happens after the story?" I feel tears but say yes with my head. Kelly hugs me close and doesn't say something for a long long time. "Well, I don't know," she says. "I kinda like it when there's something more coming but we don't know what it is. Then we can make it turn out how we want it—like in storybooks when they say, 'And they all lived...'" She stops with a smile. She wants me to say, "They all lived..." Wait, "wildly in the woods! Or they all lived..." Wait, "forever in a castle full of cotton candy. Or they all lived..." She doesn't really wait for me for this one, "on a farm with fifty horses!"

She's funny. Okay, one story. "Inside a flower!" I say. We bounce to the bed and follow clouds and I wake up with a happy ending as the sun comes in my window. It's warm.

ALEXIA

Present Day.

When Vici and I greet each other, we rock back and forth in an embrace, like we always do. It was her idea to meet up for a random "kid date," and it is something that we might keep doing, if I am not as worn out as I've been. It's been a long time since seeing her because of course her kids are always involved in something, whether it be school related or otherwise. Recently kids have been raving about a new online game, but I think Vici is more of a "get outside before you play inside" type of person. Regardless, we have carved out time, each with our two little ones, to meet up at a nearby park. These boys probably come here often, but this is our first time playing together outside of the backyard.

Vici's enthusiasm is palpable, but I'm sure it's just because we're getting a break from kids who have so much energy. I'm not as balanced as I used to be, so the hug nearly knocks me over. Then come the twins. Of course, they are bumping into everything and crashing their toys. One of the twins hits the back of Vici's leg. One has a hand in the air, with an airplane attached to the other end. His mouth makes a buzzing sound and he nearly crashes the plane into Kelly's head, who waves it off, as if she's done this several times. They talk back and forth, as intently as only kids can, and Kelly taps me on the elbow.

Kelly says, "We're strategizing with their model airplanes."

"I'm so glad they get to see each other like this." I admit to Vici. "It's good for the girls to see other people besides me and uncle Ed all the time."

Vici nods. "I was a little anxious at first for them to come over here 'cause the kids really haven't seen anyone outside of school. But they begged for an extension. And it isn't like the girls haven't seen people. I mean, we have neighbors, but since we've moved into this new area, kids are scarce. I was anticipating the worst, just waiting for something to go wrong." Vicki explained earlier. "There's being a mom for you." She colored a little but didn't add anything. In a way, she's right.

I nod back, forcing myself to look sincere. She doesn't mean to hurt with her words, but it does. Ed and I have come to terms with not having children, but in situations like this, or when my friends are all on their third and fourth kid, the pain can be acute. More than I thought possible after all this time. On another note, I motion to the kiddos, already playing together as if they were the best of friends. It definitely has been entirely too long for two people who live in the same city. That supermarket meeting was a happy coincidence. I'm not really sure how she finds the time, especially with her stuff going to all the kids' stuff. It always seems like there's one more thing to do. She's good about that, though. She chases her kids around and laughs, like she actually enjoys her kids. I wonder if that would have been me and Ed, had we ever had our own. She lets them run around kind of doing what they want, just because they already know the boundaries, so they don't usually push them. "Hey, don't go over there, Kyle," and she looks at me in exasperation. "They definitely push boundaries today,"

I take that back and laugh, a real one this time. "But it is so much fun to watch! They don't usually have such an audience."

Kade and Karl get into a running match at the beginning and Karl tells anyone who will listen that Kade was trying to take advantage of the situation, so he sits squatting in the dirt for a little bit and gets distracted. Penny walks over to him, observing and making her own figures in the dirt from a pleasant distance. Karl and Kelly head off into some sort of jumping match to see who can jump the highest. One of them scrapes their arm on a tree and seems to think nothing of it. They make up their own game of tag with new rules that change every turn they make. Vici and I get to talk about how church is going, and really just catch up on life. "I'm volunteering at church now, which is going well, but it's keeping me busier than I would have thought."

It's nice to have someone to catch up with. Sometimes I feel like I'm taking advantage of people's time when I hang out with them—everyone, not just Vici. I don't ever want to feel like I'm a burden for somebody, but Vici is always very gracious.

By the time we're nearing the end of our conversation, Penny is watching Karl create his dirt castle and I mention something about the kids having boundless energy. "All. The. Time! I can barely get them to bed each night and they wake up really, really early and they won't sleep past five thirty most days." It's conversations like this that help me remember that I *am* actually helping raise kids of my own. Hopefully it's only temporary.

Is that my hope? I want Deirdra to get better! Absolutely. These kids need their mom. But Ed and I are raising these kids together now and we've got to think about what's best for them. It's hard to relate to Vici and what seems like this perfect family. I know she means well, but her advice is hard to accept when it's coming from someone who has chosen to have her family. Really, it's true. I sound horrible and I don't mean for it to come across that way. I don't know what the best option is for these kids and I'm just hoping that I'm raising them the way that they need to be and giving them enough love.

On our way back, Kelly points out the pumpkins next to all the houses. Some even line the street in greeting. Our pumpkin festival is coming up! Kelly peppers me with questions.

"What's a pumpkin festival?"

"That's a good question, Kelly. It just means that our town gets together in the center of town and we create everything pumpkin-y that you can imagine! We have pumpkin pie eating contests, pumpkin carving, pumpkin seed spitting, decoration competitions, artwork displays. Anything pumpkin you can think of, well, it'll probably be there!"

I'm sure it looks beautiful at night, but we don't come this far into the city very often. When I turn down one of the familiar winding roads and point us home, Kelly starts again. "Woah, woah! Hold on, Penny! We're on a roller coaster! Put your hands up! How do the lights know when to come on?"

Even the trees are bowing to the inevitable autumn. Their leaves are turning red instead of green and the wind is getting more chilly. I'm not quite ready for another changing season, but it seems to be coming anyway.

"Run, run, run! Let's scurry into the house lickety-split!"

DEIRDRA

Two years and two months ago.

Every other night I leave the kids, just for a few hours. They are getting used to being by themselves, and after all, it builds responsibility, right? Kelly's nearly a pre-teen. Gotta grow up sometime. I lock the door, now holding an extra chain and bolt, just in case. They will be safe. I attempt that hollow promise. I run down the steps and march into darkness. It was supposed to be just one time. Now it's become a habit. Money is good, though, and I can't look a gift horse in the mouth. It provides for the kids. So that makes this what I need to do. It's only temporary, and sometimes temporary jobs take longer than others. This moving thing is hard. I'll have to find something more permanent. Soon.

Like what? It laughs into the crevices of questions. I push the doubt aside. I can't make it, one side argues. But I must. I must keep going. Right now the determined part is winning. I sneak past this familiar block until I'm here, a house on the corner, just ten blocks away from our house. Hard to believe. But is it? The outside looks harmless enough. I face the front door and ring the bell. A young woman, probably mid-twenties, opens the door with little more than a grunt. Then she waits expectantly when I hesitate.

"You want something?" the girl snaps.

"Um, I came to talk with Charlie?"

"What? Oh, you mean C-You?"

Clever. I shake my head at the inane nickname, mentally filing that away for a future breakup song. All of this to climb the chart. I'll be done with this soon enough. "Yep, that's him." I toss my hair like this is something I've done a million times before.

"Sure." The girl steps back once. "Well, come on!" She waves her hand impatiently, ushering me into the room. No need to be pushy. It looks clean enough, but the smell hits me hard. There's a long hall and behind that is something that looks like a bookshelf right in the middle, presumably to cut off the view to the rest of the hallway. Unfortunately, it works. It makes me feel like an animal in a cage.

"C-You, this is for you." Like I'm a telephone call. Maybe even less memorable than that. Charlie is sitting on a luxurious light couch with white and gray striped pillows. Gives off the idea that he's lived in luxury for several years. Maybe he has.

"Right..." I don't quite know where to start. "Um, I'm here to make a deal?" My hands hang inert by my side, words floating in the air like the powder that sits on the table in the next room.

He laughs, walking toward me, leaning close. A musty smell of mint oozes off his breath. Attempt at being a gentleman? "Sure, hon. You've ever done this before?" Definitely not. I blush but don't break eye contact. I've got to make this work.

"Not this part of the business, but I used to be into...back when... I'm trying to find something for my kids. I mean, something that I can help my kids..." My voice trails off as he laughs without sound. He looks away, then back at me.

The stare down seems to work. He chuckles again. "I also have dreams. I want a load of money. The problem is, first you've gotta prove that you've got what it takes." His pointing finger punctuates any question that hangs in the air. All my energy is down anyway.

I wait dumbly and exhale. What's the point? It's not worth it. I turn mechanically but he continues. "So what have you got?"

The grip on my arm tells me more than words could. I can't get out of this easily. I shrug through my hesitation, allowing my audacity to glow through the response. "Whatever you're needing. I'm willing to do anything." I reach past my silent no and toss the hundreds onto the table in front of the couch. I cringe as one of them flutters to the floor, free of the rubber band. This could have fed my kids for months. It was nearly two months of my salary. "I've got more where that came from," I bluff.

"Oh, really? Maybe the little mouse has fangs after all!"

He waves over the woman who had answered the door earlier.

"This one might be a keeper, Kenz. Give her five and let's see what she does with it." He grabs a bag from her hand and passes it to me. The lightness surprises me. Like I'm carrying something for cooking and nothing else. A cover of innocence.

"Got it. Thanks." When I leave, I have no idea where to start. Where does one, a single mother trying to deal drugs to make ends meet, sell drugs? It's not like I can look this up on Google. It would lead right back to me. Isn't that how it works? I think for a second about going back inside and asking. But the door slams behind me and I hear a man yell. Not either of the people I've just spoken to. This is a bigger operation than I thought. And I'd better figure it out quickly.

Penny

Present Day.

I hide my face behind a book. This is my castle. I found these comics a long time ago. I didn't even know what words meant. They were just like my scribble drawings. Maybe Kelsey left one lying on the floor. They shouldn't have been there. It makes the house dirty. It was in the hallway because Kelly said it was not enough room for her "stuff." The colors on the page are like butterflies. Not really butterflies, but they have pretty shapes like they flew around before landing on the page. So, like butterflies. I hold the book with pictures all in it. This is better than school. I don't even know the words, but the inside of me is happy. The itty bitty book has stories to tell me that I don't even know yet. Then the end is happy. I want that. After that book there are lots more. Kelly knows I like them and brings more. She says there are some at school, too. But then I need to ask the book lady. There are really famous ones with lots of lines and words. Lots of those. Some of them have more color pages, but not lots of words. I like those. Kelly says those are "independent authors who are looking for a way to make money but just haven't made it yet." I don't understand all her words, but it reminds me something of what Aunt Alexia told Mommy. Is Mommy in-dee-pon-dunt?

* * *

I love the dancing colors, the lines that make tracks in the story and the pretty way that the words make sounds. POW! POP! CRACK! It's like all I'm learning in school pushed in all the pages. And the story keeps going in my head, even when I have to give comics back to the library. One day before school I don't go into my classroom like I should. I go around the corner through the big doors. So many books, taller than the tallest person. All the way high. The lady who keeps books is behind a desk. It's a really big desk and I can only see the top of her head. This lady who keeps the books is always smiling. She leans over her desk and asks if she can help me. My words won't come. She needs to help, but I don't know how to ask. She smiles and shows me with her hand wave. There's a book I know, the one with the red dog and then the bears. But I tell her no with my head. I tell her, "More pictures. With words and pictures on the same page." My words come easier, like they will be kept secret with all the other words. She snaps her fingers and takes me to the books on the far side. They are back behind all my books and the others.

She shows me a shelf that is just right for me. I can sit on the floor like at home and see all the picture-word books. "They are comic books," the lady who keeps books says. And then she points to another group. "They are graphic novels," she says. "Similar to comics, only longer, like a book." I look for a long time. But I know what to choose and I get four that time. I'll come back because there are lots more.

I keep trying all the comic books. An idea POPs into my head, like the balloons in my stories. I can't let it go, like Mommy's songs in her head. Maybe she teached me that. I can draw my pictures from my head. Then when I give my books back, I can still have pictures to remember them. The first person is too hard. There is the head, the cape, the face, the feet. I turn the pages of my book I got, waiting for something just right...*there*! My finger touches that one picture. A hamburger. I don't even like hamburgers, not really, but it's easy. I can do it. I know how to make circles. This is just like a long circle. Something like I don't remember now and the shape turns into more like a table with a skirt. Not a hamburger. If I try, Kelly can help. She knows a lot about shapes and colors, but she's not as good as in this book.

PENNY

Present Day.

"My name is Mrs. Rademacher." She pronounces this in a way that I will never be able to imitate, even with all the help that I've been getting from Mrs. Sanders, this school's speech teacher. "But you can call me 'Mrs. R.' And welcome to the second semester of second grade! I get to be your teacher now, until the end of the year! We're going to learn so much." She tells us that she is from Germany, but came to the United States when she was seventeen for college. Wow! I want to go somewhere else when I grow big enough! Maybe like Chicago. I've heard lots of cool things are there.

Mrs. R. likes us "expressing our opinion through the pen" is what she calls it. We write all that week. And then the next week we are writing compost-somethings in journals, decorating the front of our notebooks, opening laptops, "only to be used while you are at school," and watching Mrs. R. draw funny pictures on the board of how to make a compound sentence. Second grade sure is harder than the last grade!

"Here you go, Penny." Mrs. R. PLOP! s a chart in front of me. It has lots of pictures and small paragraphs of explanations. I look at it only for a little bit and go back to writing my com-po-si-tion. Maybe it's called that because I have to pose in a certain way to write, like getting my picture taken. Pictures. I wonder if I can add pictures to my story when it's all finished.

But Mrs. R. sits down next to me and picks up the pictures. "These are things that can help you when you get scared. Whenever you feel anxious, choose one of these and it can help."

I look at the pictures, all combined into the shape of a wheel, and point to the one closest to me. In the picture a kid squeezes his eyes shut. I feel that expression a lot! In his hand is a big ice cube, larger than any I can find in the freezer.

"That's ice. He has ice," I say, and glance at Mrs. R.

Really quick look.

She doesn't say anything more, but I wait for her to respond. Mrs. R. stares at me for a second, like she's hoping for more.

Then she reaches under my desk and pulls out a dry erase marker. She makes a dot, dot, curve on the corner of my desk and says, "Exactly!" Then she walks over to the next group.

The mark makes a little smile.

DEIRDRA

Two years and two months ago.

"Wait, Deirdra!" A guy runs after us just outside work. I pretend like I don't hear and tell the girls, "We're going to the park! Won't that be fun!" He calls my name again. What is it with these guys? Am I

sending out an 'I'm single' vibe? Go away, annoying person. What is his name again? Dan? I grab both of my kid's hands and plaster on my determined smile, keeping an eye on the wet sidewalk. "I need..." I don't finish that sentence, but Penny looks at me. The urge to shoot up is strong. Kelly is skipping beside us. It's almost like, beyond her silence, my little one understands more than she speaks. A couple months ago I caught her with it. Left a dirty spoon on the bathroom sink. I took it from her with some lame excuse like it was hot. How long had she been in there? She tried to say something but I exploded. Yelled until the tears came. I tried to apologize, but ended up just pushing her out and doing a line. I am a phony and I want to change. But it just is. My words aren't real. Like my smile now.

"It's Dave, remember?" The guy catches up to us. "We talked yesterday. You liked my shoes." Kelly pulls Penny's sleeve and I'm glad they're easily entertained. Kelly jumps up and down. "Look how fast they move, Penny! It's like they've consumed ten billion cups of coffee!"

At first I don't say anything to the man Dave. Maybe he'll go away. But Dave has a smile and is extremely animated. I'm not buying it. "What do you need?" We're not in any hurry, but I tap my foot to emphasize that he's wasting his time. Nothing this guy can say will affect me. I've heard it all.

He takes a step back and smiles at all three of us. The girls of course are extremely interested, Kelly jumping back and forth on her feet even while trying not to look like she's listening. When he waves, she smiles. Kelly waves a little bit, but Penny stares with a frown. "How's the job coming?" he asks, turning back to me.

I just grunt. Let him interpret that.

"Uh, did *el jefe* chew you out for letting me use the phone again? I got a charger now." He pulls a still-creased phone cord from his pocket and stumbles a little as it almost flies out of his hand. Smooth. I almost snicker.

But the kids in my vision correct my focus. "It's not that. It's just…" I breathe. What a day. "I'm just not good at saying no to people."

"And I'm people?"

"And you're people."

"What do you mean? Did I do something wrong?"

"No, it's just that…" I don't finish.

Dave asks questions about the shop, but I shake my head, not in the mood to chat. Then he says, "How is your daughter?" He glances at the girls and my heart speeds up. Before I can protest that it's none of his business, he continues. "The other day, you were telling your boss that you needed to leave early to pick her up. He was…well, he wasn't very happy."

That was an understatement. But I'm not in the mood to humor him. "Both are my kids, actually. Eight and five. Well, nearly six."

Kelly smiles and nods, but thankfully, they still don't jump into the conversation. Dave doesn't get the memo.

"Are they in school?"

"Yeah, but the little one doesn't like it at all. She has some…communication trouble." Penny shakes her head, and I know she's listening. "I've been trying to get together with her teacher about it, but I don't always have the time…work and all." As the words bubble out of my mouth I berate myself. Why am I explaining to this guy?

"But what about…never mind. *No importa*." He says a word in Spanish and I nod. Sure, not important, but then, why did he ask? I've had enough of this.

"Girls, let's go." Then to Dave, a half-hearted, "Sorry."

"How many hours are you working this week?" He doesn't get it, does he?

"Fifty-two, I think. Damon is letting me pick up one of his shifts."

"Would you like to have dinner with me?"

"Uh," my voice catches. But then he wiggles his eyebrows and I laugh. Unintentional, but then I find myself replying, "Sure. Yes, I would love to go to dinner with you. Come on, girls." We walk away and I am positive Dave watches until we reach the end of the block. I whisper to the girls, "Maybe he wants to take it back?" Kelly smiles. She almost is skipping, and words to a new song form in my mind. I love trying to use these happy/sad times to inspire my writing. "Ooh, that'll make a good one!" I say it to myself, but catch myself smiling. This time, a real smile. I catch myself looking back.

* * *

"Sweetie, can you help Mommy by making the bed for me?" She carefully lays down her crayon, then hesitates and picks up the crayon box again, sliding it into one end and snapping the lid closed. Then she opens it again and closes it again. I can't help it, impatience wins. "I am constantly finding little scraps of paper covered in crayon and pencil around the house. You make smudgy marks everywhere! Is anything in this house ever going to be completely clean!" She freezes, then stands up really slowly. She doesn't smile. This catches me by surprise every time. Is she ever happy? By comparison, Kelly smiles, laughs, and chatters away constantly, but Penny rarely holds an expression and almost never laughs. Still, she seems content enough. She used to throw some outrageous tantrums and she can certainly occupy herself for hours with coloring. And at school? Who knows. My baby is new to the whole school thing, and that I wasn't even great at interacting with strangers until middle school. By high school, well...anyways, she'll grow out of it.

Penny skips to the bed, like she's radiating from the smile that I throw her way. Her face is still serious and she flicks her head back and forth and it reminds me of a tiny, wild animal.

"You're a Tigger, little bouncy-pants!" I sing the song from Winnie the Pooh and skip around with her. "Your hair has a mind of its own, Baby." She stops skipping. "Hey, why don't you smile at me? You're like a zombie!" I grab the corner of the blanket and put it in her hand. "Ouch! What was the slap for?" It surprises her, but it shouldn't. Her silence speaks volumes. "I know, I know. I'm sorry. But won't you let me help you?"

Penny shakes her head and turns back around, but when she tries again to pull up the covers, the large pillow on the end keeps them from budging.

"Wait, Penny." This time I pull up the end without touching her. It's gotten worse. I lean in close and whisper, "Do you want to play hide-and-seek for a sec?" She looks at me, but doesn't move. Does that mean yes or no? *You should know that,* the accusing voice breaks through my whisper and I rush on in an overly cheerful voice. It can't win. "Can I lift you into the bed so you can hide under the covers?"

She lifts her elbows up a little and I swing her on the bed and plop her on the mattress.

"Pfff! Like you're soaring into a cloud! You're so light, Sweetie!"

"Whee!" Penny squeals, to my delight. She lays on top of the covers, staring at the opposite wall, and then hits her head again and again on the pillow.

I frown, unsure what I'm seeing. "Penny, are you okay?" Penny blinks a couple times, then nods like she's waiting for me. I cover her with the blankets. I'm imagining things. Nothing is wrong with her.

"Penny, are you okay?" Just looking. Blink. No nod, no matter how long I wait. "Look at me, eye to eye, Penny. It's time to finish the bed!"

I thwack Penny with the pillow and I hold my breath. Will she cry? But when I peek underneath, she is grinning. My girl is actually smiling!

We do this again, up and down with the pillow. "'Toes, knees, arms, and head,'" I sing. It has always come naturally to me, and even grew after my kids were born. They get even more silly. "'It's time for my little one to go to bed! Crawl into the covers more because the dreams have already gone before. Dream of lollipops in the sky or little piglets learning to fly! Whatever your mind holds in your head: Those are the pictures you'll be dreaming in bed!' Penny, do you ever get tired of me singing?" Of course she shakes her head. But something within me wants to believe her. "I've got to practice on someone, right? And you make such better company than a smokey room full of old men! Hm-m-m." I throw the covers on top of her. She can't see my tears. I have to be strong for her. Then back to my silly voice. "There seems to be something in this bed! Maybe I should try putting this pillow up here."

I drop a pillow on her head and laugh. Sounds like a crazy laugh to me. But I'm not there yet. I have to fight it. "Hey, look! A cloud has fallen on your face!"

"Go!" a voice comes from my little child and it startles me. My mouth hangs open for a little bit. Her eyes go wide and she hunches her shoulders down, like she's trying to take it back, be invisible. She freezes and I can see her tiny breaths move the comforter, ever so slightly. I tentatively raise my hand and hover over her stomach. I pull the blanket back. She cringes away from me. Like she's trying to get away! Why is she trying to escape me?

DING-DONG!

The sound of the doorbell stops our game and Penny jumps out of bed. She follows Kelly and race down the stairs to the door. They get down the stairs and freeze while Kelly looks at me and I nod at them in consent. Kelly opens the door. Standing there is a tall man with a fancy shirt and jeans. Kelly whispers something to Penny and points at his bouquet. He has so many colorful flowers in his hands, a balloon of flowers, and he grins at my two girls.

"Hey, Dave," I echo from behind the little heads and nudge their shoulders.

"Come on in, Sir!" Kelly says, like she is bringing a King into our house.

The man steps in and I step back.

"Hola, *Chiquitas*!" He smiles at the girls first. Penny still doesn't know what to make of him. That makes two of us. "Hey," he says the last part to me and passes over the flowers. "It's good to see you." I wish he would stop looking at me. At the same time, I don't.

Kelly asks loads of questions. "Who are you? Is your name Dave? Why are you here? Can you play with us?" With each question, she hops closer to the man until she is by his feet. She hops from one foot to the other, her own little dance, though her nervous energy reminds me of my own withdrawal symptoms. It's been almost forty-eight hours and I'm doing it. Just a minute at a time.

Dave laughs and I motion towards the little group. "Kelly, honey, yes. This is Dave. Do you remember him? And Dave, this is Kelly and over there is Penny. What do you say, girls?"

"Hi. Nice to meet you!" Kelly throws out quickly. She listens almost as well as she talks.

"Nice to meet you too, Kelly. Here's a Kit Kat for each of you." He gives chocolate to Kelly and tries to pass something to Penny, but she ducks and squinches her face together, ducking behind her sister. Instead of being thrown off by this, Kelly reaches in.

"Thanks! Wow! We get candy!" says Kelly, first grabbing the candy from Dave's hand and bending down towards Penny. "Here's yours." My little one takes the candy and Kelly tells her in a stage whisper, "We can't eat these yet, Penny. We have to wait till after we eat dinner." I smile at the two of them and Dave gives the girls a wink.

I throw up my hands in resignation. "I never told them that. I don't know where she learned it." Then to them, "Girls, Dave and I are going to go out for a couple hours. Mrs. Carolyn from across the street is going to stay with you while we're gone." I glance down at my watch. "I wonder why she isn't here yet? She should have been here ten minutes ago. I better give her a call. Where's my phone?" When I charge around, I nearly bowl over Penny, who follows me like a little shadow. Maybe she doesn't want to be with Dave. Surely she's used to strangers in the house. But there's something about this one. "Okay, little shadow. Careful!"

Intending to nudge her away, I place my hands on her shoulder but she doesn't look up. She steps off to one side and won't look at me. This girl. I can never figure out quite what goes on in her head. We march up the stairs toward my bedroom.

"Dave, this won't take long. She's our neighbor, so she should be right over." My little girl bends over, tears in her eyes.

"Mom, something's wrong with Penny! She's—"

Penny throws up all over the carpet. Wonderful way to start the evening.

"Not tonight!" I can't help it. My emotions explode. I knock over my new purse and the contents spill out, some rolling under my bed. Penny doesn't get any better and before I can collect myself, Dave is beside me and scoops her into his arms.

"Do you want me to get her to bed?" Dave says. He pulls back her hair, like he might have done this a hundred times.

I'm stunned and at a loss for words. "N-no. Just maybe, um, carry her to my bathroom."

Penny is a little ragdoll and she is as white as a ghost, but when he starts talking, her little feet bounce up and down. Or maybe that bounce is just Dave. "You know what, Penny?" he says. "Whenever I was sick as a kid, I got to sit at home and watch cartoons all day!"

"The coyote and roadrunner are her favorites," Kelly says. She's so close behind them and bounces up and down like it's Christmas morning. Dave asks about how she has been earlier today and whether or not they might have eaten something bad. Then he rattles off some things that I can try with the girls to make sure they're getting the nutrition they need. Duh, Dave, I'm their mother. This type of thing comes naturally. Shouldn't it?

"These girls never get sick," I start to say. "Well, I mean, when they do, usually it's with the babysitter. They eat a lot sometimes!" Or there was that late night a few weeks ago when I was working until midnight at the bar. When I got home there was orange juice all over the floor. It looked like Kelly had tried to clean it up, but the mess was still sticky and I ended up just falling into bed anyway. I later told the girls that they don't need to get things out of the fridge, but I get the feeling that they didn't tell me the whole story. What more is there to say? I wouldn't trust a single one of my neighbors to watch these gems, and it's teaching Kelly some responsibility. I can't be everywhere at once and the extra cash does us good.

I hope my half-hearted explanation sounds convincing. "They usually sleep a lot when they're sick, but they can wake me up if they need me. She can stay in here." Surely he'll look past the holes in my story. He doesn't know me well enough yet to probe.

"Sweetie, do you want to get in your Mommy's bed? Okay, I can pick her up for you."

I ask, "Kelly, can you grab a pillow from the bed?" We step right outside, leaving Penny in the bathroom for a second.

"Hey, it's going to be alright, Deirdra. Nothing here we can't handle."

"It's just that, this doesn't happen. And then tonight! Hon, do you want me to stay here with you?" I direct this question to my daughter.

"Well, yes," Dave interrupts, "but I think you need to take care of your girls." Dave leans close to me. I punch his arm and grin, attempting to redirect, but his eyes hold me in a vice. My daughter, on the other hand, pushes my arm away when I try to rub her back to console her. Of course not.

"Fine, I'm just in the kitchen, though. I'll come back and check on you in a bit."

"Mom, what are we going to eat?" Kelly asks, and Penny grimaces as well as she can in her pitiful state.

Alexia

Present Day.

Plop into my office chair. Goodness, Deids is so much better at these writing things, but here goes. I'm trying to get my thoughts in order, and all I can think is how I failed my sister. I usually love quiet nights, but something is boiling inside. It's been seven days since we've been granted temporary custody of the girls, and though I know it's the right thing for now, something nags at me. I need to understand my sister better in order to take the best possible care of the girls. And that means doing some research. I write down a few words to direct my scattered thoughts.

What exactly goes through the mind of a drug addict? What is in her heart? I haven't been able to get the answers to these questions from Deirdra, who spends most of the time just staring dully into space or switching channels on the hospital TV set. Is this part of it? I feel like I'm in the dark here. How hard is it to look something up? Should I use a hidden tab...

I've got to get a new laptop! That took forever to boot up. Wow. That's a lot of pink! The fuzzy creature? Ed was showing the girls how to use the paint program yesterday, and they must have saved it to this background. Now where to start? Let me find out what I can. Search "effects of drug addiction"

Hallucinations
Changes in behavior
Irritableness
Lack of sleep
Chills
Paranoia
Involuntary shaking
Bloodshot eyes

Ok, wow that's a lot. Lots of information. My mind is racing. I have seen many of these symptoms in Deirdra. So, then her insistence that the whole incident was due to "one mistake" is, as I suspected, far from accurate. She's been up to something for a while. Deirdra must be a full-blown addict, but she is good at hiding it. Expert.

Though I want to look at this objectively, this the first time she has gotten in over her head. That time right before Kelly? My stolen car came back, but she and her boyfriend were high as kites. Lord, I don't think I can pray her out of this one. Not if she's spiraling back there.

"For once, can You just tell me what is best for these kids, God?"

Yes, I just asked out loud. Good for the soul. How can we take care of them when they've gone through so much? So unfair. Surely this is not God's will. Deep breath. I'm supposed to wait for an answer, right? Ok, focus. Deirdra's been lying to everyone, and the lies have to end. Underneath it all, she's a smart woman and a good mother. Or at least she tries to be. I just have to cut through the lies. Get her back on track.

PENNY

Present Day.

Kelly is riding her bike outside. I watch. The sun feels good on my face. What is it like to ride a bike? Kelly rolls by again and again. We come out here almost every day, since that first day way back when we got here. Kelly says it's been two months. I don't know if she's just joking. All of it sounds like such a long time. We each got a bike when we came and Kelly squealed. I tried riding mine then, but after falling and trying to keep up with Kelly, I decided no. It's easier with my feet on the ground. My favorite is that basket on front, even though it's red, not purple. Purple would be better.

My fingers touch the plastic. I watch Kelly and I make my eyes follow each squiggle movement, back, forth, back and forth. A couple times the front wheel wiggles back and forth, but Kelly fixes it and puts one foot touching the ground. She rides in front of me and she leans so much. She's going to crash. I take a step back, squinching my eyes shut. When I open them, Kelly grins at me.

"C'mon, Penny! Do you want to learn to ride?" She pats the top of the handles on her bike.

"No way, no how!" That new phrase I learned at school is fun to say, especially 'cause all the other kids say it, too.

Kelly stops smiling. "Why noooot? It would be fun!" I shake my head. "Fine," she mumbles so quiet and I pretend not to hear. She pushes with her foot and continues to move in a circle in front of me, turning her bike in one large circle and zooming down the sidewalk.

I move the handles on my bike and put my hand on the seat. It's smooth and cool when I touch it. It doesn't look as amazing as my sister's. It doesn't have those strings down the side. They fly in the wind the faster she goes. I want to fly one day!

"Come on, Pen!" Kelly's voice makes me jump. "Can I teach you just a little bit? Look, yours has wheels on the bottom, so it will keep you from falling so much. It keeps your balance like this." She stretches both her hands and wiggles them as her legs ride an imaginary bike. "It'll be easy, Penny, and I'll run beside you like Uncle Edmond did with me. You'll do great!" I move over so Kelly puts her bike next to me.

"Fine," I mumble. She pushes her bike out of the way and I try to follow, like I saw Kelly do, but it makes a loud SQUEAK! and the wheel feels glued into place. "Ugh!" It still doesn't move. I try pulling, then pushing. With a little more huffing and puffing, the back wheels move and I turn the front wheel easy peasy.

Kelly laughs a little bit. "You don't yank it like a stubborn mule, silly!" She points to my bike.

"That is the kickstand. It keeps your bike standing up." Then she kicks it and it's gone. A magic trick! "Okay, first you need to straddle your bike." My eyes to hers. "Put this leg—" She leans over and taps my right leg two times. "—over this middle part, so it's like you're riding a horse. At least I think so. That's what Uncle Edmond told me." I do this and Kelly gives a loud, "Yee-haw!" The corners of my mouth turn up even though I try to stop them. My heart beats in my chest, like horses running all around in there, but I don't feel the run away feeling. Kelly shows me how to use my hands and turn the wheel. I need to move my foot on the pedal to go forward. "Now let's go! Try it yourself!" She moves her arm away and I try. And then again.

It should be easy. I've watched Kelly try this a million times. When I really do push off, my leg flies in the air, a broken branch. I can't find the pedal! My foot waves wildly and the bicycle rolls down the driveway. The ground seems to keep moving when my wheels touch that part. I can do this. I can— "Ahhh!" I scream and try to jump off. I can't swing my leg over that middle bar and my foot gets caught on the back wheel. I don't know how, but I end up flat on the ground with Kelly above me.

"Penny! Penny! Are you alright? Put your foot back on the pedal every time. Are you hurt?" Her hands go up and down my legs to look for broken parts. My sister pulls the bike back up and moves down close, her face to my face. "Are you sure you're okay? That was a huge fall!"

"Again," I gulp. My heart beats fast, but happy.

"What? Really? You weren't scared?"

It's hard to explain. Yes, I'm scared, but it's a different kind of scared. It doesn't make me want to run away, it makes me want to try again. And again and again, until I figure it out. Until I learn.

I stand up and get the handles. It is easier to balance on the bike again, and I place my foot on the pedal. Inching like a caterpillar, I push with the tippy-tip of my shoe and put it back on the pedal. It works! I'm doing it! Then my front wheel hits grass and I SPLAT! beside my bike again. Human pancake. Over and over we try this, and each time, I end up on the ground after just a few seconds. Kelly teaches me how to turn, but when I try, I lean a little too much or I pull my bike around too fast and run into the grass.

I roll to a stop and put my feet back on the ground. Kelly gives me a high five. "You're getting it!" She cheers. "Pretty soon you'll be riding right beside me! I'm starving! Do you want to go in and get a sandwich?" I shake my head and "push off" with my foot like I'm supposed to, but when I try to look back...CRASH!

"Ugh!" A funny noise comes out of me.

My sister disappears into the house, so I soon get up and wipe myself off. Maybe I should get on the sidewalk. The idea takes me around the corner of the driveway and I still keep going. It works! Only a little bit of wobble. Then when I reach the end, I remember: the turn around. The grass is on one side, but maybe I can go all the way to the far side of the street. There is a small move down to the street and I brake my bike right before turning. Or try. I take a deep breath and hold on the handlebars, my hands squeezed tight. I'm rolling farther out into the street and I say to my brain, *Turn! Turn!* That's not what comes out. "Ugh!"

Stupid voice!

But I roll out past the sidewalk. Down at the end of the street, a red truck turns toward me. Oh no! My arm pulls the front of the bike around, but the truck comes closer and closer. It seems like all my movements are in slow-mo, but not as fun as the robot dance. I make my legs work and I push the air out and bite my teeth together.

If I can just...get... "Oof!"

Something hits my bike and I fly forward. My face ZOOMS toward the street, the world freezes, and I see that my left foot is caught near the wheel. I crash into the street with a SCREEEE—UMPH! Before I can figure out where I am, I hear yelling and a door CLICKS open. Loud voices talking all at the same time. One of them is my uncle's. I move to my back and see the sky. It's light blue, and there's not one cloud up there.

"I saw her the whole time! I wasn't going to hit her," says a voice I don't know. "I was slowing down until she got back to the edge of the street!"

"Penny! Penny!" says Uncle Edmond. He keeps saying it. I'm here, I tell him, but in my mind.

"Did you see what happened?" My aunt's voice comes over with the first two. My eyes are too tired to look and my head hurts. "How did she get out here?"

"She was supposed to stay by the house."

"Where's Kelly?"

"I told her to stay put!"

"Is there anything I can do?"

There's a pause and I struggle to get up, but Uncle Edmond's hand is on my arm. It's big and warm. My body isn't listening anyway, and my whole self is shaking. "Take it easy, sweetie. I'll get you." He scoops me up, a baby in his arms, a floating hot air balloon going toward the house. Aunt Alexia and the other person from the truck keep talking and Kelly is waiting inside. She doesn't say anything, staring at me with big, scared eyes.

Wander:
...to go here and there without really meaning to, just seeing where you end up...

ALEXIA

Present Day.

The day has finally come! Our first big outing. The one Penny and Kelly have been eagerly anticipating for twelve whole days now. When we stumble out of the car, Kelly squealed at her friends and ran off to join them. Ed was just as excited as the girls to be back here. He grew up in this area and it reminds him of being a kid. Reminds is an understatement.

"Alright, girls!" He says, rubbing his hands together. "Let's get those shoes on." Kelly has already vanished, so I guess today is a good day to begin letting her experience what it's like being a pre-teen. Penny finishes strapping on her skates, mostly with the help of Ed, who also insists on walking with her to the edge of the rink. Maybe not as ready to let his little bird fly as he let on! The majority of the past week has been spent listening to Kelly chatter about skating. "It's Penny's first time to go skating! Last time I went I was four, but don't they say it's just like skating a bike or something like that? Means that I can't ever forget. Like an elephant." At the mention of an animal, Penny pulled Kelly into their room where they holed up for two hours drawing animals with skates.

Ed tries giving me some directions for the day. "Sure, Ed. Yes I can. Hehe, right, right. Go get us some popcorn or something. Go!" I sidle to the rink to check on the girls. I can't help myself. I spot them over to one side. They inch toward the open portion of the rink and taller kids whiz around them. This is the largest number of wobbling little humans I've ever seen in one place!

"Now, you can hold on to the side here," Ed shows Penny the railing on both sides of the entrance. Kelly is already creeping toward the center of the rink. "When you're ready, then you can push off like this!" He makes a backwards pushing motion with his foot. "Then you stand there with your knees bent a little bit and move your feet back and forward, like this." Once again, he pretends his tennis shoe is stuck to a prickly carpet. He grins and pats her shoulder, and for once she stands there without moving away. She just looks at him with huge eyes. They don't move for a minute and then Ed bends down, then sits straight on the rink floor. He says something else to her that I can't hear and points to the whirling little humans around them. Fortunately, all are keeping their distance. Kelly is with another group of her friends and she glances over at the two. She waves and returns to talking. Good. After a few minutes, Ed picks himself up, slowly, but with a grin on his face, and heads over to me.

He plops next to me on the bench. "I don't see you out there with your skates on."

"Are you crazy? I'd crack my head open! What were you guys talking about out there?"

Ed shrugs. "Just unicorn stuff. I told her that unicorns like to skate on ice, too. It gives them good practice when they're flying. She didn't seem to buy it."

Maybe it's just my imagination, but even from our spot about twenty feet away, I know I see tears in Penny's eyes. I don't say anything, but elbow Ed and point a little farther down. The girls both tentatively stick out a foot, with Kelly taking to it like a fish to water.

It doesn't take long for Penny's wails to reach me. "I...want..." The rest of this outburst is hidden in a wave of tears. It's too much.

"Maybe this wasn't such a good idea, Ed."

"She's wanting to get out of this, Ladies and Gentleman! What is her choice going to be?" His loud announcement draws eyes.

"Stop it! You're making fun, Ed. Wasn't this your idea?" I'm so torn. Maybe I should go out there. Maybe not, oh, I don't know!

"Allie, how else is she going to learn if she doesn't try new things? I know it's hard. It is. But let her do this. At least for a while. She'll be fine." My Ed and his wisdom.

"I guess so."

"What was that?" He leans in close.

"Yes, you heard right." I poke him in the chest. "You. Were. Right! Now what about that popcorn?" I'll give her ten minutes.

After just three, Penny stops crying, though she still clings to the side with both hands. A couple of the older kids come up and talk to her, and one even tries to reach out and take her hand.

Penny shouts no and sits in a crouched camel position. She loses her grip on the side and starts rolling towards the middle of the rink. That's it. I'll go now. She'll spread her wings later.

DEIRDRA

Two years and three months ago.

"Mom, why doesn't the feather fall?" Penny bends down and does two little hops. "I'm a frog!" She's in a silly mood today, probably because of the fair, and she chats a lot more. There are so many sounds and smells. She points to a small bit of fluff hovering in the air. "It flies forever!" She sticks her arms out and zooms around like a plane, laughing the entire time. Fly away. What a concept. Maybe fly to the moon? Or to another life? An announcer gives a warning over a bullhorn and we all jump, but within a second, my oldest is pulling at her sister's hand.

"Mom, hear that? Let's go, Penny!" Kelly takes Penny's hand and she nearly stumbles. They take off in the crowd and I laugh at first, attempting to follow. Those standing in front of me don't move. Rather, they are rude and give me looks and jeers. From directly behind me, someone calls my name. "Deirdra!" The girls don't stop. Their heads bob in the crowd. I stretch to keep my eyes on them and I follow, ignoring my pursuer. Someone wins popcorn and people around them celebrate. I glance behind me and start mumbling directions to myself. How bad is it going to be if I completely ignore them? Do I need to stop? It's just for a little bit and it might be worth it to get them off my back. I wave to my kids to bring them back and Penny sees me, tugging at Kelly's elbow. Kelly glances up and they both run towards me. They barely make it before I shove them behind a building.

It smells like trash and body odor and other worse things that I can't think about or my own vomit will cover the floor. Penny screams, but we crouch beside the wall with nothing less than a couple scraped knees. "This isn't how I'm going to go," I whisper into the air, frantically looking around for the phantom belonging to the voice. They have me. They *own* me. Kelly is doing her little nervous twitching and I pull her down. There's another spot that's safer. I point it out to my kids and we do a full-on sprint. We're covered, but we're certainly not safe. I throw my hands over my kids and Penny grunts when I accidentally shove her face in the dirt. Better that than us getting shot at.

"Mom, I can't–"

"Sh-h-h!" I tap her head with my hand and she yelps. Something knocks against my palm and I know I'm going to pay for that. But we can't be seen.

"Ouch..." Penny whispers, but I whip my palm around and it connects with her mouth.

"We can't talk!" I whisper hoarsely. I wish that she could interpret how desperate our situation is right now. To be found out. With my children. It would be the worst thing.

Kelly taps her sister on the shoulder and peers into her face. "I hurt my tongue," she says and Kelly nods, putting her finger to her mouth. I snap and I am right up in her face.

"Shut up!" I hiss. Penny's eyes are globes and for a second I know that I caused this. No matter. A cop is there in a matter of minutes, waving a flashlight at us. It shines in our eyes and I'm blinded for an instant. Penny turns her head away and tears fall down her cheek. She gasps and sobs, but no more words come out. It is more pitiful than the animal that has been slinking around our house at night. Only her large eyes with tears mirror my own. And that is something I won't be able to remove for a long time. It's seared in there. Penny's hands shake as she reaches for me. This is when my motherly instinct should kick in, but I shove her down again and scream in her ear. "Go away. I'm not bothering nobody." I'm a protective mama bear crouching over my cubs. I can taste my fear and I can feel my anger roll down my cheeks in hot streams. I will either faint or throw up.

We scream at each other with no real results. That's when they call for backup and two more cars roll up. My daughters huddle next to the brick, deers in the headlight, and I find myself wishing that this place has some sort of secret door so that we would be able to sneak into the pizza restaurant next door. But it doesn't. And we don't. There is no food, only strong hands and I am yanked from my children. I scream and they scream. Kelly grabs at her sister and all I see is my world getting smaller and smaller. I'm taken in the vehicle and my children sit in the alley. By themselves. Surrounded by strangers. I won't hear my daughter's voice for a long time afterwards. And it's my fault.

Present Day.

"What else do you both have to finish?" Uncle Edmond asks me and Kelly when we come in from throwing out the trash. Cleaning days are fun! "Just the vacuuming and the rest of the dishes," Kelly says as she washes her hands in the big sink. "Then each of us has to clean our rooms."

"Alrighty then! Let's hop to it! We've got to finish those chores! Who has vacuuming?"

"I do." I go toward the hall closet where we keep the vacuum.

"She loves vacuuming," Kelly says to Uncle Edmond.

"Wait a second, girlie!" Uncle Edmond grins. "We have one more thing that we've gotta add. Now, since your aunt won't be here for another hour..." He turns the switch for the radio in the kitchen. First, the static screams and I cover my ears. But Uncle Edmond BEEPS through lots and lots of music until he stops at a fast music. It's country. Mom says, "You can always tell by the twang." She says a lot of things about music. Aunt Alexia doesn't listen to country music. Ever. He shakes his head as the guitar TWANGS! Yep. The artist sings something sad about a lost love and being in the open fields. If it's open fields, he could just run to another place, right? Maybe he needs to tell his love. Uncle Edmond turns the volume up so high that it's hard for me to even think and I can't hear all of what he says.

He laughs out loud. "NOW THAT'S WHAT I'M TALKING ABOUT! THIS CAN HELP YOU GET ALL THE CHORES FINISHED!" He dances a jig in the kitchen and goes back upstairs to finish his work.

I look at Kelly who says something with her mouth I can't hear. She points to the vacuum and swings her arm like vacuuming the air. Then she goes toward the pile of dishes in the sink. I look at the radio and really want to turn the volume down. Okay, might as well try this. I turn the vacuum on and still feel the BOOM! BOP! BOOM! CHING-a wang BOP! of the music. I smile, even if the noise does bother me a little. This is one of the first times doing this chore without Aunt Alexia's help. It feels good. I like this feeling better than the fear. I want it to stay.

"Honeybuns, I'm home!" Aunt Alexia says when she comes in the front. It's about an hour later. Telling the time is not as hard as it used to be, especially with those numbers on the digital clocks. Uncle Edmond turns the blaring music down, but my ears still hear booming in my mind. I grin and throw the pencil on my desk. The letter I am making can be for another day. I need to sharpen my pencil anyway. One of those push pencil things. We are practicing friendly letters and I am trying hard to remember all the parts. I always forget to put the date on top, which means it gets squeezed in later, and that just looks "tacky," Teacher says. I leave the unfinished paper folded, not crumbled up in a ball, because that's ugly.

"Aunt Alexia! Aunt Alexia!" Kelly yells out. "We get to go on a field trip next week!"

Aunt Alexia holds up one hand in front of her and points to her ear with the other while making a face like something is hurting her. She does this when Kelly is being too loud. I certainly like this better than Mom's method of screaming back at Kel so that she "knows how it feels."

She goes on just a little softer than before. "We're having a field trip. Aaaand..." She holds that last word out and looks around the room at Uncle Edmond, too, who watches from the doorway. "We get to go skating!" Her voice gets higher and higher and she opens her arms wide, almost like she were saying, "Tah-dah!"

"Wow," Aunt Alexia says. "That's a big deal! Who all is going? Is it just your class?"

"I think so, but I was wondering if Penny could come too, because neither of us have ever been to the skating place before and I think it would be tons of fun!" Kelly must be really excited because she makes huge motions when she says this.

I can't believe it! I get to go skating? I hold my breath and watch my aunt.

"Well, I don't know, Kelly. Penny's teacher might have something else planned for her class, and besides, don't you want to have fun with your friends?"

"Well, yeah, but Penny is my best friend." She puts her hands together with fingers, like she is begging or praying or something.

"What do you think, Penny? If it is okay with Kelly's teacher and with yours, too, do you want to go?" School is getting harder, and even though I've never been skating, the figure skaters on TV are amazing.

"Yes, I want to!"

Aunt Alexia claps her hands once, like she always does when she's made the final decision. "Alright. I'll let your teacher know, and we'll see." Kelly pumps her fist and I jump up and down. "C'mon little monkeys. Let's get ready for supper.

When we're getting in bed at night, my mind thinks so many thoughts. Another new thing! What is this one going to be like? Then another one grows right on top of that thought. Kelly wants me to go. She wants me there, so I will try. I feel a little flutter of something.

"Pst. Penny!" Kelly leans over in her bed. "I betcha I can eat more popcorn than you! Kyle says there's a stand and they make it hot!"

No way, no how!

Present Day.

They finally asked. The question that the girls have not been giving me but that I have dreaded since the moment that they first got here. Because in reality? I don't know how to answer.

"Aunt Alexia, why doesn't Mommy come back for us? Is she in trouble?" Kelly has huge, beautiful eyes, that girl.

I hesitate on how to phrase this in my mind. This is the first time she's said it out loud. One wrong word and the girls could end up hating their mother. Or me. Edmond and I have talked about it. We've whispered about it together, just the two of us, how to tell Kelly and Penny, for a while. It's still a puzzle and I want to tell them the truth, but only in a manner that they can handle. They're still so

young, almost babies. Yet they've already seen so much of the world!
I search for the right words to explain something like this.

Dark and dreary. My mind is cobwebs.
I can't take the H. Not now.
I've got to get out of this ebb
   and flow of my lifestyle.
Who knows what day it is because I've slept
   some days away,
Not working like I need to for my girls
Even if they're not here, I've kept
A close eye on them and remind them, "I love you."
I'm trying hard, but some days....
   Where is that drive in me?
I can't make it through
   but then—
A small envelope of hope is beneath my door
My neighbor starts and stammers because
   we don't talk
But she shows me something she's never given before
And I have a card, a gift card for my kids.
I take it, but shrug away the gesture.
I don't need her pity—what a waste.
Into the pile of bills, hidden among all the other pressures.
   But wait!
Picking up the phone, I dial a number by heart.
—Al? It's me.
I have something.

"Your mommy loves you, both of you, very much! You do know that, right?" I think this is probably the most important thing to convey. "But before Penny was even born, Mommy started taking medicine to feel better. Then she took more. More than she should have, than she needed."

Kelly asked if she was sick.

"No honey, she was sad. She was upset when she broke up with a guy and she decided instead of talking about it, she wanted to forget about it. So she didn't take just a few pieces of medicine. She took enough that she started thinking not like Mommy, but whatever the drugs told her." The girls sit there wide-eyed, and don't say a word. They are listening. Okay, now comes the part where I really have to be careful on how I phrase it. "When a person takes certain types of drugs for a long time, that person can get addicted. This means that it is really hard for that person to stop taking them."

Kelly says, "Like what happened with Mommy."

"Yes. So Mommy might have wanted to stop after a while, because she loves you both so much. And she did for a bit, when Penny was born. But her body wanted more drugs, so it told her to start taking them again." I'm still trying to gauge how the girls are taking it, so at this point I am watching them carefully.

"Why can't she tell herself 'No'?" Kelly is starting to get upset here. I've watched her with Penny and she seems to hold it together fine, so this surprises me. Maybe trying to come to grips with her own emotions is more overwhelming than citing off facts for someone else. Besides, I can't just sweep this under the rug! I still think this is the best. Cautiously.

I tell them, "She tries to, but it's hard with certain types of drugs because they're strong. I have talked to her a whole lot, but sometimes the drug makes it so Mommy doesn't want to listen. She can get mean sometimes, but it's the drugs talking. She loves you."

"She yells." Penny actually says this out loud. Even Kelly looks surprised. But I keep reminding myself to act neutral. She won't come out of her shell with me getting too excited every time she says something. What I really want to do is pick her up and swing her around, and do a happy dance with those girls, right there!

I will myself to focus. Calm. What are they asking? I explain some more. "She gets upset because her body is frustrated. She doesn't know how to handle things well. And..." I wonder for a second how much detail to give, but then I realize these girls needed to know. From everything I've studied, she gets upset when she's trying her hardest and it still doesn't work. But I decide to tell them, "Your mommy having those drugs is getting in the way of her taking care of you. And the law says that someone else needs to take care of you instead, for some time."

Kelly is crying by now, but she still stands up and faces me. I reach out my arm and she hugs me. Penny comes close enough for me to touch her. "You girls are so special! And your mom knows that too. She just can't take care of you right now. I can't be like your Mommy, but I can be your Aunt Alexia." I want to never let these girls go! "I am so extremely glad you are a part of my family."

A loud wail of music hits us right then and we all cover our ears. "Sorry! Sorry!" Ed runs in to explain that that's the loudspeakers. That he's working on the surround system and there's a glitch. He promises to get that done.

Kelly wipes her face. We don't need any more tears right now, so I ask if the girls want to make cookies. They might be able to do it by themselves by now.

"With frosting!"

Another blurt of music vibrates in my body.

Alexia

Present Day.

Kelly went outside to see her sister. Penny's still a little unsure of her feet as her wheels wobble under her. She tripped over the rubber stopper a couple times and fell once. I can't help it. I get tears when Kelly offers her hand. True sisterhood. I know this will change as they grow, but they are there for each other. They are learning this together.

Get a grip Allie! It reminds me of Deirdra and me as kids. Have I ever shown her that kind of care? Oh, surely we did growing up, but when we got older, we just went our separate ways. I had my drama club, volunteering, and other things, and I guess I left my sis behind!

She was so strong-headed I thought she didn't want me. But maybe—

"Aunt Alexia!"

...

"Well, how are you doing out there?"

"Can I talk on this?" she asks, pointing to my work headset.

"Oh, the mic? Sure. I use that for work. Do you want to tell me a story? What do you think of skating today?"

"Um, well, I think it is okay, but I kept slipping! And then...ooh! Popcorn is over there! Can we get some popcorn? Pen! Remember when we used to play Frankenstein? This is like that! We just gotta keep trying until we find steps that work! WHOOO! Let's go back out."

Frankenstein was the scientist, but I won't tell her that. They wobble back out, not graceful, but their skating is a little more functional. They are so much like Deirdra. Determination. They're waving me over. So much for the journaling.

"Wait, we've got to record this! How are they doing out there?"

"Ed, you can't just cut in like that! Haha. Not bad. It reminds me of Deirdra and me. When we used to play together. It's like—hmm, Oh, I can't get emotional here."

"Yep, you're right. Whooo-ee! Yep, that looks just like you, too. Ah! They're up! There you are, Al! In case you didn't catch it, folks, that right there was a wink. Those kiddos aren't the only ones who learned something new today."

That just happened. When did the youngest member in my family get so wise?

The girls' laughter echoes as I finish washing dishes. It can get disturbing to envision what is going on with all those bumps and giggles, but it is a blessing to hear that wonderful sound in our house. It has been so long since we've had such beautiful music here. Maybe it's time to do something together as a family. The last outing with the school didn't go well, so maybe just something for the four of us. The last time we were even remotely successful was when Dave came over again for Jenga and pizza. Not sure if we'll see him again because he got promoted! It sounds like he's finally moving on. "It's time," he acknowledged quietly. Kelly had declared in that moment that her favorite food was pizza, and I assume Penny must have liked it as well, since she ate her entire slice! It's so hard to get that girl to eat anything, much less any sort of food that is good for her, unless we count carrots. For some reason, every time carrots are placed on her plate, Penny devours them. That's one thing at least.

One of our neighbors called this morning, so we're going to go check out her new puppies! She usually calls to check up on the weather, or talk about her kids' newest award. This time it was something different. She was way more distracted than normal and kept interrupting the conversation. I was about to end it when she cut in, "Hey, Al, I know chores are tonight after dinner, but would the girls be able to put off housekeeping a little longer? I have something I need two little girls to help me with."

So two minutes later I choose to ignore as the girls innocently plop back on Penny's bed after jumping on the mattress like a trampoline.

Baby steps.

"Alrighty, girls! Guess what! Do you remember Miss Megan from down the street?" I try to sound chipper, because I am worried about throwing them off their schedule.

"No," Kelly says.

So much for that. "Well, her dog just had puppies, and she said that she needs two girls named Kelly and Penny to come check them out. They were born a couple weeks ago, so they're still a little unsteady, but I promised her that you both could be very gentle. I'll even take pictures so that we can show Uncle Edmond when he gets back tonight."

"Yeah! Puppies! Can we bring one to Uncle Edmond's work?"

"No. That's not happening." I ignore the Edmond-sounding voice in my head that tells me to say yes as much as possible. He says it builds flexibility in my life.

When we get over to Megan's house, we go to the back room. Kelly insists on bringing her jump rope "in case a pup wants to play," but she drops it the second she sees those wiggling fluff-balls. There's a crate with the mother dog, a sheltie, and her five tiny puppies. Since my old Bugs Bunny died, we haven't had much new excitement in the way of animals, unless we count the gray fox that has been nosing around lately.

Kelly immediately picks up a little puppy and it snuggles into her shoulder. She lets out a little giggle and looks at her sister to ask if she wants to hold one. Penny takes a step back. I wonder what she is thinking, whether she's scared of the dog or just doesn't want to hold it.

"Look, Aunt Alexia! It's licking me!" Kelly laughs. Lots of loving, licking, hugs, and fur. We get our fill of puppy love, but Penny hangs back. Kelly is ready to adopt the whole litter and Penny sits in a corner, quite a ways from everything. I am holding a wriggly little pup that bounds out of my arms, over to Penny. She watches it warily and tenses her arms, but seems to realize she can't make any big moves. It sniffs her hand. She moves her body and it jumps onto her leg. Penny gives a little yelp and closes her eyes. It is like the pup runs out of energy right there! It curls up and naps for ten minutes! Kelly rushes over to pet it, but I warn her not to take it out of her lap. The two sit, petting the sleeping beauty.

Lord, please bring joy into their life. Help Penny to smile. I'm constantly praying for both of these girls. They have been through so much.

I promise that we can make pizza that evening. That is a great trick to get the two girls back home. While the dough is rising and the girls watch a movie or something, I want to get some computer work finished. Since the last pandemic, it's been functional to work from home, sending emails and making calls from my corner office. I am so glad for their sake.

Kelly skips all the way home, chattering about the puppies, exclaiming every two seconds, "Aren't they a-DOOR-able?" Even while we're getting ready to make dinner, her excitement doesn't stop.

I'm surprised that when I pour out the flour for the quick dough into a bowl, the girls jump up to help. Kelly offers it to Penny, who grasps the handle of the spoon. I watch carefully. She stands there for more than a second. Most of the time Penny just watches from the sidelines. *Okay, Allie, keep working or the girls are going to notice,* I tell myself. I found Penny sitting on the bathroom counter yesterday morning making faces at herself in the mirror. When we're ready for the movie night, Penny disappears upstairs.

It is unusual, but I decide to give her a few minutes instead of going after her like I normally do. Maybe she needs a little less hovering. Maybe everyone does.

I know that in my head, but actually letting go is another thing.

PENNY

Present Day.

I grab my blanket. My cape is tight around me. But right now I can't put it on my head. I don't want them to know yet. I try to stay hiding a lot because I can only play when it's me. The grownups don't understand. I lie on my back in the grass, some of the sky showing in the middle of the branches. All the clouds look different. They all have their own shapes. What are we building today? I build new places in my head by looking at the sky. They look alive, and sometimes even with my eyes real tight, I can imagine they're really around me and I can explore new places. This place I don't really know is better. Except for Kelly. And Mommy. And most times, Aunt Alexia and Uncle Edmond. They are nice. But my real home is

Mommy. She doesn't really know about this place either. Only the purple bear on my bed because I whisper it to him before I sleep at night.

ALEXIA

Present Day.

She is listening to me. I laugh to myself at the revelation. D makes it so easy to be frustrated with her. So many stupid decisions–selfish decisions really–with barely a thought for her kids. And then she gives me the puppy eyes with the I-have-learned-my-lesson promise. One easily broken. Though for some unknown reason, I love her through the ruins. She has essentially ruined her life and there is nothing that I can do because she won't let me.

Then today, Deids drops in after who knows how many weeks of silence and she has a gift card! Who knows where she got it, and by the looks of her, she should have kept it for her own food. But she let me have it instead. To give something to the girls. Of course I let her stay and I wish I could have done more, but she looked decently clean and told me she was trying. She had a neighbor who had been helping her organize a room in her house, to keep her occupied. She just passed another month mark clean. "And seven days," she reminded me, when I marveled at her accomplishment. "It's a daily process. And then it starts over the next morning."

We finished off two boxes of pizza. She looked thin and haggard, like she hasn't been getting much sleep, but here it is, in solid proof. Fifty dollars on a gift card. She is thinking about her girls! It is an amazement to me! Somewhere in her drug-induced, praise-seeking mental state right now, she still has Penny and Kelly on her mind. That is what makes her a good mother in the first place, and the reason why I can see myself giving her chance after chance.

Rumble of an engine grows inside my head;
a party full of life, but I should be home instead.
I need to escape, to get out of this cage;
making friends and dancing the night away.
The kids will be fine. They're growing up, after all;
I missed Penny's last birthday and when did she get so tall?
This new type of drug will keep me going strong;
I need to finish my job and to prove the voices wrong.
Making time for this life means I'm missing out on another;
I need a hit, I need one like no other.
One part of me knows that my friends only hang around
because of this line of powder I've found
My girls were asleep. My girls were fine;
but there's something that nags me at the back of my mind.
What have I missed? What did I miss?
I don't remember; navigating through this storm
makes me tremble
And I tremble and curl up, hoping it will pass; when did this start?
When did I start dwelling on the past?
I must focus on the here and now, the present is alive;
this is truly the only way that I'm going to survive.

Penny

Present Day.

In my room I bury myself under covers, glad winter is cold. I stop doing everything, except breathe, the heavy part of the blankets pulling on my head. My thoughts are moving all around me. I have a picture of my friends in class flying inside my head, only I imagine they are all little chicks, like in that show. I think of all the things from this new school. My mind goes around and around, like Carla and her space spinning. Maybe I can figure this out, like that puzzle that me and Uncle Edmond are working on. He says, "Sit back and look at it every now and then. Figure out how you want to arrange it. Sometimes you might sort by color, or shape, or sides." Size? "Then you have to be okay with little moves, one moment at a time.

Every little step will lead to the end. *Voila!*" Maybe after a while here, I will be part of this family. School. Friends. Maybe I can fit, too.

"Okay, okay, I've got one for you!" Kelly's voice echoes in my room and my entire body jumps. My sister climbs on the bed with her all-teeth smile. I play punch her arm and Kelly bounces on the bed, squishing my feet.

"Ouch!" I say, but I laugh. She laughs, too. "I'm waiting for you to ask what it is!" I try to roll my eyes. Other kids do. It's like saying,

A phone call can change a life.
I was lounging in my PJs, playing with my three-month clean pin
A sharp ring cuts into my Lost rerun. Forgotten.
Pausing the moment I jump up
Into a new life.
I got the job! On a whim
I applied and that was the call; I'm in!
Life can be funny, one minute dead to the world
The next, jumping into the unknown.
I start in a week.
I'm so excited I'm shaking and wiggle my feet.
I want to dance around
I feel so weak...

"I don't believe it!" or "This is dumb." But I don't really think it's dumb. I want her to keep going. "What?"

"Where do cows go for entertainment? That means to have fun. Do you know, huh?" I shake my head. Kelly waits most times until I speak. Like a game in a game. She tells me a joke. I try to answer. But she keeps going this time. "They go to the moo-vies!" Kelly is not even finished before she's laughing really hard and bends over to laugh in the covers.

We should be doing homework, but papers are everywhere on the bed with empty places where answers should be. "Here's another one! Why do bees have sticky hair?" She looks at me, waiting an extra long time. Must mean she's excited about this one. "What do you think?"

I guess she's going to wait for me every time we start a new joke. "What?" This time I don't wait long. I really do want to hear. The ending is worth it. "Because they use honey combs!" This time Kelly snorts while she's laughing and I giggle. I don't really understand, but this is so fun. I take her joke book. A lot of the words are hard to read, but I find a picture that I like. I point to that tall giraffe. "Do you want me to read this?" she asks. "No, not shaking your head. Do you want to hear this one?"

"Yes." I smile at Kelly.

"Yes, whaaat?" My smile comes off my face and I just look at my sister, hoping she'll keep going. I haven't said the word "please" in a long time. I've practiced with my mouth, just no voice. It reminds me of all those guys that were mean and made Mommy say, "please" before they would do something. I have a funny taste in my mouth and it makes me want to cry.

I can't.

Kelly must see me because she starts reading, loud and fast, "Can a kangaroo jump higher than the Empire State Building? Hmmm, let me explain. We learned about this in a book on New York last year. The Empire State Building is a really, really tall building in New York, which is one of the states in the U.S."

I point at the picture of the kangaroo again and Kelly hops off the bed and starts bouncing around the room, stretching her hands up high. It's so funny! A laugh slips out of my mouth.

DIERDRA

Three years ago.

The girls are a constant surprise. Even after I came in late last night and accidentally knocked over an entire bucket of markers that Penny had left in the middle of the floor. We stayed up for another hour after that. I was starving so I made popcorn and we arranged markers in rainbow order. Moments like these, even at midnight, makes it fun to be around my girls.

"You're it!" Followed by a round of giggles. Penny ducks behind a bush and Kelly takes giant steps in the middle of the playground, exaggerating her movements as she moves alternatively closer and farther away from her sister's hiding place. More giggles from the bush.

An overwhelming wave of sadness crashes over me. It's just me coming off my last high, that's all. It might become my life, where I'm hiding half of myself from the girls. Nothing I can worry about now. I just take a little bit, to help me be here with them, in this moment. *It will run out soon, and then where will you be?* The voice in my head plagues me. It's wrong! But it's also right. There are ways to get off, but this is the best way right now to get them what they need, to be sure they're being taken care of. It's the only thing and it pays better than both my jobs combined! Sometimes they stay at home for a little bit, but they're fine. They're getting better. And really, I'm preparing them for real life.

Life's not nearly as cut and dried as they think it is. Not as much as I used to think, either. I was so innocent, and I didn't see what was right in front of me. Here I am, a druggie and estranged from my family. Never would have imagined it, even a month ago. But then again, a fire is something that disrupts many areas of life. It has blown up in my face. And I am powerless. I must prevail over this! I will do whatever it takes! Only...

What other fires will I have to put out?

ALEXIA
Present Day.

Dear Deirdra,

I hope you are doing well. Enclosed is something that Penny wrote, along with one of Kelly's essays. She's already writing two pages in fifth grade, can you believe it. I hope you can contact us soon.

Lots of love from the girls.

Alexia.

Making slime
How-to, step by step.

Name: Penny Bonner

Glue
Baking soda
Contact solution, like in math!
Yum! FOOD coloring
baby oil
One of the 1st things, we got a big bowl and put
a hole bottle! of glue and olso the baking soda,
which Teacher gives us these little Tspoons to use.
And then we put in just 2 drops of food color, and I
chews the red, but it looked like pink. That's OK and
after this she said that we could pot snells in ours
so I foud 1 that was a smell like cokies bakeing. I
still think mines' the best. She gav us words on the
bored to help us with the writing. Lots of writing.
    Then teacher came and would squirt the 3.
contact solution in our bowl but she wouldn't let us do

it ourselves. Thats OK because evry time I stired my mix it would snell like cokieys bakeing Yum! my favorite smell, 1 of my favorites. She did this a lot and everything got mixed and mixed and after that she put in some more 3. contact solution until it was redy she said hands up! and we couldnt touch until the baby oil she put in at the end. Just a little bit. Then we got to play with it and pull. It felt weird + sticky but lots were smiling so I wanted to like it. I didnt hold it, but I did touch it. With 1 fingr. I will show this to Kelly and see if I can send som to Mom because I know she's geting better and it would make her feel good to play with some. This is an awesome Experiment and this is how-to do it if you want to make slime you should!!!

PENNY

Present Day.

"Look what I found!" Karl raises a beetle in the air, waving it like a prize. I wrinkle my nose, but squat next to him anyway. I want to see how he makes this castle. Aunt Alexia and Vici go back over to the truck to look at something. Uncle Edmond said that she had to bring it so that she could put our bikes in the back. It doesn't matter. I'm not riding that thing. The castle that Kelly and me made before never looked how I wanted. The dirt slid down into a lump. There has to be a way to make the castle stand up. I look over to one

side, then the other, and a beetle POPs right in front of my nose! I jump back, not being very careful. I twist my ankle, but Karl doesn't notice because his grin disappears in a blur. WHUMP! His brother tackles him to the ground. They fall, two dominoes on grass.

"Hey! Hey!" SWING-SWING. He never hits for reals. "I found a beetle! Aw, you made me drop it!"

"Oh, here it is." Kade grabs something and holds it up, waving at his brother. His hand is really full of dirt and the wind blows right then. Dirt flies into my face. Weather likes to attack me. I blink to get it out and make tears in my eyes, but nobody sees. The boys laugh and Kelly pulls Kade's hand closer.

"Let me see that. Ew, that is sooooo gross!" she says. "It looks like a living rock! Only shiny and with legs. Ew! Look how it moves like that!"

"Hey, Karl, you made me drop it again! That was going to be my special bug!" He pushes his brother. Kelly is frozen and watches as they both push back. She opens her mouth and points, but Karl is on top of Kade! They don't even say words; they just move, wrestling with kicking, sometimes throwing in a hand, but mostly using their arms and legs to hold each other down. They wrestle and grunt for a few minutes, one leg going this way, arm grabbing at hair, and a small yelp. An UGH! escapes before my brain can stop it.

One of them says, "Ouch! Hey, you can't do that!"

Karl raises his hands to give up, then he is sideswiped with an arm and they keep going.

"Boys, no wrestling here! We're not at home! You came to play with the girls!" When they hear their mom, they both stop, standing up not too fast. Kade gives Karl one shove before running towards the street. He stops right before the edge. Aunt Alexia always tells us to stay out of the street.

"Hey, Karl! Let's ride bikes!" Then he looks at me. "You have bikes, right?" he says. I am just about to open my mouth when Kelly replies.

"Yeah." She points to the truck. "They're in there."

"Great. Let's go! Can I ride first?" Kelly nods and gets her own bike. I don't want him riding my bike, but I don't want to ride it. I think they might ask the grownups, but one of them, Karl or Kade, I'm not sure, jumps in and starts rolling it. He keeps rolling it until one wheel is close to the ground. Kade or Karl on the ground grabs the handles and then the one in the truck sits down with the other wheel. Then they have both bikes on the ground! Quick as a wink!

I close my eyes and hear yelling and screaming. My mind fills with the last time I got on that bike. Nope. I won't. The two circle the driveway, yelling at each other, and Kade even tries to take his hands off his bike handles. He's not very good because he keeps twisting one way and then the other. But I really can't do it at all. I sit down and put my back against the brick. The concrete is cold, but I won't sit in the grass. It will get me all dirty.

"You don't want to ride?" Kade asks me. I freeze. Is this a time for running? No. I stare at him for a second. I need to be polite. He is our friend. I guess he is, anyway. I shake my head and stare at the bikes again. "Are you sure? It's super fun to go fast!" I just listen. "But then again, you don't have to go fast like Flash. You can go slow." Flash? What is he talking about? A camera? "One time I went so slow that I fell off my bike! Well, not really fell down because my foot caught me, but it was almost like, for a second, the world was spinning backwards." Like SGN? Some Good News, that YouTube video with the smiley guy I used to watch?

He doesn't say anything else, but sits down, just staring at the bikes with me. He makes one loud sigh. Then he is quiet and I want to look over at him to see if he is still breathing. But I'm scared of that because I don't really know him. His foot is wiggling. But he still doesn't say anything.

I could get used to this.

PENNY

Present Day.

"Well, let's see here. What have you drawn today?"

Mrs. Rademacher has her teacher voice on, but she gets next to me, holding my paper. She looks at it the wrong way up. Then there's the color. It's all wrong and I don't know how to make it right.

"It's a—" She turns into a grinch and crumbles up the paper. "Do it again!" she roars, her eyebrows volcanoes shooting unfun says. I blink and it's just her, smiling at me. The daymare flies away. "Did you draw a forest? Look, I see lots of trees. I like the orange one. It looks like a tree in my backyard when I was a little girl. I loved climbing it. Can you write a sentence about your picture? What's your favorite part?" My head says no way. Touches two times and gets up. "Oh, look," her voice talks to the top of my head. "It looks like there's a bear in those woods." Her finger comes down a tree to touch my scribble. I give her eye to eye. She is already going but gives thumbs up. She speaks my same imagine language!

Present Day.

"They might be more like her than you think."

I sit down hard on the bed, the weight of his words sinking into my soul. I don't want to believe it, but he is right. Small things that the girls do; movements or even their looks when they're annoyed. These make me mad and miss her at the same time. And I don't want to ever admit it, but he is right. Most times he is. However, this is something completely different! He takes a step closer to me and his words echo through my head, trying to settle on my very unsettled heart. "You are trying to raise these kids to be like you. And that is a good thing. But maybe they're just a little bit more like your sister. You've got to open up with them about her." Up to this point, their mom has been a shadow, only creating the space that I've needed to pacify the girls' curious minds. "This won't work anymore. They are growing up."

"They're only seven and barely ten years old!"

He shrugs and for a minute I don't think he will say anything. "They are having to grow up quickly, yes. But don't you think the truth is better handled by those who love them? They're going to find out some way eventually."

Penny

Present Day.

I stare at the pencil in my hand. The yellow butterflies glow back at me. If they fly away, can they take me with them? Back to Mom? Back to how life was? I wish that they could just come to life and chew this pencil to bits, so I won't have to finish this project. Every day my teacher asks me to speak a little more. She tells me that she isn't forcing me. "I would love to hear your voice, Penny!" is what she says. The butterflies don't say anything and they get along just fine. Except that one in Alice and Wonderland, but he's kind of creepy anyways, so it doesn't count!

Sometimes I do want to talk. I speak more with just Kelly, and even with Aunt Alexia and Uncle Edmond. But when I get to class, my voice hides in my throat. My brain knows I am going to say the wrong thing, or that I will get in trouble. Or that my tongue will get all tied up.

One teacher said something that scares me. "If you don't practice what you want to say, your mind is going to forget what it means." Is that true? It doesn't feel like my brain is forgetting, and I have lots of conversations inside my head. Maybe they're not enough, not for an almost third-grader. But then I have to sit and think about more, and everyone always says, "Speak!" I can't speak if I don't know the words.

Over there, on that Proud Projects part above her desk, Mrs. R. pinned our writing for the monster project. It's pitiful. "Pit-iii-full" is a word that means exactly how it sounds. Like the pits. Like I've fallen into a big hole and I can't dig myself out. Maybe it's better to stay down here. When Mrs. R. was standing there, right next to me, she was nice, but it made my hand cramp up and my brain freeze. She wanted something awesome and it's awful! But it's still there, above her desk. I don't know why she used it.

Monsters in a deep forest.

That's it. I scrunch up my nose like the old witch on TV, wishing it would go away. I only wrote these words because I found all of them in

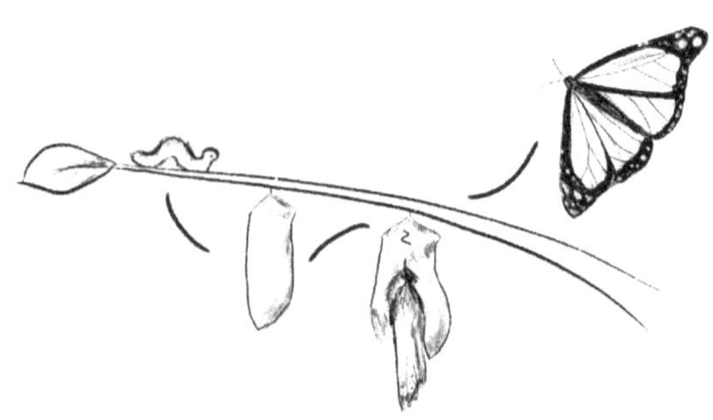

our books here in class or on the word wall. I made sure not to make any mistakes, because she wants it to be our best. I hate my writing. I wanted to use the word "giant," not deep, but it wasn't one of the words on the board.

Why is it so hard to spell? I know exactly what I want to say in my mind, but I can't ever seem to make it look right on paper. It should be one of those spring shows where the words fall right into the part of my brain meant for those words, but in my head, it comes out in a thunderstorm.

I hate thunderstorms, too.

What Mrs. R. doesn't know is that when I got home after that pitiful writing, I opened up my new drawing notebook and finished a story that was almost a half page! But I can't show that one. Only the class work is allowed on the board, at least I think so. And it's wrong. I just made the words sound good, and it looks good to me, but I know Mrs. R. will just say that it isn't right.

The clay sits on my desk: the lump of a frog without arms, part of our put-together project. This art project might turn me into a lump of human without arms. It is called Di-oh-whatever-word, but I can't say that. I roll out my clay to form a snake and take another color to roll a second one. Second is a word that we learned for a special sort of counting, like "second grade!" I wonder if I could use this to count how many days until we see Mommy. I love using that word as much as I can. I'm the second child, the second person in line, that is the second time Mrs. R. has talked to me. Yes, I will take pancakes tomorrow, on the second school day in the week. The list flies through my head. I was the second person who found that word from the word wall, even though Ronnie got to find the next word because Mrs. R. didn't hear me.

I "concentrate" which means my mind is thinking hard and roll my clay into a ball. I always think of my brain turning to orange juice, that slushy stuff in a can. This clay circle is always hard for me to get absolutely right because it always seems like one side goes flat. Pretty soon I create my monster, or blob, as one of the kids says it looks like. A colorful lump with character is what Mrs. R. Might say. She likes character. The body is red even though I wanted pink, with blue arms that are too long. My monster needed to have lots of spikes, but every time I try to stick the yellow spikes on its back, they fall off onto the table. So now there are just yellow dots. These I can press into the clay, even though my monster looks like a little—

"Wow! That looks a little sad, doesn't it?" I might have been thinking that, but to hear it out loud is different. I hold my breath. Is she going to smash it? I never like it when Teacher just starts speaking right beside me. Like she had been invisible and shows up because I got it wrong.

"Can I see if I can help? To make it rounder?"

I put my head down and Mrs. R. puts her arm in front of me and speaks while she is working. She should just smash my monster. Are teachers allowed to do that?

"Okay, we're going to take these arms off. Very...carefully..."

She speaks like I am doing something to help her. She puts the blue strings beside my hand, so I hide my hand in my lap.

"There. Can we make a new body here? It will look just like this. But this way, it won't fall apart when I put it in the oven." She pulls a silver, wrinkly ball out of nowhere. Like magic! "This is the aluminum foil that we need to put inside your ball so that the clay will dry when we put it in the oven."

She wants to destroy my monster! I thought it, but now I really don't want it to happen. I took forever to build this monster and it's exactly how I want it. Almost. Maybe if I make something really good Mommy will like it and want to keep me. I don't need any help to change it. I don't. I don't need help from her! Instead of saying all of this, I squeeze my eyes shut and hear a slap. When I open my eyes right after, Mrs. R. is rubbing her cheek. I didn't feel my hand hit her face, but her face is red and my hand is up in the air. My heart beats really fast and it's like my monster is building inside me, waiting for Mrs. R. to yell. The new kid is right there and I push him. He's sitting too close. Plus, why is his monster so great? Why doesn't Mrs. R. tell *him* what to do, instead of me? Can't I just do this all by myself?

Mrs. R. brings me over to the desk that's all by itself, right next to the supplies. She says to think more and reminds me, "We don't hit in our class because we want to show kindness to everyone, even when we're frustrated."

I am not listening, just thinking about how my teacher will destroy my monster. Destroy is to completely make disappear. To get rid of forever. I don't even like monsters, really. But it was mine. It was supposed to be Mommy's. I lay my head down on my arms over the desk. The tears are hurting my eyes, but I am not going to cry. I am not going to cry. I won't cry! Why can't I figure out how to do things like everyone else? All the other kids have great monsters. Why is mine so bad that the teacher has to tear it up?

When Mrs. R. comes over again, I blink until I can see her. "Penny, let me tell you something." She squats down so that her face is right in front of mine, like a baseball person ready to catch the ball that flies at her. She is probably waiting for me to hit her again. "I'm sorry I had to move you away from everybody else. You don't normally get into trouble, and you've gotten so much better at expressing yourself. But one of our main rules is that we can't hit. We have to use our hands to help others." If I'm quiet she might go away, so I listen. But I don't have to be happy about it. I give the biggest frown I have. Not going to look at her. "Now, you know that when you hit someone, you have to sit out for a while. I need to make sure that you're not going to hurt anyone else." She pauses. Will she go away now? I put my head on my arms. "Penny, I need to see your eyes." So she won't go away. "I need to see your eyes, please." I still show a frown, but look eye to eye. "Penny, I am so proud of you." What? "You put together a monster, and that shows me that you know how to follow what I ask the class to do. But we have rules here that you need to follow, too. Look at me." My eyes hurt when I look. "I make those rules because I need to make sure that everyone in my classroom is safe. And that includes you."

I'm listening now, for reals.

"Penny, I think you need to try harder to make friends. And that means no hitting. What do you say? High five?" She holds up her hand. I kinda want to. But I just can't. I don't want to touch anyone right now. Mrs. R. gives a little nod and tells me that I can go back. I look at the crumple of foil on my desk and then at my clay. I wish that my teacher would come over to help again, but she's with another group. I PLOP! down in my desk. She probably doesn't even remember that I haven't finished Spikey yet. Monster Spikey. No, Mr. Spikey.

My eyes touch places in our classroom, wander from thing to thing. That's another fun word. Wander means to walk, but not really know where you're going, to go here and there without really meaning to. They wander over to the cage with our butterflies. Well, it's not really a cage, it's just a large net where we're keeping all the baby caterpillars. What if one escapes? Or gets into the science lab and starts to glow in the dark? "They're pretty, aren't they?" Mrs. R. is doing it again. She appears so quick that it makes me jump. "Do you want me to get them down so your group can see them?" I point to them, just one finger. I know Mrs. R. doesn't see my hands under my desk, at least I don't think so, but she gets the cage down anyway. She points to some crawling ones.

"Oh, look! That one's clinging to the side!"

The fuzzy thing wiggles back and forth as it crawls up the side of the cage. But then it gets stuck on the side and PWOPS! to the floor. I gasp.

"Don't worry. They do that all the time. It didn't get hurt. Sometimes they only want to try. Yesterday when you were all gone I watched them, and they were all over the place!" Her hands move crazy-like in all directions, like the butterflies are already flying around her. Now the rest of the kids are excited. They throw out questions.

"How many are there?"

"Are they going to be green?"

"No, brown!"

She answers a few questions about the butterflies and another group comes to see. I'm going to see them all, real butterflies, real soon! Pretty ones with different colors. It'll be so much better than those ugly worms now. Or caterpillars. Whatever. They make my skin feel creepy. When they grow, they wave their wings. My whole face smiles. And those colors! They're bee-YOU-ti-full, as Kelly says. Butterflies are like Kelly, who bounces up and down when she's excited.

Mrs. R. reads my mind. I figure that she has some sort of silent understanding of what's going on in my brain. She does that with lots of us. "Each of you in this class is like a butterfly. You are learning new things each day, and by the time summer comes and you move on to the next grade, you'll be someone different!" What does that mean? Like a secret identity? I look next to me, trying to imagine me like Keisha, with fuzzy black hair and freckles. I can't do it. Someone different?

She sends us all back to our desks. Before I know it, Mrs. R. picks up my red ball of clay and says, "Can I help you fix your monster?" I nod once. "Okay, well, we're going to flatten the ball here so that we can wrap it around your foil. Now, I want you to keep the spots, so I will try to peel them off and I'll put them here on the table so that we can use them again." I don't understand what she's talking about and I try to shake my head, but it comes out in-between a yes and no.

I watch as Mrs. R. takes off almost all the spots and lays them next to the stringy arms. There are two stuck in the clay and she only gets part of them off, leaving a mark. But then she grabs a little piece on the edge and flattens it into a pancake. We've practiced doing that, and it's a lot easier to make something flat. She pulls off a little more and adds it to the fat clay pancake.

Then she takes some off and passes it to me. "Now can you try? We need to make several of these, so you can add yours to mine." I take the clay and press into a pancake. "It's really fun to smash something, isn't it?" Mrs. R. hands me another and I push it down again. She picks up her end and puts the tips together. "Can you press here? We need to make it one big piece." Quick as a blink, we make a giant pancake that Mrs. R. wraps around the foil ball. Then she hands it to me. Something is getting made out of this mess!

"Next we need to smush it all around the foil so that we don't see any silver. Can you do that? Like this." She uses her fingers to push down the clay on one side. I do the same a couple times, but only use one finger to poke at the ball. It feels funny. "Now here's the hard part. We need to make this round, so that it looks like a monster's belly." She gives me another lump of clay, and I press it onto the foil, very careful. Then Mrs. R. rolls it in her hands...and it is a ball of clay! "Well look at that!" Mrs. R. smiles and holds it up. "Now it's ready for you to add the dots of yellow!" Okay, maybe this tearing apart thing isn't so bad after all.

DEIRDRA

Three years and five months ago.

"Okay, let's try this! I can do this." I give a little hop for imagination and grab my paper and a pencil. It's so much easier than the computer when I have no idea what to write! At the top I scribble a new signature. Not quite. I lean back, tilt my head, then write another, this one with a large flourish on the D. That looks much more elegant! But do I want to appear elegant? Nope. What's better for someone popular? I attempt another, and that one is better, more lines than loops. I make one more mark, straight through my first two signatures, then copy the last one that I wrote. No, not that one. Another scribble. Better. And a third new signature. No! I scrawl out all of the signatures, making one big blob of pencil marks.

That won't work. And I'm not supposed to be working on signatures anyway. Now, time to figure out what I'm feeling. That's the best direction.

Anger.

Frustration.

Perfect. Solid emotions always work well for moody songs. I write out a few lines and reread what I have. It's okay, but not epic. I can't quite put my finger on it. There has to be something that I feel that will resonate solidly with these people! They've been at work all day, anyways, and they need something to help them get through the night so they can then get through the day. I do, too, for that matter.

Making a new thought is harder ~~to come by~~ to achieve

Scraping by to make a living…what is left of me?

Creating chances for everyone I know, yet

    the resulting promises just seem overgrown.

~~Pulled along by the whims of the wind. It just~~

No, no, and no! Overgrown. Wind. I'm not planting a garden! There is no way this dribble will be ready for tomorrow night! I've got to have a good set. All these covers and old songs won't cut it. They don't want to hear nursery rhymes. They want to be *moved* by something! To be shocked. To…

"Mom, I want it!" Penny jumps up and down in the doorway, pointing accusingly at her sister.

"But it's mine!" Kelly whines. "It really is, Mom."

"Nuh-uh!" Penny bursts into tears.

"Mom, I don't want to watch one of her ABC kids shows again! What about that movie we watched last night? It's better."

"No! No! NOOOOOOOOO!" Penny grabs her sister's arm and Kelly squeals.

I pull Penny off her sister and bend down. "Penny. Look at my face. My face, here. You don't grab Kelly. Kelly, let your sister have this now. We'll watch something later." I wink. The stormcloud passes as quickly as it came, though neither smile. The girls disappear and I turn toward my papers, now scattered on the floor. What else is new?

"Mom!"

"Penny! Not now! Go away. You're making Mommy frustrated." I grunt. "I'm mad, hon, and you're making it worse. Leave Mommy alone. Now." I put my hand over my face, and when I feel her hand on my leg, I swat it away. "No! Mommy needs quiet right now. Not your incessant babbling! Please. Kelly! Come help with your sister." I call my oldest into the room. Both of the girls watch me in silence. I feel myself crumble. There's something about both pairs of eyes looking at me, worse than if they actually said anything. *Breathe. You've got this.* "Okay, girls. Please give Mommy five minutes of quiet and I will be there soon. I have to write this really important song and I have to really focus hard. Okay?"

They nod, and Kelly runs her finger across her mouth like she's zipping her lips. Penny's eyes follow the motion and she does the same, just in three-year-old fashion. Her sister whispers, "Now throw away the key!" Kelly punches her fist in the air, like she's sending her key out into the sky.

Penny tries, throwing an open hand in the air above her head. Then she slams her pointer finger into my hand. "There! That's for you!"

She gave me the key.

PENNY

Present Day.

When I see Aunt Alexia nod for permission, I take one of the cookies on the kitchen table and run up the stairs. I like helping her make cookies. It makes me not remember the scared things, but I have a happy feeling in my stomach. Then I get to eat my happiness, too, and that's fun!

We can eat snacks in our room now, but we also have to clean it up, too. Kelly and me decided to take turns with the big vacuum but most times she does it anyway. The lines on the carpet have to look right! It's like a plane landing road, I guess. I take too long, she says. If I do it well enough, maybe Mommy will come back for us and we can go back to our house.

I shut my room door as quietly as I can and go to a corner of the room, sitting with my legs bent under me, my favorite way of sitting. My hummingbird book is under my nightstand somewhere. Here it is! Aunt Alexia gave me this book after she found one of my drawings. She found it at a book fair, which I guess is probably like the school fair we had that one time. I wish that the hummingbird in my dream was really here, and that it could be with me though all of this. Aunt Alexia tells me that because Mom has not been able to take care of us like she should, she and Uncle Edmond are going to court to try to get cust-ody. That even sounds bad.

When Kelly asks what that means, Aunt Alexia explains that the man that had come over to the house on Monday is one of their lawyers. Aunt Alexia says that this man helps them get what they need. He asks questions because he wants to hear what goes on at home and how we are being taken care of. Aunt Alexia tells me that if they get something called "sole cust-ody" they will let Mom visit, but that we will not live with her anymore. Kelly and me. I play with the edge of the pillow on the couch. I really want to be with Mom, but I want to make cookies with Aunt Alexia and play games or sing silly songs with Uncle Edmond. Not see them ever-ever? Why do I have to choose?

The middle part of the book is my favorite. This is where I put my own drawing of the hummingbird, the one Aunt Alexia saw in the backyard. I use a pencil to trace through the paper. The new teacher here showed me how to do this. But we haven't done anything yet to start drawing. He's afraid we'll make messes, maybe like Mom does. I've tried a lot, but I don't know how to make it look like a real, live pet. No way that I am going to draw in front of all those people. Just draw at home 'cause the school kids will only stare at me more!

The court day comes fast. Before I can say, "Supercalifragilisticexpialidocious," it is here and Vici comes over to watch us while Aunt Alexia, Uncle Edmond, and Mommy go to an important meeting. It's long. It's about us, I know, because everyone had those frowny faces before they left, and when Kelly asked about where they were going, Uncle Edmond says only, "Obey Vici, and we'll see you girls in a little bit."

We have lots of fun playing dominoes, a board game, and a new game I've never heard of called Twister. This is a fun one that I don't know how to play, but somehow we end up in a tickle fight pile on the floor. Then, after a really, really long time, someone comes in the front.

"Penny, Kelly! I'm here!"

Is it Mom?

Is she really here?

"Mommy!" At the same time, Kelly jumps up. We were counting the number of times that the fan went around in circles and talking about this "hearing." I guess that's a place where they get their hearing checked, like at school. They must be finding out if we are healthy enough to stay in a family. Vici goes and talks with Aunt Alexia in the other room.

Before I can hear what they're talking about, Mom bends down to hug both of us and strokes my hair. She is crying. Why is she crying? Is she sad? Does that mean it went wrong?

"You are mine, Babies!" she says. "You get to come home with Mommy! Isn't it great?" She pulls us back and looks in our eyes. Then hugs again. Back and forth, back and forth. Mommy is smiling even with tears, so I know that it has to be okay. She hugs us a second time.

Kelly pulls me up toward our rooms. Mommy's voice gets louder and Aunt Alexia has a high speaking voice like when she is mad.

"Did you hear that?" Kelly whispers. "We get to go home with Mommy! Finally!" She squeaks out the last word and clenches her fist tight in a ball, her face smiling. "Let's go get our stuff ready!" I cover my ears to get away from voices in the room downstairs where Mom and Aunt Alexia talk about Very Important Things. Loud talking.

More like yelling.

Did we do something wrong?

Does this mean now we won't see Aunt Alexia and Uncle Edmond? Ever again?

Family is hard.

PENNY

Present Day.

"Are you all ready for dinner?" says Aunt Alexia.

Uncle Edmond holds up three fingers. "Just three more minutes, hon, okay? Kelly is about to crush me!" He pats his hand over his chest and closes his eyes tight with a funny look on his face and Kelly laughs.

"Oh, really? Well, girls, make sure to let your Uncle win at least one." She places one hand next to her mouth and pretends to whisper, "We don't want to hurt his feelings." Then she points at me and Kelly seems to get the hint.

She leans over to me. "Can you help me, Penny? Should I ask for this one or this one? Which is better?" I look at the cards, but they have pictures and numbers. What do I do? I've never played this, just watched. The card in the middle has a two, so I point to the next number. Three. "Good job, Penny! Let's use the triangle. Hey, Uncle Edmond, do you have any triangles?" Uncle Edmond looks like he is sad, but it's not really real, 'cause he can't keep a sad face. He smiles when he gives over the card. Kelly cheers and hugs me. I let her. "We did it!" she yells. "We beat Uncle Edmond!" I smile then, and I see Aunt Alexia does, too. She winks and looks away.

"Hey, you got a wink from Aunt Alexia!" Uncle Edmond says. "Alexia, I've taught them too well!" He pokes Kelly in the side. She squeals real loud and tries to bury her face in the biggest pillow. When he reaches toward me, I push his arm away. "Okay, I get it! Sorry about that. My bad. Have patience with me, okay?" I don't move and he's not smiling. But he's not yelling either.

"Guys, your playtime is up," says Aunt Alexia. "Now get in here before dinner gets cold. And remember, after dinner, you've got to finish that picture you've been working on for Mommy. You're going home tomorrow!"

"Yessss!" Kelly pumps her fist and gives a little skip before she moves over to her seat at the table.

Aunt Alexia and Uncle Edmond look at each other. "I'm going to miss you girls," she says.

"Here, these are yours now."

"Al, what——"

"The girls made them. They're some drawings that they've worked on while they were here. There's plenty of space back here to add more."

"Oh, Al! That's so thoughtful! What's this? Popcorn?"

"I told Penny it probably wouldn't stay attached. But she insisted."

"She said that?"

"Penny has a way of communicating if you learn to listen."

Silence.

"Don't worry, Deids, you'll get there."

"It's so hard. You've gotten all this together and I just——"

"I had help. I have a couple friends who helped enormously. They taught me what it was like to raise two little ones. And they encouraged me when it was rough."

"That would be nice."

"You just have to ask. I learned that the hard way. So many mistakes. And these papers here? Well, that's the first step."

"Ask a friend..."

"Oh, and Deirdra?"

"Hmm?"

"You can always ask me, too."

"I know, Al. I've always known."

Present Day.

Okay, now I'm awake. Whatever fairyland I have been visiting, it was just a dream. It's just a dream. Where is Ed? Still here. There's a hard sleeping snore echoing in the quiet room. Good.

I move down the hall to our guest room, so I can talk out loud again. So much waste here, all to add to what? There's a lamp, random pictures from years past that I never look at, and several piles of books. The majority of them are how-to books. I like to stay up on things. How to cook, sew, knit, build birdhouses. I've actually done that last one, too. And cooking of course. Knitting frustrates me and sewing takes up too much of my time. I prefer the kitchen mostly, where I can smell my success and relish the faces of people as they eat my creations. Penny and Kelly don't quite appreciate it.

Didn't.

And my favorite, the olive green, overstuffed chair. Ah!

Deirdra.

That's all I can think of. The dream is fading, but it was about something that we used to do as kids. In that dream we were adults, but it still reminded me of where we used to be. How did we wander so far away to where we are now? How did I let her...

Oh! I know! Wow, how did I not see this? I am trying to do all of this—everything—for her. That's what Deirdra must have been trying to tell me! Even as she was going off into la la land, or wherever she goes when she's high, Deirdra was trying to explain that she doesn't need her sister. Well, she does. And her kids certainly do.

So I'm gathering all these little tidbits of information, something she's been trying to tell me for a long time and it finally makes some sense. I'm getting in the way. That hurts. I've been pushing her further over the edge. She's been so desperately trying to prove that she can make it. Desperate for—

To take care of her kids? To manage on her own? What does she need to do? There I go again! Trying to control this. Okay, Allie, get a grip. Don't worry about the future or what to do.

I need to let Deirdra do this.

There is nothing that I will say or do that will speed up the process.

But I want to.

I can't.

I have to ignore those locked drawers in the house. She has the right to keep things secure, right? It doesn't mean that drugs are there. Everything looks so spotless, even her bathroom. The scent diffuser in the wall squirted lavender and the bathroom almost hid that unpleasant scent.

I've reached a dead end. How to combat this? How to—

I can't control her. I can't control Deirdra. Not really. Sure, I can pop in, call her, text her, or even follow her if I'm desperate, but nothing will change her mind. I can control the way I react and that's it. Is that some old saying? I've got to look this up.

Power on my laptop is good. Fully charged. Okay, what am I going to input for a search? There it is. I've faced this question for so long, for so many years. Nearly ten of them, wow. It's time for me to do something now, something that doesn't involve trying to fix her. I have got to put some trust in my sister. I love her. Now I've got to support her and I need some idea of where to start..

There. It's done. This Friday. Okay, my calendar...set.

NARCONON, Family members.

PENNY

Present Day.

"Deids, you can't keep going on like this. Please. Just take it. It's just a small thing. Make my day. It is my six month gift and for the whole family being together again."

I'm not sure what six months means, but it's not long enough. Mom pushes at the lady's hand, who is trying to give her some paper or something. "Kara, I just can't. It's too much. I don't need a guardian angel."

"Sure you do! I got this as a gift for that shower that I worked last Saturday. So, essentially, I'm regifting it. It's not even that nice of a gift on my part."

"Ughh! Look, you're making me cry." Mom always gets mad because she says that she won't show weakness.

"D, you sound like your kids. Worse, actually, because Kelly wouldn't throw a fit, and Penny of course doesn't. I know what that's like. Believe me, I used to—"

I walk back into the house. I've started seeing that most people think just because I'm not talking that I don't get into trouble ever. I have been especially careful lately. I have even given Mommy some extra drawings for the fridge. So she doesn't forget us. I try to keep an eye on those pictures, but Mom said that she is going to put them all in a book or something. This one is my favorite. It looks like a horse that is running away in the wind.

"We're going to have a little artist on our hands, aren't we? Better than what I was doing at your age. I was too busy chasing boys, really, when I was not much older than Kelly. Barely a teen and I was always writing the name of my latest crush on the backs of my notebooks." A beeping comes from upstairs. Must be Mom's alarm. "Oh! NarcAnon! That's right! Good thing I set that." She keeps talking when she goes upstairs. "Yeah, not sure what I was thinking as a teen. I was so dense at that point in my life." She peeks her head into Kelly's room because I can see her feet. "Girls, promise me that you'll focus on the moment. I am going to focus on the moment with you girls!" Um, okay.

"Girl power!" Kelly shouts.

"That's the spirit! No gifts needed. Just our own talent." Mom grins and does a little dance.

DEIRDRA

Three years and six months ago.

I'm creeping in from work when I overhear my little ones. They've barricaded themselves in my closet – for some reason one of their favorite spots. Kids and their fortresses. I edge into my room, getting just within the doorway so that I can hear them without them knowing that I'm standing there. A sound rattles downstairs, but I ignore it.

"It's too dark in here!" Kelly's hand shoots out of the closet, but she's immediately pulled back in. Penny must have grabbed her arm. I can't see Penny, but I can imagine her shaking her head in the dark. A flashlight blinks on, one that I keep beneath my dresses for emergencies. It must be story time.

"Well, thank you!" She giggles and I watch the shadow of her head emerge grotesquely in the middle of my room, like she holds the flashlight up to her chin. Two little giggles and I can't help but smile.

"Now...let's tell ghost stories!"

Penny is definitely not going to agree to that. She has a hard enough time without a nightlight, but we simply can't waste electricity every night with that. Plus, Marc keeps bringing up that the girls have to grow up sometime. But do they?

Kelly begins her story in a spooky voice. She always does this with stories, and especially likes the kinds that someone would tell around a campfire during the summer. I close my eyes and listen to the ridiculous little story, one that I'm sure they will tell over and over in the days to come.

"Once there was a giant bear..." she says, then stops to hit a PUUM! PUUM! PUUM! on a box lid. Probably one of my nice shoes, but they love the sound effects because it puts them in a story. Kelly calls it "the experience". More giggles, then, "This was a very hairy, very large bear. Extra large because he did not come from our world. He came from an aaa-lee-un world!" Her voice comes out all wiggly and Penny laughs again. She must do this a lot with her sister. "Now, in his world, the bear was not so big. Everything there, all the animals, were giant. How did he get here? Well one night the little girl forgot one thing. You know what it was? It was the window! She left it wide open! She didn't know that that night, when the sky was just right, an alien bear could crawl into her room. Yep, it's just like that book with little monsters, or the one in the forest with the three bears. But this bear wasn't looking for the little girl. It just wanted to eat. And it ate fish, like one called salmon. One day it was hunting for fish in the river and fell right through the window into the little girl's room. The girl was scared at first, but it started to talk. It said—"

"That brown bear," I stick my head in and whisper, "creeps and the brown bear crawls. The brown bear searches above all—" I walk around the bed. "—to hunt and search for one specific dish. A slippery, slimy, and wiggly fish!"

Kelly claps her hands and laughs. So does Penny. They haven't heard the new poem yet. It will be a song soon. I can feel it in my bones. The dream is still there to create my songs into something more.

"It's supper time, girls." I wink at them and Kelly does it back. Penny reaches toward me, but at the same time, Marc steps in, grumbling gruffly about what is taking me so long. Then he says something about letting the girls just stay in their room. I moved in with him after the fire, and ever since, he thinks he has a right to run my life. Not much longer now. It looks like Penny is about to duck back in the closet, but Kelly grabs her arm and guides her down after us. It's time to rethink this whole situation.

PENNY

Present Day.

"Hey, Penny!" Mrs. Graff, the speech teacher, smiles at me. She is so tall! Sometimes it's weird being back here, in my old school, after spending lots of the year with Aunt Alexia and Uncle Edmond. Kelly calls some of her friends on the phone from here, but I don't really have any. This is almost the same as back there. Teachers though are different here. Mrs. Graff was here before, but now she's in a different office. The little areas have walls, not real walls, but little pretend walls that are tall enough so we don't see each other even though sometimes it's noisy with kids.

"Hi." Earlier that morning I practiced raising my eyebrows. Kelly and me laughed about it so hard.

Kelly said, "Pen, you should act happier. You can do something. Let's see, hmmm, What about raising your eyebrows? Show excitement! Like this." Kelly tried and her whole face got happier. So I tried it. "That's it! You look so much less formidable. It means scary. Perfect!"

I showed my sister again and Kelly wiggled her eyebrows. A little FIZZ of laughter came out of me. I couldn't help it. We laughed a lot, raising eyebrows and making silly faces.

Mrs. Graff does smile at my eyebrows now. But I can't. It's learning time.

"Let's sit here," Mrs. Graff says and sits on a stool by the table. She wobbles, then puts her foot by my chair. Too close. The book in front of me is the same we've used since I got back. Almost. Not the color. But the same words are on the front. Like she's reading my mind, Mrs. Graff says, "You've switched over to a new book. Now we'll be at the next level! I've heard that you've been doing a lot of good speaking at home, so we're going to try something different. Maybe songs?" I don't even know what to say. I just sing with Kelly. And maybe Mommy. And Uncle Edmond. Okay, lots of people, but not a teacher! "Penny, I know that sometimes it's scary to talk. It's like something is going to attack you and that's your way of hiding from it. By not speaking at all, you don't have to confront it." She shakes her head. "What I mean is that you can find a way to fight that fear. It's going to come. We all get scared, but if we have ways to fight it, it makes it not quite so scary. Now to the fun stuff! Tell me, 'Mrs. Graff, you're so serious!'"

She makes a serious face, but it's not really serious. It's almost funny. Then she smiles for real. She puts a soft thing on the table and it's right next to my hand. She leans forward, like she's going to tell a secret. And she pulls out a long, black stick, like a stiff snake, a blue plastic phone, and a red cup. Like the cups we use at home! I reach toward it but think maybe not and put my hands down. Where they should be.

"Okay. We are going to try something different today. I know we need to work on sounding out more challenging words and expressing ourselves because that's really important. But today we're going to look at something that I think is just as important. Do you know a lot about feelings, Penny?"

I stare. What does she mean? I nod when she just sits there. Smiling. She's waiting for me. I need to do something, but I don't know what. My mind gives a shrug.

"Great!" She pretends like I answered or she saw something that was okay. Did she see me? "There are lots of feelings. Would you be able to draw them for me?" She passes a marker to me. "Now when I give you an emotion, or feeling, I want you to draw it here." She points right in the middle of the table! "This is a dry erase marker, so you'll be fine." Wow, lots of surprises! I haven't done this since maybe all the way back to the very first time in school.

"Now, here's how we're going to do this. I want you to use the marker to draw a scene that matches the word I say. For example, if I say, 'happy,' you draw something that makes you happy. You think you can do that? Okay, here we go. First one. What is something that makes you mad?"

I stare at the table, the lid still on the marker. I want to write, but the BUZZES are in me again. My thoughts are frozen. Breathe. Like Mommy says. But there's a voice in my head that says, "C'mon, Pen! You've got to do this! You can do it. Do the picture." I shake my head. Can't.

"What is it, Penny? Can you not think of anything? Okay, let me give you a hint. You can draw a mean face. Start with a circle, like this..." She draws on her part of the table. "Then you add eyes, and a frowning mouth. I'm also going to make eyebrows. Don't worry. It'll come off, see?" She wipes it away. "*Voila!*" That funny word again. She touches her eyebrow when talking and some of the marker comes off on top of her forehead. "Or I can even draw a picture of my dog. Like so! It makes me really mad when he is up at night barking when I just want to sleep. Can I help you with this?" Her hand waits, not touching mine. "Can I show you how to draw the face?"

I shake my head and put down my marker. Mom won't like it if my clothes get messy.

She tries drawing faces more times but I don't want to do this. I don't know how to draw faces. My world is butterflies and hummingbirds. Mrs. Graff goes to the squishy ball. I have been watching it since the beginning and Mrs. Graff throws the ball in the air. She bounces it from one hand to her other and then the table in front. I don't touch it, so Mrs. Graff grabs it up and says, "I got it!

Now, can you try this? Here, catch!" She throws the ball toward me and I just look, not moving. Not a single inch. The ball crashes into the table and rolls onto the floor. Mrs. Graff's laughs. "Well, how about that? It doesn't bounce like I thought it would." Another giggle and she sits. Why is she laughing? "Oh, Penny, can you throw the ball back to me? I need to practice my throwing abilities apparently." I don't move. Mrs. Graff picks up the ball and puts it right there in front of me. "Penny, I know you can do this. Can you throw the ball back to me?"

No. I don't do anything. I wait but then push the tip-top of the ball with my finger. It moves, but only a very little bit. Mrs. Graff smiles and claps her hands like it was the best ever. "Good job!" I want to be mad. It's just a ball. So I roll my eyes in my head. I don't really do that when I'm with a teacher.

"Penny, thank you for helping me. I wanted to show you that this is a stress ball. Do you see?" She squeezes it in one hand. "This means that when you are upset, you can squeeze this really hard, and it can make you feel better. I know your teachers at your other school might have told you some things about this. Or, if you're scared about something, you can do this." She closes her hand really hard, opens, then closes again, lots of times. I do smile when she makes a silly face.

"See, that's it!" She smiles, too. "The best thing that you can do when you're under stress, or worried about something, is to laugh. It makes you feel so much better and gives you something else to think about." Mrs. Graff opens her hand and the ball is there. "Here. This is yours. It's your very own. I want you to remember to squeeze it anytime you need. I've already told your teachers that you can have this. But you must remember, when you're not using it ,you need to keep it in your backpack." I take it.

Next, she pulls out the long black thing. So weird. But there's no head, so it's not a snake. "This is my magic wand. Can you help me by saying it out loud?"

I'm listening now. My mouth makes the word and I whisper, "Wand." It is just the most tiny tiny sound, and I don't even know if she hears it, but I said it.

"Yep, that's right!" No clapping or jumping for joy this time. Still smiles. "But look, it's broken." She moves the wand to the other side and gives it to me. "Can you fix this? Can you tell me what's wrong?" What am I supposed to do? I'm not touching that! "Here. Take this end. It has to have someone special touch it. Only then does it straighten up." I make a deep breath and hold it as I reach out and take the end. The wand makes a stick in my hand!

"Oh!" I don't know what happened and I'm close to dropping it.

"Oh, wow! Great job! Are you sure you're not a magician? You figured it out!"

Mr. Peters walks in. And I let the wand go on the table. "I'm sorry to cut in on your time," he says. "I know you still have about five more minutes, but we're going to go outside once more before the weekend. And I want to make sure that Penny gets to play today."

"Absolutely!" Mrs. Graff stands and puts the bag on her shoulder. I stand, too, and watch as she puts the cup and phone back in the giant bag. "I have another campus to get to, anyways. We'll come back to these. Don't let me forget! You'll remind me, right?" I nod and follow Mr. Peters.

She still has a smudge of marker on her face.

Playing in the front, running back and forth, I am spent.

My mind goes to bills unpaid, desperate calls

back and forth, everything spent

Since my relapse back

I'm taking one step forward

Eighteen days clean

And ten hours.

Just two more. Then ten more. Then a million.

Never-ending cycle to salvation.

I'm not as sharp without my H

Harder to make a point because I feel like

I'm missing part of my mind

My mind tears apart where I've been

Like a tunnel

With no light.

"Mom, catch!" And I grab a ball thrown across the yard

Have I finally caught the A-train, making it across this mire?

My sister and Edmond drive up to have a chat

Oh no, their talk drives me crazy, such a tirade

Tired of their judgements; since the judge ruling they've retired

from my life

I just can't.

Let us in! Let us try.

I shut myself in. And I cry.

They deserve more.

I can't serve any more.

"Mom? Can we say hi?"

No, Deids. No, I can't get high.

I can't!

What else can go wrong? What else is there? for me?

My hope was lost a long time ago.

Time is not on my side.

PENNY
Present Day.

"Penny, you are going to fail this project! I gave you since last week to get some equations turned in for me, and you've given me nothing. Tell me, are you close?"

I don't know which is definitely not going to happen: finishing the math or talking with my teacher. Mr. Peters makes a sigh noise. "Figure out a way to get it done, Penny. You have until next week. Make sure you've put your name down for presentations on Monday and Tuesday." My head hits my desk. I don't even know what to think. I don't understand these equations because I didn't come to school those days. Mom said it was a brain break. It's easier to pretend like I know what it is in class and I can just copy all the things from the board.

"Psst!" Where is that voice coming from? I don't see anyone looking at me, but the boy next to me, Danny, I think his name is, sticks his head in his backpack and it almost disappears all the way. His hand moves the bag from the inside. "Psst! Penny! Look what I've got!" He has a giant notebook, lots of extra papers stuffed inside, and PLOP! s it on his desk. With one hand. "I've written it all down. My dad's an engineer, so he helps." Mr. Peters isn't watching, he's helping someone with seatwork. Not much time but Danny talks in a softest voice and speaks faster. "Wecanworkontheproject. Together. I'veseenyou. Doodling. Onyourmaathpageandthat-woooooould—make a greeeeeaat project!" His eyes go as big as disks. I think I smile.

"Danny, are you and Penny ready to listen?" He caught us.

Ooh, good, he has the video for social studies. These short videos are great. We're talking about the American Revolution, and each movie keeps going from the one before.

Danny says, "We'll talk later! Talk to your folks. I'll ask again." He leans back in his chair, his front legs off the ground. Mr. Peters has told us not to do this lots of times, but most boys still do and even girls. Not me. I definitely won't. But Danny's different. Really good at math, 'cause Mr. Peters always asks, "Come show how you got that, please?" He writes all the steps, even the really long ones and they're just how they're supposed to be. Even the new ones, he gets those.

Right after school Danny grabs my backpack and I stop. Kelly is right there. So close. "Hey, Pen! I asked Mr. Peters. He said that we could! Only since we're doing it as a group project and no one else is, we're going to write five problems instead of three."

That doesn't sound good. More math?

"Do you think you can do that?"

No.

"Get your scribbling hand ready!"

"What are you talking about?" No, don't tell Kelly!

Danny doesn't hear my mind yell. "We're doing a math project, and Penny's going to help me. We're gonna work together and present it next week. About the new equations we've been learning in class. Can I come over tomorrow after school?"

I feel hiccupy and my neck feels like there's a scarf wrapped around it. He's doing it again. Asking me direct questions. I don't answer in class. Why would I when I'm here? I don't even try.

Kelly jumps in. "I'll ask Mom. Wait just a sec." She texts on her new phone and I peek. One word answer. No. "Can we meet at yours? Our house is...messy."

Danny shrugs. "Sure. That should be no problem." He doesn't say anything else, but runs full speed back to the group and chest bumps another boy. One of his friends that he is always with. I can't remember his name, but I always call him One with the Glasses in my mind. Danny is Wild Hair Dude because it always seems like his hair is about to fly off his head. I wonder if he ever combs it. Maybe boys don't do that.

At Danny's house we talk a lot, about favorite candy and other stuff, then about our math problems. I don't understand it, but Danny is a good teacher. After a really long time talking, we finish. We decide to use real things for each problem, to show how they work. That's the fun part. All of it we put together in a pile. Danny explains well. Mommy comes to pick me up. It's already been two hours! He asks if I can stay for dinner but Mom says no. She doesn't want to come back again.

I wave at him and we drive away. I thought it was fun but hard. Oh, no! I forgot my hat and scarf. "Mom?"

"Hm, hon?"

"Nothing."

Just four more days then the presentation. Not much of a present.

The morning it comes, he is nowhere...just like everyone in my life...He was here yesterday, but I need him now.

"Good morning, Mr. Peters," a voice I know comes from the hall and Danny's face comes in and he's holding a red hat covering his head. And he's holding—my hat! He puts the huge paper of our project on his arm and tosses my purple scarf. In my face. But it's so soft and I don't care. He's here. He says, "You make me do all the work." But he has a big grin. "Sorry I forgot." He sits down and opens the package of pancakes and eats them all without saying anything else.

"Alright, class, announcements are coming on so I need everyone seated." Mr. Peters looks right at me, waiting. I sit down. On our project.

"Oops, sorry!" Danny moves the paper and I sit again, for real this time. I don't eat the pancakes, but the chocolate milk is pretty good. These pancakes can't be as good as Mommy's.

Our turn is after Jose and Kanara's. I am shaking, my hand and my teeth, when we get up there, but when the kids laugh at my drawing of Danny throwing the ball to his big dog and then jumping in the air, I laugh, too. We used a string here to show the length and pretend that fifteen inches is fifteen feet. It's my favorite one of all of them. The class claps really loud after we finish, and lots of kids want to see my drawings or figure out the math puzzle. There are answers on the back. I smile at Danny, who tries a high five. My smile disappears. No. I duck my head and go really fast back to my desk. I pat the top of his desk after he sits and I think he knows. We did good.

DEIRDRA

Three years and seven months ago.

"Listen to this, Penny! I've got a new one for you!" She grins at me. Not even in kindergarten yet, but she loves the songs, no matter how silly they are.

"What do you have, Mom?" Kelly bounces into the room. These girls are great for a first audience. I start humming the first few bars of a new song and wiggle back and forth.

Penny laughs out loud. "Dance mama?"

"Absolutely, Miss Penny! Let's go!" I grab her hands and dance. She nearly falls over, but grins and hops up and down. She gets the zoomies and runs around me, squealing with delight. Just then the phone rings and I rush to grab it. Not now.

Yes, now.

"Hey, guess what, girls?" I catch them right as they're about to play a game with their fort. I grab the edge of the blanket from Penny, who looks at me. "We've got to take this down for now. Mom is going to have a guest. We are going to have to go upstairs. Well, not me, but the two of you." I fold it quickly as I ramble. I know I'm not making much sense, but Kelly nods. She's used to this sort of thing.

"But what if–" Penny starts.

"Hush, hon. Not now. Kelly, can you take her?"

Kelly nods and they head up the stairs. Good.

I thought I was done with this. It's hard to pay for three of us. Besides, I won't use. Five minutes later, there's a sharp rap on the door.

PENNY

Present Day.

At the park I watch Kelly. This is the first in a long time that we've been here. We play the tag from school and Kelly goes up the slide, running. I don't follow, but Kelly does a little dance at the top and makes me laugh. It feels good. Mom goes back and forth, not looking at us, just around, but I don't see anyone. Maybe another friend is coming. Wait, where's Kelly? Oh. Over there. What does Kelly call that place? A spider web. And she's the spider. No way! No how! But maybe these rocks? I go up to them. The rocks are right there in front of me.

"Penny? Kelly?" Mommy says. Kelly drops, crouched under the spider web, and plays in the dirt. "Penny, be careful! You could fall."

My toe does slip and I hang, but my foot is super close to the ground. My heart beats fast and I want to get down a little. But I want to get up. I want to cry.

Will Mommy come get me? I try to call, but my voice won't work. Then Kelly's head peeks over at me. She's at the top. I have to get there. I climb up. All by myself. I made it! Then we run around and back down.

"Let's make a sand castle!" I like that much better than climbing. Kelly sings a silly song about monsters and princesses, making up her own tune as she goes along. "Monsters crunch and swipe, but the princesses will always hide. Monsters attack, then the princesses fight back!" Kelly knows how to make up songs like this 'cause she does all the time. Maybe she'll be a singer like Mommy when she grows big. Mommy is trying and she can teach Kelly. We just get our castle almost done but Mom calls us. First normal, then her serious voice. She gets louder.

"C'mon. C'mon, hurry!" She says it again at the car, but to herself 'cause her words are super quiet. Like someone will hear us. Is someone here? I look around, but don't see anything. Nobody. When we drive home Mom looks back a lot of times. "Get inside! We shouldn't have done that. We shouldn't have been there. It's too much. They'll see!"

She gets food in the kitchen and doesn't say anything else. "Who is it?" Kelly asks my wonderings. I haven't moved from the floor in case there are cameras. I know spies work sneaky.

"Nothing. Nothing. It was nothing, Sweetie. We just won't do that again and it won't happen again. There are just people that I don't want to scc right now. I'm going to keep you. I will. You'll be safe. Let's have dinner." She fills a big bucket for the stove with water. "Let's sing one of your silly songs, Kelly!" Mom moves everything off the table. "Are both of you going to help? You know, you could sing those songs like you both were singing on the playground." She changes her voice, making it low. "Monsters can't win the princess's jewels when, um...the prince riiiides in! Pitiful attempt at a poem, but it's on the spot. Still a success!"

"That was good, Mom! Don't you want to hear another one, Pen?"

I nod. "Yes, Mom sing!" Mom's mouth is open, and I know I surprised her. But I'm really happy! And our yummy food tonight!

"Then let's finish this story. The prince started to hum! There was a favorite song that his mom taught him, before he was even able to walk. Now he couldn't call out because it was dangerous, but he hummed as loud as he could!"

Kelly taps her arm. "And what is the song?"

"It went something like this." Mom's eyes move back and forth, like she is reading something in the air where there's nothing. She smiles and puts all her fingers in the air. "I got it!" Mom hums some music.

"It's our fun song!" Kelly pretend-whispers to me over Mom's lap. She hums along in a higher voice, but Mommy looks like she's crying. She looks at me. I don't hum, but find her eye to eye, like she says. She pushes our shoulders nice-like and sings the last song with us.

DEIRDRA

Three years and eight months ago.

I look around my room and sigh. It is a sorry place. It is 11:30 the night before both school and daycare starts and the girls aren't even close to tired. Not a great way to start the week, but otherwise I might not get to see them. The corner of the room where we've crashed as a last adieu to the summer lounges like a rumpled hug. I move to my own bed, hoping to get some actual sleep before work – another double shift at the hardware store. Too early. My body is complaining after today's shift and aching from muscles I didn't even know I had. Probably lifting all those boxes. I'll walk out eventually. No doubt. But long-term goals are nothing compared to getting food on the table. I kind of like the job, anyway, even if

Shiela can be a pain and Jerry complains more about inventory than he actually stocks. The people who chat while waiting for their car or who search for the latest and greatest gadget really are the best. The stories I overhear! Their lives are little disasters, too, like mine. They just hide it better.

My two darlings munch chips and giggle at an inside joke, attempting whisper voices. They crawl to the foot of the bed, with Kelly's elbows nearly squishing my feet. Their laughter echoes into the hollow worries. Even here in my own home, I'm out of it. I sigh at the mess on the bed covers. The decision to allow popcorn for dinner either makes me the greatest mom in the world or the worst. Every day it is a toss-up. I run my fingers through my newly chopped-off hair. Practical or perfection? These days it's hard to tell. My whole life is a mess.

"Mom, where does the moon come from? Kelly here, she says that it, um, that it..." My youngest, Penny, pauses for a moment to look at her sister, who nods in encouragement. Kelly has displayed a motherly vibe from birth, something that definitely was not inherited from me. Patience has never been a virtue of mine, and I have to physically pinch my lips together as I remind myself of the "wait time" Penny's teacher suggests. It's torture, and my brain wanders as Penny traces her finger on the floor. As usual, she doesn't look up. "Kels said it doesn't really shine. Not really." My littlest rubs her eyes from the corner, refusing to sleep even as she nearly falls over. Her personality is shining out big, even at four, already hinting at a defiant streak. Such an attitude is directly opposed to

Kelly's laid-back personality. And yet somehow our little family fits, like a well-timed coincidental accident. That pretty much describes us to a T.

"Hm." How to explain this for little ones? I turn on my flashlight, shining it toward the bathroom mirror. "Come here a minute." My youngest plops into bed next to me. "Do you see this light over there in the mirror?" Something in the angle causes a flashback to the morning excursion I made before the girls were up. Early morning rewards.

"Yep," she chirps.

"That is like what the moon does. Where is the light really coming from?"

She points to the mirror and I shake my head.

"No, where is the light coming from before it goes over there?"

"Right there! Right there!" Kelly waves her arm and jumps in front of us, putting her finger over the bulb. The room goes completely dark for a moment. Two tiny screams ring out and I can feel Penny's heart speed up.

"That's it, Baby! You got it. The moon is like the mirror. We can see the light over there in the mirror, but it's not really where it comes from. The light in the moon really and truly comes from the sun."

"Really and truly?" both girls echo the familiar saying.

"Really and truly."

Penny puts a hand on top of her head. To me it looks like she's trying to become the moon. Maybe she is.

"Like that." She points to the beam hovering in the room.

I nod. "Just like that."

"What happens if the sun can't reach the moon?" Kelly adds.

I shake my head. Where do these questions come from? We don't even watch TV. The electricity went out several days back and our entertainment options are limited. Hence the reason for watching the movie on the iPad and candles in the dark. I charge all the devices when I'm at work. But mostly it's just waiting, constantly waiting. Usually with the windows open.

It's always been like that. Waiting for acceptance, waiting for their hopeless dad to come back, and now, waiting for electricity. I sigh a hundredth sigh of the day. Dark surrounds me. These girls are the brightest stars in my universe. I switch to my sing-song voice, "If I can't reach the moon / Will you come to me? / One thousand years apart / Then together we'll be." They giggle at the lyrics, a song I had written eons ago. The early years after high school when I attempted a musical career seem like a distant memory. With a toddler on my hip, most studios wouldn't give me the time of day. I haven't written anything substantial in ages, other than a couple local hits. I tap each girl on the head and they jump down to the floor. "Kelly, I think that is a question for your teacher!" The two of them giggle in response. For tonight, this is enough.

I drift off nearly two hours later, listening to their soft snores.

A blaring fire alarm slices into my dreams.

DEIRDRA

Three years and eight months ago.

"Ma'am, the wiring in your house is shot. You're going to have to replace it." I cannot do anything but nod, numb to everything substantial, like my bare feet on the asphalt and the pair of children clinging to me, unusually calm for such a highly intense situation.

This can't be it. No! This is not how it was supposed to turn out. "I—um, what are my options?" I shove hair behind my ear and try to fake nonchalance, despite trembling.

The firefighter shakes his head, mirroring my desperate hope. "There is no other option. Perhaps your landlord will cover it?"

Another hope dashed. There was no way. The landlord had already visited my apartment last week, harping that rent and everything else was due. This is the end of me. What am I supposed to do now? My sister? No, that is unthinkable. What about...every option is no. I shake myself out of my reverie, nodding toward the firefighter. He walks away and I barely notice. I'm on my own now. The next step is up to me, right now an empty hole of options. I am not going to grovel to my sister. She'll only rub in my face what a failure I am. I gather my children, the lost blooms in my garden, the rest turned to charred rubble.

My children. These are the only things in my life that I have left. Until I figure it out, because I will. The only things that matter. I fish my phone out of my nightgown, silently thanking heaven that I had the sense to grab it from the nightstand before rushing out with the kids.

I don't even think before walking down the street. I leave my home, my broken car, my friends, my yard that we just played football in. All of it is obsolete, crumbled like so many discarded songs that are piled next to my bed. Were. My dreams are dead. I cling to my girls, one in either hand. They drag along behind me, Penny continuously looking back as if wondering when it will be time to go to bed. Keep hoping, girls. Even Kelly is yawning. I had better find a spot to stop before they completely collapse. I stop and smile while my brain is whirling.

Where in the world can we go? The very last semblance of home has just gone up in smoke. What are my other options? Think. What about the bridge next to the park we played at yesterday? Yeah, that seems like it will be good, away from the elements, yet not secluded enough to be scary. I nearly tear up while looking at my kids, now playing an impromptu game of tag. They are oblivious to what is going on in their little lives. Kids don't notice what adults do. Right? Something nags, but no time. Gotta keep going. "C'mon, kids, let's go just a little farther," I tell them. It's probably only a mile or so.

If only my phone battery hadn't died. Kelly skips behind me and Penny run-hops, trying to copy her sis. Not too successfully, but she looks like a cute little duckling and she squeals with delight.

Nearly an hour later we wander into the park, having gotten sidetracked by construction and a couple wrong turns. Directions have never been my strong suit. I am frustrated with myself and beyond the point of exhaustion by the time we reach our destination. I lay down my flannel coat and motion to the girls. For tonight, this is home sweet home. "Girls, how would you like to go camping under the stars tonight?"

"Oh, goody!" Kelly says. "You mean with s'mores and everything? I've always wanted to do that!" I arrange our makeshift cot and wish for a couple more layers between us and the cold ground. "Mommy, where's the chocolate?"

"Mmmm? Um, we don't have any tonight. We'll have to get some tomorrow morning."

"Marshmallows?"

"No."

"But I want some now," Kelly pouts.

"Soon, hon, I promise." How many of these promises am I going to break in the upcoming days? We curl together for warmth.

* * *

The next morning I spend my last few bucks on McDonald's, forgoing my breakfast so the girls can fill up on pancakes. Then I'm beyond thinking. I step toward the intersection, by one side where the girls have space to play without getting too close to traffic. I explain to them that I'm going to stay and "rest" for a while and the girls need to play some tag or build some mud castles. Under no circumstances are they to come close to the street. I scribble onto the lid of a used to-go box:

HELP NEEDED. I HAVE KIDS. PLEASE.

I can't even bear the words, but I have to try something. This is the only way I can think of to get some immediate cash. It's not like I can just drop them in the back while I go back to work. I might have to. This is not a permanent solution. Just for today. The cars whiz by, barely noticing me and honking more often than not. I feel like the burden to society I am and understand with greater clarity the folks who do this every day because they must. This isn't for forever, I remind myself. Only one or two days until I can figure something out. Another solution nags at me, but I can't. There is no way I'll make that call. It would be too humiliating.

By the end of the day I have developed a new way to catch attention. When the cars are slowing down to the next light, I smile and wave, and usually there are one or two cars in the span of a couple lights who will give me change or even a dollar or two. One moment Kelly and Penny start jumping up and down next to me and a man leans out, handing me five dollars. "Go get yourself some ice cream." He smiles at them and continues driving. The girls cheer at that and Kelly starts turning cartwheels. They probably think that this is a great day.

"Mommy, this is the first job that I've had ever! Can we do this every day?" My heart sinks to my stomach and leaps into my throat at the same time.

I can't do this. I make a phone call to my neighbor, the one who gives us Christmas cards, and ask for her to bring her car to the park. I hang up, pausing for more than a minute. "Deep breath, Deirdra," I say out loud and follow my own advice.

Then I dial another number. "Hey, it's me. About your offer yesterday. Still interested?"

This is going to be a long night. "Mom, when can we go back to our bed?" Kelly's tiny voice cuts into my motherly worry. How do I talk to her without adding worry? How do I hide the realities of this night from them?

"Girls, tonight is going to be an adventure. We're going to go over to a friend of Mommy's and then I'm going to run an errand." Never mind that it is a place that no child has probably ever entered. Desperate times. And I have to give them somewhere. No way that I'm going to sleep on the ground again with these sweet bugs in my possession. Once was enough.

Possession. I grimace at my own words. Well, here goes nothing. Next step forward.

PENNY

Present Day.

"No, no, no! That's not what it's supposed to look like. C'mon, Penny! You can do this. You did it yesterday. Think, Penny! What is that little rhyme that you use to practice adding numbers?" Mom looks around the room. "Kelly! What is that chant you learned in second grade? To help remember addition problems?"

She doesn't say.

"Kelly!"

"I don't know!" Kelly yells really loud. Like, extra loud.

"But you have to! You remember...like, um, the doubles go together." Mommy laughs a little and stops singing. I wish she would keep going. I like her singing.

"I told you, I don't know! That was forever ago!" Kelly says.

"Hey, *that* rhyme might work!"

My sister rolls her eyes.

"Please come over here, Kelly, and help your sis." Mom pats the couch next to us.

"Aagh! Why do I always have to help? I'm doing stuff!" She crosses her arms and stomps with big steps all the way to her room. That means she doesn't want to work. The new Kelly motions. Mom follows her, and so does her loud voice.

"Because Penny's not in a talking mood right now, and I'd like her to work on her math skills."

"Mom, I'm just a kid, not a mom. Leave me alone. Get out!"

Mom comes back and leans against a chair in the room, closing her eyes. She's done this a lot today and other days, too. "Um, let's see. I—" Mommy puts the paper on the table in the middle and her hand shakes. She uses her other hand for her eyes and takes another breath. Not like a normal breath. Water falls onto the paper, just little drops. Mommy is crying. I sit, watching the tiny ponds like I might see fish swim around. What made Mommy sad?

She goes back to her room and puts the blanket on, just over her feet, like she's trying to stay here in this room. Her eyes always look around, like for an escape. I learned that big word from "Finding Nemo," the fish movie. I stand outside the room. Well, really, it's Kelly's, but we sleep in the same room ever since when I had more nightmares. That was every night for a long time, when Mommy wasn't home. Now we mostly sleep together anyway. It's better for talking and I like it. So I call it our room. Kelly is doing homework in our room, and I don't know how I'll finish mine. Mom can't figure it out and it seems like it's written in words I can't read. I try to sound out, but I can't put the words together.

Present Day.

It was the girls' idea, really. They were so excited to come see us, and Kelly said she was so excited it felt like a party! They were quick to volunteer and helped us last week when we got to see them for a couple hours. It's not the same, but it's good to see the kids again, to laugh with them. Now if we can only get Deids to come around...anyways, she is today!

The girls picked the colors of the balloons in their favorites: pink for Kelly and purple for Penny. Of course Deidra would choose black. But it's her day, so who am I to stand in her way? We were able to arch them over the porch so that they formed a wreath of some sort over the doorway. It really did look elegant, and even though Deids isn't one of those over the top gals, I'm sure she will like it. I laughed when Kelly said that it looked like a castle. Well now that the work is done, I can see what she's talking about. It is elegant, in its own way. I remember the first time those girls walked through those doors. They must have been terrified to come live in a strange place, with people they didn't really know. Them? What about me? I had the weight of the world that first week when it felt like everything I did could break these kids and yet I was the one responsible for keeping them safe and healthy, not just keeping them alive. Once I realized they weren't as fragile as I thought, it got better. Deids' not as fragile as I thought, either.

Speaking of, "There you are, girls! We were waiting for you!" Ed rumbles up the driveway and the girls leap out, running towards the porch. He had requested to pick them all up because he thought it would give Deirdra a chance to take it all in. It takes a second for her to soak in everything, as she gazes first at the balloon arch and the girls twirling in the yard. Then she burst into tears. Ed comes up behind her and awkwardly pats her back. I step toward her and embrace her. Penny sidles up beside her and gingerly takes her hand.

Deirdra laughs and swipes at her eyes with her free hand.

"*Voila!*" Edmond turns toward the kids with a flourish and plays his circus master impression. in a funny voice.

"Look! Balloons are everywhere!" Kelly is lost in her own moment. "It looks even better than I thought!" She flings her hands in the air like she can stir up the magic in the day. Ed passes out a box of stuff he insisted that the girls would need and they certainly seem to enjoy it! Just little trinkets, like wind-up finger toys, feather boas, and princess crowns. Who couldn't feel privileged to rule such a kingdom as ours? Maybe this place is a castle, after all. He steps up toward Deirdra and passes her a feathery wand.

"For you, meh lady!" He flourishes the wand in the air before placing it in her hand and winking at her.

Deirdra flashes him a smile then she walks over towards me, leaning against the porch rail. Deirdra has a way of making me feel like a stranger in my own house. And yet, those tears in her eyes remind me that I would do it all over again. I would watch the girls, I would probably fight with her again, but I would continue loving her despite it all. It's just the way that we're going to be. Forever and always. She tilts her head towards me and I raise my eyebrows. She's up to something. "You have your thinking face on."

She just shrugs. "Why now? The ruling was months ago."

"I realized— " A feather from the crown flies into my mouth when I begin. I spit it out and almost choke. Dierdra tries to say something here, but I put my hand on hers and keep going, trying not to snort. "I realized that I didn't ever celebrate the fact that you and your little ones were all together again, as a family. All I was focused on was that they weren't going to be with me. And that's not fair to you. Or to your girls. They are excited, and we're going to celebrate. A homecoming!" I wave my bag of chips in the air.

"I have no problem with a celebration any time! Let's get this party started!" Deidra plucks up my phone and tweaks something with our music.

"It's our song!" Penny cheers.

You must run, you must fly, you must twirl all around the place...

PENNY

Present day.

A doorbell's **RING!**! then **KNOCK!**-knock-knock-knock-knock! **KNOCK!**-knock-knock-knock! Mom laughs. "It's your Aunt Alexia, Kels. She'll be excited to see you!" Kelly squeals and runs toward the door. Kelly pushes her face into the door to hear the voices then bounces up and down to see through the peek hole, but she's too short.

"I'm getting taller!" she says all the time. I turn the lock thing and Aunt Alexia and Uncle Edmond step in.

"Why, hello, Penny! It's good to see you! And Kelly, come and give me a hug!"

"Hey girls, you've both grown so much!" Uncle Edmond uses his loud voice.

"Deirdra? Are you here?" Aunt Alexia tries the kitchen but Mommy is in the living room.

"Of course I'm here," Mom says.

"It's good to see you. What? No hug?"

"How's it going on your side of the world? The girls are doing great." The words are happy, so I pretend Mom has a real smile.

"Um, sure. It's going well. Pretty quiet without you two running around." Aunt Alexia smiles at both of us. "But yes, I definitely see the girls are in good hands. How are you doing, Deids?"

"I'm fine."

"Aunt Alexia, come look at my room!" Kelly says. "I got a new bedspread! And I want to read you a report from school. I made a craft the other day..." They go up the stairs and their voices go away. Oh, yeah! My picture! I forgot! Mommy hasn't seen this one.

"What have you got there, Penny? Is that a unicorn?" Uncle Edmond sits to look at it and Mommy sits, then stands, then mostly sits again. She's not looking at my picture. She puts her hands on her knees and takes a calm-down breath, just like she taught us.

But after a while she moves to sit next to me. "She's been learning a lot in her new art class, and she gives me tons of pictures all the time."

"Well, you've definitely got to send one to us! That is, if your mom will help with the address," Uncle Edward says.

"I'm sure we could work something out," Mommy tells him.

Aunt Alexia comes back downstairs. "D, you've done up Penny and Kelly's rooms so nicely! How did you manage it?"

"I didn't take out a loan, if that's what you're asking."

That was a long day of shopping! We had all spent all day on a Saturday going to tons and tons of garage sales and then Mom needed to fill up the car with gas and we were both hungry and whining and Mom said we were driving her crazy. But she was the one driving. We had some peanut butter crackers at the gas station and they were pretty good.

"Why are you here? Checking up on me?" Mom asks.

"I, uh, no. It's been weeks since we last saw you. We wanted to come because we hadn't seen you and the girls for a while," Aunt Alexia says.

"Yeah, right. You could have just called. You always do. All the time! You know I can handle them without you nosing yourself into our business!" Mom is yelling now.

"We wanted to see your place, and how the girls are getting along."

"You wanted to check up on me!"

"D, that's not it at all. If we wanted to check up on you, there are better ways to do that. It's why they invented Google."

"I'm doing fine." Mom shakes her head like Aunt Alexia asked something.

"Are you sure about that?" Aunt Alexia shows Mom some envelopes. Then she looks over at me and puts them back down, tapping them again.

"Oh, leave it! We're doing just great. Great. Nearing the end of the month and everything is always tough. I know things are *way* easier at your house!" Mommy takes the envelopes and puts them in a cabinet. That's a loud door. "Quit trying to fix me." Deep breath. Mommy doesn't say it, but I can see her thinking it in her mind because she closes her eyes.

"Deidra." Aunt Alexia does a deep breath, too. Then she keeps talking. "Let's—"

"Hey, Uncle Edmond, Aunt Alexia, tonight's game night! Can you stay?" Kelly comes back in.

"Kelly, not now!" says Mommy. "Go with Penny and—"

"Please, Deirdra?" Then they have a silent conversation only with their eyes. I wish I could learn to do that. Maybe it's a sort of adult super power.

"Fine." Mommy pushes me to follow Kelly and turns to the kitchen. I can hear her getting out things for us to eat. "It'll be an early supper!" she yells out to us.

"WHOOP!" and "YEAH!" from us. Kelly pulls out her favorite deck of UNO!, of course. I thought maybe they would already know how to play. But Uncle Ed asks on every turn.

"Okay, so if I have this blue, I can match it to that one?"

"Only if that one is here, in the middle pile," Kelly says.

"And what about this six?"

"You have to find another six that's down here."

I hear a CLUNK of Mommy pulling something out of the cabinet. It's not an envelope. Mommy is sad or worried or whatever she is when she pulls out the Things. But she's not going to use it, right? 'Cause she promised to keep us, not that Thing, right?

"D, can you help us out here?" Aunt Alexia asks. "Kelly's trying to show us that song she says you play all the time. Ed tried to pluck it out on the guitar when the girls were staying with us, but Penny said it just didn't sound the same."

Mommy comes in and hugs me. "You are my girl. Mine. You, too, Kels."

"Please, Mommy?" Kelly jumps up and down.

"Um, okay. Let me see. Oops, bad key." I love hearing Mom sing again! She even gets up and dances with us!

"See, you should have become a professional singer, Deirdra, instead—"

"What? Instead of what? Instead of wasting my life away? Instead of giving up my two precious girls? Because—" Mommy starts to cry. Kelly looks like she's going to cry, too. "Because I am trying. I am trying hard! And you have no idea what that's like! You have everything that you could ever want!"

"Wait a minute!"

"You couldn't have your own kids so you decided to take mine, is that it? Now I see how it is!"

"Stop it! You are completely—"

"Right? 'Cause I know that's what you're thinking. Even if your perfect life doesn't look like it. You want to take the one thing I have away from me."

"How dare you! You have no idea—"

"What you've been through? Because I'm sure what I have been through has been hell compared to what you've been through. You've never had a worry in your life and you have no right to judge me. I..." Mommy really starts to cry now.

"D, I didn't mean—"

"No, of course you didn't mean! You never mean to. You're the good one, the one who stayed in school and didn't get pregnant with that deadbeat." Nobody says anything for a while. "But you know what, Al? That's why I did it. All of it, the drugs, everything. It's even why I didn't take as good of care of them as I should've sometimes. I was trying to remember. To hang onto that moment. And I didn't want to mess it up. I thought...I thought if I got too close it would fall away. And it did. And now I have nothing." Mommy smiles, but tears are still on her cheeks. "But you know what? It's not nothing." She looks at me and then Kelly. "I got you back. And I'm going to keep you here." Kelly hugs her.

"So what about that song? You want to hear it again?"

Alexia talks really quietly to Mom. "I think we can do that."

It's one of those days where you just want to play
And the day is spraying problems in your face
So squeeze your eyes shut and shout to the sky.
Ker-SWISH!, ker-SWASH! I'm going to fly!

I'm going to jump and dance all over the place
'Cause troubles will come almost any day
It's my turn to look my enemy in the eyes.
La-la-la-di-la! No matter what, I'm going to try!

I'm going to la-di-la, BUM shi-BOO
And when it gets bad a little shimmy-YAH too!
BUM shi-BUM and BOP shi-BOO
A little la-la-la and MOO! QUACK! MOO!

Dance around and ignore the worries 'cause I'll
KOP di-BAM and SHOO di-SLIDE! with a
BOPPITY-BAP BAM! my troubles will all hide AWAAAAY
SWISH di-SWISH and KICK! and SLIDE!
Do a little shimmy and JUMP!

Screaming seems to be the only communication I am capable of.
I push away all those who try to help, even my family.
My responsibilities call and knock and flood my conscience.
How can I become all that they need?
Missing deadlines and replying with pitiful reasons--so heavy...
That's all I'm left with when I'm confronted.
I ignore those who care and make excuses without cause.

This time will be my last--I will tell myself again and again.
But the temptation is real and I ignore my own determination.
Is my love for my kids not enough for me?
What is going to happen to them if I'm gone?
Really, though,

What.
About.
Me?

PENNY

Present Day.

What are you looking at? I don't say this out loud, but my shoulder touches Kelly's shoulder and we look out the window together. My voice doesn't say, but she answers me.

"Look down there, Penny." She points her finger. At the car, I think. I nod. "Mom has been down there for a really long time and it looks like she's talking on the phone, but she's not. She keeps laughing and one time it looked like she fell asleep." I don't know what that means, so I just watch. "I think she's gotten it again. The drugs. She acts funny, like she's scared of something that's not there, and she talks to herself."

"Why?" I've learned not to ask many questions, but with Kelly it's always okay.

"She wants to...oh, I don't know, Penny. She says that the stuff makes her do her job better. I don't think she always knows what is happening when she is taking the drugs."

"Like sleepwalking?"

"Maybe a little like sleepwalking. Like Frankenstein! Ooooh!" Kelly sticks her arms out like she's a zombie monster. She tickles me and I try to run but she holds my arms.

"Stop! Stop!" She tickles me more but then lets me go. I like her playing with me. She is always there. Maybe Mom can be there, too. If the drugs stop being her friend first. Then she could see us, not the pictures in her mind. Kelly shows a silly face and wiggles her fingers. I laugh and move back.

It's just for tonight. Just a slip-up.
It has to be.

I can't be falling…

Present Day.

"Hey, Kelly, you know what?"

"Hmmm?"

Kelly's fingers touch the bench. I'm on the other side and stare at kids on the playground. We finished walking around the playground and saw ducks, but Mommy said that we're not going home yet, and Kelly is in one of her moods. Mom calls it being a teenager, but I think she's just being mean. She won't play and she won't tell stories. This park is not a long walk from our house and Mommy told us we're big enough to go to the park, just us. She said a time to go back home, but I don't know it.

"Kelly?"

"Hang on just a minute. Let me finish this chapter. We're supposed to have our books turned in tomorrow." Kelly always has a book on the playground. She puts one finger in the air and won't look at me. Still reading. Is it a song book? Maybe one for exercising? It has a bike on the blue front and it looks like it's floating in clouds. That's silly, like my mind pictures. Why would she be reading that? She glares at me and puts the book in her lap so I can only see the words. But I saw it! It has the name of the song we used to sing and dance way back when we were really little, like maybe kindergarten. One where you turn yourself around. Hokey Pokey or something?

"Is—"

"Shh!"

I turn away from her and then decide really fast I'm going to walk home anyway, even if it's not time to. One street we have to cross at and I stop. A car slows down and the driver inside waves at me, just like they do when Mommy is with us. I must look older! I kinda hop skip, still just a teensy bit afraid the car will start driving before I get all the way across.

At home I know I'm supposed to wait in my room, but I go over to Mom's room. The door is closed and it looks like the light is off. I **KNOCK!** super quiet, and again just in case. Nothing inside, so I open the door. The room is dark and the window doesn't have much light. If I stay here long enough I could forget that it's daytime. "Mom?" I blink a couple times and someone is in bed. Mom? I step closer and maybe Mom's sleeping. One arm is out on top of the covers. I almost run from the room and something stops in my throat. There is something...is that? Yes. In the middle of her arm there's a needle, like the one before, but it is still in her arm. I don't know. Do I need to wake her up or call the police or leave it? Nothing works. I can't move, I can't think, I can't breathe. I can't even blink. I've got to get out! Get help! Kelly would know what to do.

Then a huge fear hand grabs me and I'm shaking and running as fast as I can back to my room. No place to hide. I jump on my bed and pull back the covers, my bright purple pillow staring at me. I squeeze it tight, wishing that it would bring me to a world far away from here. I curl up under my covers and don't think about anything except squeezing my eyes shut and getting far away but the needle shows up in my brain. I almost scream.

And it's my fault.

She told us she was good, that she wasn't going to do the drugs because she loves us. So if she's doing them, what does that mean? Why does Mommy hate us? Is she mad at me because I didn't do anything? Just left her there sleeping? I'm a scaredy cat. She is always sad and doesn't want to play with us anymore. We have to do it ourselves. I am alone—

"What is it, Penny?" Kelly sounds like she's mad, too. She is already here, so she must have followed me from the park right after. I didn't hear her come in. She makes a HUFF noise and I can't see her but her voice is so close she must be in my room. This is the first time we've had our own rooms so she doesn't normally come in here. Is she going to be mad at me, too? "Penny?" She sounds different now. I don't hear anything, but it feels like something is on top of me, then it gets heavier. I move the blanket. Kelly is sitting next to me. "Did something happen? Are you okay?"

I have that stuck-throat feeling again and my eyes almost cry tears. Then I do. The knot in my stomach grows tighter and tighter. "Mommy—" I GULP some air, but can't breathe. "Mommy got..." My teeth are closed together tight, not letting words out. "Why...does...Mommy...hurt...?" And then more crying. I have hiccups. Kelly rubs my back and that helps. Kelly never hiccup cries.

"I know. Mommy is doing her drugs right now. Did you see that? With the..." She can't even say.

I nod. We both know.

A noise comes out of Kelly. "I—um, it's why I stay in my room. I want to just read so that I don't have to see. All that she's doing. That day that Mom wouldn't get up and all those people came. Do you remember? All I did was scream. I couldn't even help her! It made me so mad."   I don't remember. Kelly doesn't get mad. She's always happy. Maybe "moody" like Mom says, but not mad. She's always super patient.

"Well, I did. And I thought about throwing things, but I didn't. I wanted to. I was so mad at Mom. I thought she loved drugs more than loving me. And I was afraid that she would leave us all alone. Aunt Alexia and me talked for a long, long time. On the bathroom floor where I wanted to hide. It was a good talk and she said it wasn't my fault. She said when I think it's my fault, I need to look that ugly thought in the eye and say, 'I am worth it. I am worth being loved. I need to find the good.' She said saying it out loud would help my brain to get it quicker. Most of the time when I do say it I don't want others to hear, so it's usually in my mind." I breathe deep, my ears still listening.

"I was even mad at Aunt Alexia and Uncle Edmond because I wanted them to figure out how to help. They're our family, so why didn't they help?" She stops and stares into the air. Does she think about fairy creatures and hummingbirds, too, when she does this? I lean on Kelly's shoulder. She says, "We can't tell because we'll have to go away again. We have to keep it a secret. And now with the baby...we're going to figure this out." She sounds like Mom when she says this. "I don't know how, but we will." Then silence. I like that. "I'm glad you're my sister," she says.

I really like that.

DiERDRA

Present Day.

I pace nervously back and forth in my room. I can't get a grip, but I'm trying desperately. "Just do it. It's what I need to do. Okay, this'll help." A swallow. "I don't have to worry, and I don't need to let it bother me. Just one slip. Won't even count it if I get right back on the program. It shouldn't even affect me if I don't use it for too long, and I can deal better. I'm gonna get caught." I sigh and am startled by the sight of my youngest daughter in the doorway. Did she catch me?

"Mom?"

"Do you ever have those voices in your head that talk?" I'm past the point of caring that I'm taking advice from a seven year old. She swallows, her huge eyes boring holes into me. I didn't think so. "Well, mine are arguing with me."

"What are you going to do?" She asks quietly. I smile at her, pausing at the significance of this moment. She's making steps.

"Well, I'm going to listen to you! Now why did I agree to do this? Girls!" My voice comes out loud and commanding, a product of my nerves. "It's time to go! We're already late and have a long drive!" I glance at Penny. "I'll drive a little faster than normal," I say and I give her an almost-smile. She reaches her hand toward me, almost like she knows that I need this. "Okay, sweetie. Are you ready?"

"Yep!" Kelly answers. "We have our Bibles and everything!"

"Church, really? Is there a better way to make it up to Al?"

They don't answer and I wasn't really looking for a response. We woosh off to the car, as Penny would say, if she were in a talking mood. I plaster on a smile. This is for the girls. For my sister, really. "Off we go!"

The sun shines on my face and arm, but I grip the wheel and swerve back and forth on the road. I can't do this. "That one looks like a star!" Kelly yells out, pointing at a cloud somewhere outside the back window. They love this game, but they've played it two days in a row and I'm getting tired of it. "And that one's a unicorn!" Penny whispers. "Look! What is that?"

"Kelly, you don't have to—" I start.

"A cat." It came out in a normal voice this time. For everyone. She did it! Penny grins, like she knows.

"Hmm, that's a good one. Oh! A frog!" The game keeps going, and I glance in the rearview mirror. She's not watching my face. I check the book in the passenger's seat, with some unknown philosopher on the spine. It's not the type of book that interests me, but one that suits my purposes. My plans have changed, and the longer my girls are here, the more I think about why I'm doing this.

"I have one of those!" Kelly breaks through my thoughts. She holds up her Bible and waves it in my face. I wave her off and try to get back in my own lane.

"Yes, I see that, Kelly. Good job." Then to get their mind on something else, I say, "Girls, do you remember the church Aunt Alexia and Uncle Edmond took you to whenever you were staying at their house?" I look through the rearview mirror and they both nod at my reflection. "We're going to meet at the church and then go to the house for lunch," The girls squeal and pump their fists.

"Maybe we will get to play with one of the animals!" Kelly remarks. "Have you ever been here, Mom, like when you were mine and Penny's age?"

"Yes, Kelly, a couple times. Maybe just once. But not a lot. We weren't very religious, but sometimes we went to some church with...with someone."

"Then why do they go to church?"

"Al and Ed? Well, maybe because they know that they need something to believe in. There's nothing worse than feeling so small because you realize that you can't do it on your own. That's not a good feeling."

Kelly shakes her head, but Penny questions me with her eyes. We arrive within a few minutes and Kelly runs to the large building with Penny hurrying close behind. "Maybe I can play with one of my friends there!" Kelly says, bouncing back and forth on her toes while she pulls open the door with one hand. Penny looks about as excited as I am to be there. I shoo my kids into the classroom that Kelly says they went to last time and I step out into the hallway. There is no way I'm going to one of these groups and talk to tons of people I don't know. Fortunately there is a bench close by, against the wall. It'll be okay, I tell myself for the umpteenth time that day. It isn't all bad. Less than an hour later, the girls come out, with Penny straggling behind the kids and Kelly shooting forward to catch someone else that she knows. Penny stuffs a slightly-chewed-on handful of pretzels in my hand, which tells me that she must not have liked it, but was trying to be polite. Besides my kids, everyone else lines up in the hall like they are in school. The regulars must have practiced this.

"Thanks, Penny! Yummy!" I attempt enthusiasm. Kelly skips off to talk to another little girl with a brown ponytail. Maybe they're in the same class. They whisper together and look friendly. Penny stares at my handful of food, but doesn't make an attempt to take them back.

"My girl with big thoughts!" I rub her head. "Who is that?" I signal to Kelly and the other girl, but Penny just shrugs. "Hey, I know that lady. She looks familiar." A woman passes the gaggle of girls and I try calling the woman's name, hoping she's not going to think I'm a lunatic. "Anvi?" I clear my throat and try again. "Hey, Anvi! It's—" The woman and I make eye contact. "Hey—hi! Aren't you a nurse? My name is Deirdra."

"Yes, I am. Sorry, I—" She hesitates. I knew it! Lunatic here. I rush to clarify.

"No, no, it's not you. I was one of your patients a while back. About seven years, actually. Wow. I came in after, well, some time before this one was born," pointing at Penny. I keep my eye on her as I explain the next part. "Something…bad…happened, and you really helped me. It meant a lot at that time in my life." *I found someone I could trust.* But I can't quite say that yet to her, a virtual stranger.

Anvi smiles but doesn't say anything else, and I rush on before she turns away. "You had been laughing and joking with people outside the room right before you came in."

She laughs. "Yeah, I like to give those guys a hard time. Keep their spirits up, you know? It's tough to be in a job like that day after day. We see some really sad scenarios, and it's good to bring some sunshine into the place. I—well, I think I remember you. You wore the Millennium Falcon T-shirt, right?"

"Never wore it again after that. Yep, that was me."

A kid-sized blur whizzes past us and grabs the lady's leg. He seems to be about three or four years old and stares at Penny. Like really stares. Without blinking. He has glasses wrapped against his head, which seems to be a good idea with the speed that he moves. The little guppy ducks under his mom's arm and scoots to the other side. His face is right next to Penny's, two little kids that remind me of where I was just a few short years ago. Then he looks at Anvi and taps her elbow.

"Mommy, that girl Kels took the last donut today. I didn't get to have my favorite. I think red is my favorite color because we got to use red today in our picture. Is it going to be hot outside today and can we go swing again?"

"Car, Mommy is talking to someone. Sorry, Deirdra. This is my youngest, Carson. We haven't exactly learned about interrupting yet. You know how young kids are! Speaking of, I see one of my others just picked something off the ground. I'd better go make sure it's not a cockroach or anything." I nod and Anvi touches my arm and leans in. "It was good catching up. Take care of yourself. I'm glad to see that you're here today." Anvi hurries to her other kid and I watch. The past just caught up with me.

"Ah ha! I knew I'd find you!"

"Aunt Alexia!" Penny says.

"Well, go on, Penny! Go say hi!" I tell her. Surely she missed them! I can almost say the same about her.

PENNY
Present Day.

The service is pretty short, and I listen politely to the music like I'm supposed to, though Mom doesn't sing along. The words are on the screen and the band is giant—different from the kid's part in the little rooms this morning. I'm not here to worship the Lord. Just watch the bunches of people and stare with Mom. She's looking around, too. She takes her book and says that she has to go to the bathroom, but won't take me with her.

After the service we all have lunch together and Mom answers questions about her and other stuff that Aunt Alexia says really soft. Kelly and me play together and Uncle Edmond gives us a hug as we're about to go. "What about group dishes? Then we can have dessert after we clean up." Mom tries to say something, but Aunt Alexia pulls her into the kitchen. I remember this. We did these chores when we stayed here. I didn't like doing the dishes, but the bubbles are fun.

"Okay, fine. Penny, Kelly, we're going to stay and do dishes," she says in a way that makes me not believe her.

"Goody! Penny knows how to, too!" Kelly yells.

"What?" I haven't seen Mommy look like that since the last time she was here. "What do you mean? You really want to?" I look at the big bunch of dishes in the sink. No I don't, but if it means staying here longer, then I guess it's an okay idea.

Kelly scrunches her nose. "Well, you'll have to help me with the soap because it's pretty hard to reach, but I know how to scrub them. Then we can just let them dry and put them up later."

"Well okay, let's hop to it!" Aunt Alexia says.

"Where has the time gone? How did they learn this? Without me? What have I ever truly taught them?"

"Hush, Deids. It's something that they learned. I can teach or you can teach, but they don't pick up on it unless they really want to know it. You've raised some pretty great kids."

"And I really want to tell you something else—"

"Incoming!" Kelly splashes bubbles all over Aunt Alexia. Uncle Edmond on the other side joins in and hits Mommy.

"Hey, Mister! I thought you were doing the drying, not the sopping soap bubbles!" Aunt Alexia scolds. Uncle Edmond just winks at her.

"This is the best day ever!" Kelly yells. I think I agree with her.

"Why?" Mommy asks.

"Because we get to spend it with you. And with everyone!"

"Now don't you two go turning this into a sappy cry-fest!" She scoops up bubbles and taps Kelly's head with bubbles, making it look like the top of an ice cream cone!

I watch Mommy pat her hand on her stomach, like I've seen in her old pictures when I was in there. Is that what she has to tell Aunt Alexia and Uncle Edmond?

I have something to tell her, too.

Deirdra

Four years ago.

Finally! Finished! Penny proudly holds up her newest drawing, one where I'm a combination of a head and limbs, holding a bouquet of flowers on my birthday. I splurged on that one indulgence and it was the beginning of my hopeless love of the very useless sentiment. I hold my finger up to tell her to wait as I finish my conversation. I'm being told in no uncertain terms that if I'm late again to my job I can just kiss it goodbye. Well good riddance. I give him some platitude about how I am going to be a model employee from now on and then hang up, turning my phone off for good measure. These kids deserve my attention more. Penny is standing next to some of my books by the wall and she looks like a little scholar. I'm quite proud of my little collection of books, but the neat little rows only serve to remind me that I am not my own. We're renting this house for now and it gives me a little comfort to know that we can soon leave all that behind. Penny reaches for one that is closest to her. It's my own dumb fault for leaving it out after my last client transaction. I stop her before she uncovers something drastic.

"Penny, come here. Leave the books alone. What are you going to show me?" She holds her picture close and turns toward me, her eyes on me, but seemingly wary. She's a kid. She doesn't know. I bend down to gaze at her masterpiece. It definitely has a head and lots of colors. "Oh, Penny! It's so—" So what? "You've done a great job! And you know how much I love flowers." She smiles shyly.

"Hon, listen to me. Don't ever be discouraged by all this going on around you. You have so much talent, and I know it's hard for you to say your thoughts to me sometimes. But you know what? Keep being you." She had started gurgling like any little kid, but within the last month or so, I've noticed that she keeps more to herself. Maybe she's the type of kid who needs to internalize things. Still, she has tears in her eyes and it breaks my heart.

"Drop all of that mumbo jumbo that says you've gotta do this or that. That doesn't matter. They don't know what they're talking about anyways." Penny blinks, but I keep going. My thoughts fly and I have to get this out. "Ignore all that," I say. "Keep your head up and be proud of you. Who this person Penny is! Same for your sister. You and your sister are so much better than me. I don't deserve what I've got. Allie keeps giving everything up for me. But you wanna hear a secret? She is really doing this for you, hon, not for me. I want you to remember that you're awesome, you hear?"

She's listening. I grab her in a tight hug.

"Penny, I'm so proud of you and your sis. You are going to be someone great. I can feel it in my bones." I love this feeling. I wrap her in my arms, like a soft blanket and all my love beating within my heart.

PENNY

Present Day.

Me and Kelly sit in the back seat watching the poles WHIZ past. The radio THUMP! THUMPS! with drum beats, just as excited as we are to be done with school. Kelly leans forward to tap Mom. "Mom! Mom! Turn it up!" She grins at us and points to the front seat. "Listen to this one! It's the best!" I smile and look back out the window. There are lots of guitar parts in this song! Like those Uncle Edmond plays! On Kelly's last birthday he made her a birthday song. I move my head to hear the words that have become so familiar.

You've got to give it your best, though it feels foreign in this exact moment DEE-de-DUM!

Maybe it will hurt, but someday you will soar!

"What does 'foreign' mean, Mama?" Kelly asks.

"Like an ay-lee-un..." Mom's voice shakes like she's retelling an old, scary story from the TV. "Someone from a different place," she adds. "Like us!" Mommy starts to smile, but she gets serious fast and doesn't look at me. "Sometimes it's better to be away than to be at home." Mom now does a lot more thinking than talking, which is not normal for her. I haven't seen her smile in a long time. I try to imagine Mom, Kelly, and me in green-skinned jumpsuits with antennas, and a horrible dream from the night before comes back. I'd rather not be foreign. Foreign is too scary.

Maybe it's like that time on the playground. That's why I never step past the edge marked, even when my teachers let us. Like on days before a vacation or field days. Unless I absolutely have to. It's not safe. But Aunt and Uncle's house, it was different.

What is going to happen when I tell Mommy? What will she say? She responds so differently on good or bad days. Sometimes she listens to the sadness, loneliness, or des-pair-a-tion, like Kelly said. That's when someone really, really wants something and will do everything they can to get it. Is that where Mommy is now? She doesn't look like it, but maybe like my imagination, it's inside.

I think this hard and look at Mom, humming to the new song that just came on the radio. When the car swerves a little bit, I grab onto the armrest. Mom chuckles and asks, "Are you scared that we're going to crash? There's nothing to it." She puts one hand over the back of the seat and the other on the steering wheel. Now I can't see the front except if I lean real close to the window. Mom jerks the steering wheel to the right real fast then left, right and left again, like the car is a ship in waves. We've never done this before. Mom has a grin, but she doesn't usually play like this with us. Kelly WHOOPS! beside me, but I can't breathe. Any words that I've practiced are stuck in my throat. My heart feels like it's jumping up into my brain. There's something wrong with me! I clutch Mom's hand and try to say something. Anything! I get frustrated because even though my mouth is open and I feel like I should be screaming, nothing comes out. Mom's arm is right in front of me. I feel like it's forcing me to stay in this wild ride. I can't escape!

I want to close my eyes but can't. Tears are there in my eyes, ready to fall down my face. I try to imagine something beautiful, anything that will take my mind off what is happening right now. Like...mountains! But this time I can only imagine the mountain is going to crash into me. What about fairies from Kelly's book?

With the speed of the car, I know that the fairies are just carrying it along without thought to who is inside. My voice finally comes back up in my throat. "Mom!"

She looks back and laughs. "See, beautiful girl? I knew you had some vocal chords in you!" I can only look at my mom and try. Try to say something that breaks this fear. Stop the car. Please please. Stop the car. You're going to kill us! But nothing comes out when I try to tell her no. Her eyes get wide open when she glances at me and nods. "Alright, hon. I'll stop." Mom stops rocking the car back and forth and pats my leg. Like that's going to make it better. "You know I didn't mean to scare you. I was just playing. Just trying to have fun." She waits a moment, enough for me to take a small breath, before she continues. "You need to lighten up. You're too serious. I just want to see you smile."

Nothing about what Mom says stays. That was so scary. Like we were really going to crash. Way faster than Aunt Alexia or Uncle Edmond drives. I don't like that feeling. Ever. I know that I should say something to try to make Mom feel better, but all I can do is grip the seat and look out the window, waiting for the exact time when we roll to a stop.

It takes the entire car ride to wipe it out of my mind and I don't feel like I'm breathing right until we are walking into the store and far away from that terrifying car. Am I really too serious? Is Mom just doing that to play with us? What am I doing wrong? I can't help it as a couple tears sneak out of my eyes and down my cheek, which I wipe away quickly. It's going to be—

Breathe.

Okay.

Isn't that supposed to make me feel better?

We finish shopping and get back in the car. No crazy moves. Our dragon roars as Mom starts it. Mom turns on the radio again. It's Mom's song. The only one that the music guys would take. Back when she was trying to be famous. "Turn it up! Turn it up! They used to play that at school!" Kelly yells from the back. She always does that with this song.

You there! Feel like you can't measure up to the conformity—BAM! Cymbals are here—*of society. BUM! BUM! Now the drums. Two beats. Low.*

The rain just keeps coming. BOOM! BOOM! BOOM!

Whatever this instrument is, it is low and makes me shiver. It sounds like real thunder. In the next part, with just the band playing, I think again about the words. Conformity. Holler. Society. Expectant. Those are big words. They sound kinda silly.

Society. I think that means people. Measure people. Like those marks we put in the garage every birthday? And the rain. Maybe it's like those big thunderstorms. Not with the rainbows. But in the song it's maybe talking about those sad times. Like when Mommy locks herself in her room or takes some "alone time" and we stay with Aunt Alexia and Uncle Edmond. Does this person have that kind of sadness? A deep, dark sadness. He sends words the other person doesn't want to listen to and she pushes them away like I pushed Aunt Alexia at first. He's trying to talk to her, like Teacher sitting next to my desk. A serious talk. Maybe those silly words mean he's trying to make the other person laugh.

PENNY

Four Years Ago.

I think really hard, but can't quite make my drawing look right. SCRIBBLE, CRUMBLE, THUMP in the trash. I want to make another like that one I gave Mommy. Where is it? I enter the kitchen. No, it isn't here on the fridge, and not on the table. What color? Maybe purple? That is one of my first hummingbirds. It reminds me so much of Mom because it is in a garden. Mom loves flowers, even flowers that the plant guy, J-Dog, gave her the other day. Not his real name, I don't think, but it's funny. He lets us call him that. I look over to the counter by the mail, where she always puts it and it stays for a long time. There it is! The tail of my little hummingbird sticking over the edge. I pull at the paper and it looks like I tore the page. It is ripped on one side and has some edges that are not right. I check my hand, then the paper again. No, I don't think my hand would do that, even if I pulled hard in accident.

I get my knees on the chair. Now I can see better. Mom always starts yelling if I do this, and Aunt Alexia explained many times that the chair can tip over if I am standing. So I'm not standing. Small little pieces are next to the hummingbird picture, all around the mail. Some are rolled into a tiny roll shape. Little pieces of paper stuff are dirty and have some other stuff, but I can't tell what it is, all on them. Only like four bits of my paper is here. Not a lot, but it's like the time that Aunt Alexia cooked pancakes and had to leave the

Got a fix and good to go
Kids are oblivious. They shouldn't know.
I'm getting restless and need a break
Grabbing breakfast and we should head out to the lake.
Road trip with the girls; they won't know what hit 'em
They will flip! There's a favorite disk that we'll bring to listen.
Penny pushes when I want to help; some things don't change
I give a yelp and wait outside; I must release these chains
Of expectations, haughty looks and bills. I can't stay here
All of this part of life can wait until we get back 'cause we're on an adventure
Singing at the top of our lungs, adrenaline spiking. Is it the drug?
By the side of the road we stop to play and I get more hugs.
This is how it's supposed to be; the real life
Why is it no matter the most I have is strife?
I can't get a break unless I push everyone away.
I've got to escape! This false kindness I can't take.
One more hit, just this time. "Go and play over there."
I sit in my car with elation and guilt. It's over.
Penny and Kelly climb in ready for a vacation! They are my four-leaf clovers.

ingredients on the counter 'cause someone called her next door for an emergency. Like flour. I make a smile.

What kind of emergency would make Mom leave pieces from my picture? One has been really important to her. The monster. She once told me that she tries her hardest to stay awake—what Mom calls "alert." In my mind, the word makes Mom's eyes really large, where she doesn't sleep at all. Sometimes I hear her walking around at night, so that must be it. Why did she tear my picture? Maybe she doesn't know. Some of the kids at school say they have cousins or moms, too, who don't know when they do bad things. Why does the monster steal all her focus?

DEIRDRA

Four years and two months ago.

I self-consciously tug my borrowed sweater to my chest, aware of the hole beneath the armpit. Just one more paycheck and I can get a couple new things. The current apartment has the bare minimum, but at least it's keeping a roof over our heads! For now. Penny's rattling cough shadow boxes with any remaining money due at the end of the month. Another week of cash gobbled up by life, along with everything else. A tune floats around my head, reminding me of the ever-empty balance in my bank.

"I'm going to make it as a musician one of these days," my daydreaming voice bubbles without consulting me.

Al looks away, barely suppressing a guffaw. If Alexia wasn't so stuffy, I'm pretty sure she would laugh us right out of the house. Instead, my sister leans over and ruffles Penny's hair, grinning at her niece.

"Mommy sings really good!" Penny confirms and I've never been more grateful for my youngest's carefully chosen words.

"I'm sure lullabies are a little different than hit songs that actually earn money. She had her chance and she squandered it," Al replies to Penny, but directs her eyes to me. The doubt stings. "You can't even care for your own kids." Kels must have mentioned the cold hamburger for breakfast right before we hopped on the road. The statement is true, but it adds fuel to the fire.

"I'm not squandering my dream. I'm merely elevating the concept of composition." I use hard-earned vocabulary to shoot back verbal daggers. I might not have graduated college, but I got through two years of an English/Music double major before quitting, until I realized it wasn't what I wanted. My vocabulary has always been exceptional, but little help it is when attempting to cling to my dignity. "And I don't need your approval, though some sort of acknowledgement might be best on this day of giving thanks."

"Well, I'm thankful that you are finding something that you care about, though I don't know if it is going to pan out like you want it to. You have an agent yet?"

I stare her down, tears stinging my eyes. I refuse to let her best me, but something within prods that she is right. Needles in my soul. But not now. I can't listen. I open my mouth and Ed moves near my elbow.

"Anyone up for ice cream?" Ed swings his legs over to Kelly and nudges her knee. His tone suggests he might have winked, but I'm too busy staring Al down to notice. Alexia blinks and summons a small smile toward the two of them. The fight set aside until the next time. Then we'll measure bank accounts or religion or something else in which Alexia is far superior. Good thing she doesn't know the cost of my new employment. Again. The clock in the hall chimes and I breathe a sigh of relief. Only one hour more promised before we can escape.

PENNY

Present Day.

"Hey, let me show you something." Kelly PLOP!s on my bed and my stuffed bear sails to the floor, ka-PUFF! "This book is soooo interesting!" Kelly squeals and puts a small book by my leg. "It's all part of one big, long story, but it's filled with tons of little stories in between. We've been talking about it in class."

It really doesn't look too impressive. Maybe it will be way too hard. I shake my head. "I can't. It's too hard." I hope Kelly can't hear my upsetness. Kelly is the only one that I try to tell what I'm thinking. She's always been a good listener. But I still don't tell her everything. I hate the way that I stutter out words while I read, even when I'm by myself. Like my voice wants to stay inside.

Kelly stops her excited voice, but still has a grin. "No worries." She tries to toss her head like the girls in her class do, but her hair goes all wild like a lion. She hops off the bed and goes to her mirror next to the bathroom. She stops talking long enough to see her hair fall back onto her head right. Not cool yet.

I laugh even when she sticks her tongue out at me. Kelly has acted like some of her friends lately, not talking to me as much. What do her friends talk about? She hops back onto the bed and I catch myself when I go up and down. "Here's what I can do. I'll read it to you. And then we can both hear it at the same time. Plus—" She takes the book back and puts it in her lap, like she is thinking again about the plan. "I need to read at least thirty minutes at home anyway, so this will be good practice. Miss Caroline says I am a good reader."

My sister looks at the book not me and I take the book and try to read the front. One word I don't understand. "What is 'gables'?" I point to a word on the front.

"Just a fancy word for part of the roof. It's 'Anne. Of. Green. Gables.'" She points to each word in the title, just like my teacher does. "Miss Caroline read the first chapter to us during class, and I think it is talking about the house that she lives in. I don't know. I didn't ask her. She doesn't like it when we interrupt. It's really for next year's grade, but Miss Caroline said that I can take it home to practice since we've read some of it. We can do that. But this one—" She grabs the book. "—has some awesome pictures. Here." I try to see the pictures over her shoulder. "You can look at it for a while. Just a little bit."

Kelly jumps off the bed and goes toward the stairs. "I've got dishes tonight before I start homework." Her face disappears and then *POP* s back in. "You are soooo lucky to take out trash this week! Maybe I can get the trash next time. Maybe." Then she's gone.

I don't like dishes either, but I push that far from my mind. When I open the book there is a picture of a little girl in a small room with weird-looking walls, like flowers or something glued on them. Then that same girl hugging a tree in another. She's right. I like these pictures. They're different, but they all seem so happy. The whole book doesn't have any color. This is strange. What in the world is this book about? That's what Teacher always asks when we start books. I turn to the next picture that I find and it looks like the girl is talking in front of a lot of people. On a stage. My stomach tightens at the thought of doing that. Even worse than when I got told to help with a math problem because Mr. Peters says we have to move around when we're learning new things. No way! No how! Nothing is worth being alone with other people looking!

DEIRDRA

Four years and six months ago.

"What do you mean, 'Get a sitter'? You think money grows on trees?" I have a feeling Marc is "otherwise occupied" and is only thinking about the blond sitting in front of him doing whatever, hoping I can help him out with another hit. I know that he likes to see other women, and I told him that I understood. It still rubs me the wrong way. Boyfriends aren't supposed to be forever, but still…I guess I'm asking for too much.

"C'mon, babe, this'll be the time of your life!" He whines and my resolve grows like a wall. "I've found the best location for our next escapade. Those maps of the world in your room, huh? Who needs to travel in reality when I can give you the trip of your life beyond that, right?"

He has a habit of putting unnecessary words at the end of his sentences. I never should have brought him back to the house. Even though the girls had been out most of the time, it still gives me the creeps to have them return to our mess. Their innocent eyes catching everything I left seems that much more acute. "Marc, I can't go clubbing with you all the time. I have the kids to think about. This means that sometimes I have to think of my girls. They're going to get taken away if I don't get serious." I say it as a threat, but it dawns on me that this could be reality if I keep on this path. Woah.

Marc remains persistent. "Can you make it even for a little bit? This means that it will be something that you will never forget, just something that will carry you through the week. How old is your biggest girl, anyway? They can take care of themselves by now."

I can't believe he's giving me parenting advice. I don't think he's ever held a baby or cared for another human younger than eighteen. Sixteen, at least. I shiver at the thought. "She's five years old! She barely knows how to turn on the TV by herself!" There is no way. Right? His persuasiveness is getting to me, and at his next joke, the edges of my mouth resist a smile. He always tries these horrible jokes that don't even mean anything, but then I end up laughing and lowering my defenses. Sometimes I hate myself for that...weakness. "No, it's not possible. I can't do that to them. They're just babies."

I don't even convince myself, but Marc seems to take me at my word. The frustration creeps into his voice and he doesn't even try to hide it. He gets louder and I hold the phone away from my face as his voice turns to squeaks and high demands.

"I got it!" I yell back, "You don't have to yell, geez. No, I—Yeah, I know, but—"

Another guilt trip about this pleasure I'm deliberately ignoring, apparently. "No, it's not. I can't." Words from the street that have become familiar form in my mind, but I can't pronounce them here, not with the kids. *Stop it.* I shake my head so the words disappear into the air. I laugh a little louder to show that nothing he says bothers me. "I know, but it's important. Maybe tomorrow...It's not like that... Listen—"

Tears sting my eyes. This is just insulting. "Well, then you should, too! How dare—Hello? Marc? Hello? Are you there?"

I slam the phone down with a loud CRASH and watch the girls cringe, with Penny covering her ears. The emotions are too much, but I won't. I won't cry. Not now.

I am going to be strong. I am going to love on these kids. I am going to prove it to myself.

How in the world, though, when I feel my body breaking down? I need a hit! My newest obsession consumes me. But I can't, not with the girls. Not if I want to do this for real. I'm their mother. I will do this. Put a good face on.

But really? The dark cloud is coming. It's coming.

Penny

Present Day.

"Penny! Look over here!" Kelly motions out the car window at the bushes on the side of the road. Only these are weird. They have something that looks like snow on them, but it isn't. Fluffy clouds, maybe? No, I've seen fog on the ground before and it doesn't look like this.

"It's cotton bushes! They are growing cotton! Isn't that cool?" I don't know what my sister is so excited about, and I get mad when she picks at my shirt. I push her hand away. "Don't you see? That cotton is what goes into our clothes. That's what it starts off as." Maybe she has a point. I look at my striped shirt, this orange one that Mom grabbed on our way out the door. I don't wear it much, and there's this thread that hangs off the end of my sleeve that I can't quite ever get rid of, no matter how many times I grab it with my teeth. Mom goes to the side of the road and stops, but says it's just for us to look. We're not getting out until later.

I wait for Kelly to finish her story, but she looks at Mom. Mommy? What is she doing? Mommy doesn't say anything and sniffs a bit, glancing back at us every now and then. We don't move so I don't know why she keeps watching. We start the car after some quiet minutes, and Kelly starts the cloud game again. I get distracted by a pony-looking cloud and wave my hand around in the air, pretending like I'm "soaring over fields on my wild stallion!" Road trips are fun, but I really want to be quiet. I do like seeing Kelly smile even if she's a little too excited.

Mom turns around and says to Kelly, "Be quiet! Mommy has to concentrate!" Maybe she's mad because we had to leave our house, but I don't know why. Mom wipes her nose and looks in all sorts of directions, even though we're the only ones driving on this road. Pretty soon I don't notice what she does because I fall asleep and don't hear anything except quiet.

When I wake up, Kelly lays on my shoulder. I shrug her off, gentle this time. It reminds me of when I fell asleep on Aunt Alexia while the man was talking in church. I sure miss them. We haven't seen them in such a long time!

"Okay, girls, we're stopping here." We stop and get a sandwich. Kelly and me split ours and Mommy drinks a Coke. She even lets us have a couple sips. It makes my nose burn. "You both go into the bathroom now while Mommy steps outside and takes care of a couple things. Kelly, you remember to help your sister okay? Remember that she's little and you need to watch her." She looks at Kelly for a long time, and I know it's supposed to mean something. Kelly doesn't respond, but she shakes her head. I sure wish I could understand these things better. Besides, I'm not so little.

We go to the bathroom and I even remember to wash my hands. I love the way the blow dryer shoots hot air into my hands and on my face, too. Kelly lets me push the button twice and my face has a burning feeling from the hot air when we go outside. Kelly sticks her arm out really fast and I run into it. What is she doing? "Let's...um..." She looks the other way, where there are lots of snacks and bottles of soda that we never get. "Let's go this way. Maybe Mom will buy us a snack before we get back in the car."

She won't do that. We already had a sandwich and she keeps saying we have to watch our money. Why is Kelly like this? Why won't she let me go? Kelly
walks near the front, where there's big big windows and all the cars are out front. Mom is beside the car and the door is open. She doesn't move for a really long time, and I wonder if she's frozen. Kelly's hand touches my back and I let her lead me. Anywhere else. What's wrong with Mommy? Is she going to leave us? Why doesn't she want to be with us? What is in those drugs that makes her love them more than us?

I finally receive the long-awaited news: My song has been requested. All I have to do is show up and do my best

Creating stories with my words is something that has become more than a hobby; it's worth

More. I create worlds so that others who hear realize they are not the only ones out there.

The only ones going through the same experiences; this is my chance to stand up with my voice.

A connection that I can form solely by the power of my imagination.

I hope to pass this on to my little trooper, the baby who rests inside, waiting to be introduced

into the world, my life. A scary thought twisting within me like a knife.

I have tried to do my best, but every time I am failing, falling, not enough.

Making steps to success only to slam back down again.

The beginning of all. The end of everything.

Will it ever change? Can I emerge from this mess?

Here's my chance.

Sitting on the stool and in front of me looms the mic.

Something that I have longed for seemingly forever; then why the fright?

A wave of terror hits me with the first verse; then I know. It's not terror—worse.

It's nausea. Not now! I have to do this; what's the first rhyme? I take a breath. This just takes time.

Too late, my chance is ruined. I should have listened to my body before I stepped into this.

Walking home with no money. No song. How in the world is my family going to get along?

My family, growing inside me. Is there no way that we can be free

of this oppression and doubt? It seems like I catch a drift and then can't ever figure it out.

PENNY

Present Day.

Today is a good day! I get up and comb through my hair. It's harder to do now that it's getting longer, and I have to put a section over my shoulder to reach the very ends. I don't really know how it goes in a ponytail, so I always have to ask Kelly, or she sometimes braids it. I love my braids.

The thing is, Kelly doesn't always have time. "I've got to get ready for school!" she says, especially when I ask really late, right before it's time to go. So that's why today I want to get up early. It is going to be the day we get to see the new baby chicks at school!

I remember this from the first time in kindergarten, when we got to line up and Teacher said, "Look only with your eyes. Do not touch with your hands!" But this year I am in third and I get to hold the baby chicks. Finally. They're going to be at our school one whole week!

I look in my closet and really want a new dress. One with pockets where I can maybe hide some chicks. I'd bring them home and put them in a chicken pen we could build out of cardboard boxes from the dumpster in the back. Then I'd get to feed them myself every day! But maybe it's better now. If I had a new dress, it would get dirty.

Kelly tells me to hurry up. I grab my hair thingy and go to her door. But I stop there and don't go in because she doesn't always want me to come into her room. She says that quiet space is good. I guess I like quiet space, too, so I understand. It's just really weird. She motions for me to come in and I jump on her bed. She holds out her hand and I put the hair pieces in her hand, like always. Before she starts combing my hair, she takes a pink gum wrapper from the bed and throws it toward the trash in the corner. It misses. Kelly hums some song to herself. I don't know that one, but I like to hear it. It reminds me of the times in the car whenever Mom turns the music up really loud. She hasn't done that in a while.

Kelly is done in a really short time and I look in the mirror at myself. Not my real self, but the reflection of myself. The one that looks like me. I am a little bit, but not all the way sad, but still kinda sad when I see that Kelly braided my hair on the side, not in the back. But she did it, and I can be the snow queen today. I smile and remember to thank her and then she asks me to come to the bathroom. We talk about grownup stuff and things that she says that I need to know for when I get older. She said that it is not to be scared of, but that it will happen to me soon. I sure hope not. Sounds painful. Then she points to my feet. I forgot my shoes! "Finish getting ready! What about those shoes that Mom found for you yesterday?"

I run back, but my mind goes back to the "grownup" stuff. Is it really happening? Do I need to get ready for being grown up? Does that mean I can really make this decision and it can be a grownup decision? I'm not even a teen yet.

Why do things have to be so hard? Now I just need to figure out what I will say.

DEIRDRA

Ten years ago.

"Let's go, Kevin! It's time for the show to start!" This is my favorite band and I've saved up forever to see them. At first my boyfriend had told me no. And he definitely didn't pay for the tickets. We've only been going out for a few weeks, but it has been super intense. The best three weeks I've ever had with anyone. He'd opened up my world and I've never felt such emotions before. It's like a new way of feeling alive! Maybe I'm in love. I've never been in love before, but there's a first time for everything.

But when I told him about this awesome concert I'd scheduled, he flat out refused to go to the show. Some lame excuse about the noise or crowds or something. I tried to see if Frankie or Ribs would go, but they both backed out with other excuses that they had to work or whatever. We all have jobs, don't we? Some things are just more important! We're in that sweet spot, official adults now. I can't miss out on The Redfish, best rock band on this side of the state! Gotta live a little! I check my phone again for the row number. We definitely got nosebleed seats. Both of us. Kevin called last night and said he'd go, even when he doesn't really like this band. He thinks they're just noise. Just noise? Who would say that? Though they're nearly sold out, it's the fact that we're here that matters. This is going to be great! It starts with a bang and I sing my heart out, ignoring that Kevin is sitting down, staring at his phone. Some date. The least he could do is turn down the brightness. Instead, I pull out my own phone and wave it around with the crowd. He's not going to ruin my night.

The next song that they play is my favorite and I belt out every single word, feeling more and more excited. It has all been completely worth this night! The crowd around me agrees. I lose myself. Right as the last notes resolve, they slow it down to another song I've heard before on the radio. It must be one of their newer ones. Maybe this one is better for Kevin. "How about this one, huh?"

But he pops up from his seat, leaning into my ear to say, "Hey, I'll be back." Nothing else. Kevin heads toward the exit before I can ask why. I'm stunned for a second, but the lead singer begins the song and I hum along, somewhat familiar, yet not knowing the words. Instead, I review in my head over and over again the lyrics I've been working on for my own next greatest hit. It's gotta be, surely. And I'm going to have lots of creative juice after a concert like this! Someone in the crowd whoops and the couple next to me starts clapping. I yell out, too, joining the group of strangers. We all have a love of this group's sound in common. A group of familiar strangers. Well, most of us. Kevin's absence is a sour taste in my mouth, but I swallow past it and blink back tears. I'm not alone. I'm with my closest friends here. They know what it's like to appreciate music.

The nausea comes right back and I figure I shouldn't have had so much spaghetti before coming here. I roll my eyes as I shuffle towards the end of the row. Only a moron would order spaghetti on a date. Well, it was supposed to be one, anyway. When I reach the hallway, I look for Kevin, but he has disappeared. Not right outside like I thought he'd be. I harumph and open the bathroom door. My dinner comes up before I can even make it to the stall. Oh, great. Then I feel even worse and rush to get the door closed. A few minutes later, I splash myself with the sink water and try to wipe off my skirt. I just wanted to enjoy the night and here I'm left without a date and my outfit ruined. I stare at myself in the mirror. I've never been one of those teens who shines with the robustness of a tan, but I look especially gaunt tonight. "Staring at the possibilities/No friends within sight of me..." I hum a nonsensical tune, but smile at myself, wiping off a smudge from my mouth with a paper towel.

When I open the door, I ram into Kevin's shoulder. "There you are! I thought these guys were your favorite and here you are camping out in the bathroom."

"I wasn't even in there for ten minutes. Geez!" I brush past him, adding, "Besides, I got food poisoning or something from that awful restaurant. C'mon. They're nearly done. Let's go catch the last song." I motion toward the sound of the roaring audience, but he shakes his head.

"Nope. I'll be out here when you get out. Besides, I'm your ride home."

"Forget it. Will you make it up to me by picking up a strawberry shake on the way home?"

"Let's make that two." We go through the drive through and he grabs my hand. "I just want to get back as quickly as possible." He squeezes my hand and I lean over to kiss him. But he pulls his head back and grabs the two shakes that are passed through the car window. "Here."

I expectantly sip and it's perfect, my favorite flavor oozing through the straw as he drives away. But the feeling of nausea quickly emerges. "Pull over!" and I open the passenger door just in time. At the same moment it hits me like a ton of bricks. This is not just food poisoning. More retching. Another thought quickly follows: What will Al say?

PENNY

Present Day.

I walk around the backyard again and again, until I lose count of my steps. I only know that the sun has almost gone down, so it's been at least an hour. I think. This right here is all I know. I don't want to face all this! I don't want to face them again. "What to do?" This is just a whisper, and it bounces around and sinks into the grass under my feet. Nobody will hear it because it's just me.

But I do. I know what to do.

One of the first books I remember reading at school was about a giraffe that wanted to dance more than anything. Then there was that book about the boy who was friends with a bear. We read that just this year. Maybe books can do that. They use objects that aren't real or even alive and have them talk to humans. Like that tree and the little boy. The girl who was so strong she could carry a horse. I keep all of these stories piled in my brain and pull them out sometimes to bring me to happier places. Words like these aren't just for school.

Everything is so different from the way it was those first days of school. I was always crying and screaming and afraid that I was going to be left behind. I guess I am still like that, now, but I am trying to learn to think, to plan, to find other ways to deal with it all. I hold my tears inside. But I also hold something else inside me. Inside here, my brain or my heart or something that I can't quite see, is my voice. Maybe there is something different. Kids have laughed at me, and adults have pointed. I've gotten called names, whispered about or even pushed around. But nothing has changed how sure I am.

I need to protect. Protect who? Myself? My mom? My words? However this turns out, it's going to be different. Because I am different.

And I am going to find a way to show them.

Maybe in my drawings? I have been doodling since that last time we moved to the house we're in now, and I like being able to show Kelly and Mom these crazy worlds in my brain. Maybe they will show where I am going. This new school might be different, too.

I hope so.

Present Day.

"What do you think would happen if we lived in a castle?"

Kelly lies across my bed, our favorite place to talk. "We could each have king-sized beds! With lots and lots of pillows!" We both giggle and I WHACK! my sister with a pillow. This one has been with me through all the moves that we've made last month and all the months before. This new house is my favorite, though. But we're farther from Aunt Alexia and Uncle Edmond. And I don't like that.

"You think we're going to move again?" Kelly is completely quiet afterwards until I say something. She's really good at that.

"We always do."

Kelly doesn't say much, just turns the pillow over in her hands. After a long time waiting, she says, "Yes, I think you're right. I hope not too far. Mom has been gone a lot more, but she's also been a lot happier. She says good night to me every night now. Usually she does that when she's not thinking about work anymore. When she's…" She almost says something, but she doesn't. "Anyways, I keep thinking, even though we'll move again, maybe this time, this one place will be perfect. We will find a great place where she gets a really good job and we can just stay there forever and ever! Then Mommy will be happy all the time and she won't have to take any drugs to feel better." She waits for a little time, then says, "We can't tell anyone. They'll take us away again. Maybe for good. It's not so bad, anyway. She's better more times than she used to be."

I have nothing. It's easier. I don't want to move again. I want somewhere to stay. My eyes go to the pictures on the wall, right where Mom put them. Also there are pictures of hummingbirds and flowers and even that little puppy that we never got. Kelly sniffs and I look at her. I know what I have to do.

"Kelly, I have to go."

"You what? Go where? What are you talking about?"

The plan slips out. It's been in my head for weeks. "I want to go back to Aunt Alexia and Uncle Edmond's." It's strange hearing my own voice saying it out loud, but it helps. That's exactly what I want.

"What do you mean? Will Mom let you?"

I shrug and swallow the fear taste in my throat. My heart beats fast. I know Kelly is thinking hard because her face is all scrunched up, but she doesn't say anything. Her finger goes over and over the pattern on the bed covers. Like me with my coloring pattern, trying to get it just right.

"Smile," I say. I don't know at first if I am talking to Kelly or to me. Then she nods. Okay, for Kelly. She doesn't need to be sad. She's always been the one showing me the WOW in every day.

Kelly nods. "What is going to happen?" I shrug again. I haven't thought that far, I guess. "Are we ever going to see each other again? What is Mom going to say? Do you think she's going to make you stay?" I hold my breath. I don't know which to answer. She could. Kelly says it again. "What is going to happen to us?"

"I will write you." I say this like I know it, because I do, but don't know how. They do have computers at school. I put all my pictures in a pile, and my mind is thinking of places in Aunt Alexia and Uncle Edmond's house, where I will write some stories, like the one with the hummingbird. "We will..." Will what? See each other again? Even now Mommy's almost ready to move! Always a new place, finding new people and getting away from the old people. And what about the...monster? It used to be something for me to say when I was little, but seems right for now. It's scary. I can't look at Kelly then, and I can't say anything more.

"Mom will listen to you, Penny," Kelly says, then stops. Just when I am trying to figure out the right words, she says, "I love you,

Penny." She stretches out her fingers until they just touch the tips of mine.

"If ever there is tomorrow when we're not together...there is something you must always remember. You are braver than you believe, stronger than you seem, and smarter than you think. But the most important thing is, even if we're apart..." My favorite Winnie the Pooh quote.

Deirdra

Eighteen years ago.

The sun is bright in my eyes when I follow my sister outside. She said something about us finding buried treasure, but this looks more fun to me! I climb onto a barrel that's outside, the one that dad used to use. But he doesn't anymore. He hasn't come around for lots of weeks. Al says that it's because we are trying something new. Like just us. By ourselves. Well, and also Mom, but not right now. I put my foot right where I tried the last time and I climb up, all the way to the top! I'm on top of the mountain! Allie frowns up at me, but it makes me smile even bigger.

"What am I going to do with you, little one?" she says. I shake my head and stand like a superhero. You can't catch me! I'm going to fly away when it gets dark. Al follows my look and says yes with her head.

"It's almost that time, and Mom said that we need to get in bed before eight. That gives you," she checks the time on her wrist, "Twenty minutes. Then we can play a game for a little bit before we get in bed."

I won't go to sleep until Mommy gets home. At least, I'm going to try. I don't want to go in now. "I'm going to fly away, all the way off this island. Watch me!"

"No, Deids! Don't do that!" I stop for a second, my hands still stretched out, but I'm pulled back by her frowny look. "Mommy doesn't want you to get hurt."

I shake my head and jump and Al does this little breathe in. She didn't think I could do it, but I can. I did! "I did it! I did it!" I run around her, round and round, just out of reach of her fingers. She isn't too mad because she laughs. I go again to my sing-song voice. "I'm running in the grass with my toes. My feet love the grass and they run to you. Here, catch me!" Then I jump toward her – and land on her foot.

"Ouch!" She sits on the ground and gives me a mad face. She puts her legs up turns around, not looking at me. I stand still where I am, seeing if she's really, really upset, or if it's just Alexia time. She mumbles something and I jump over closer.

"What–" Then her hand reaches out and grabs my wrist. "Hey!" She jumps up and laughs and I move back and back, trying to get away. She lets me go and runs. I do my song again. "Look, I'm going to fly away! Zoom around and around before I land to you."

Al laughs. "That's right, Deids! 'Zoom' and 'you'! They rhyme!" She stops chasing after me. Then she puts her hands on her hips. Like she's a superhero, too. "I'm thinking of a number between one and ten..."

Ooh, this game's my favorite!

PENNY

Present Day.

I don't sleep good and Mom is already in the kitchen when I wake up the next morning. "Hey, baby! C'mere and come sit with your mama." Mommy pats the corner of the chair, but there's not very much space there. I try to squeeze onto the edge. I'm a little big to be sitting in her lap now, especially with her growing tummy. I think it's a girl, but Mom says it'll be a boy. Mom is very awake and she smells good like she put on perfume. We sit with no talking for a few minutes and the TV sounds get loud and soft, loud and soft. Mom turns up the volume, but the noise doesn't change.

"What do you have here? Another picture?" She takes the sheet from my hands. I have messed it up because my hand has been so tight holding it, but she makes it look pretty and flat. "Oh! You wrote me a poem!" Then she reads it out loud.

"My love for you is big and wide/ I know it's so big that it can't hide/ It makes me happy and sad to know/ That I want to find a place to grow / It doesn't mean my love is small/ But—

"What is the rest of it, Penny? What did you mean to write here?"

I take a deep breath, then another one, just to be sure. I want to tell so much. To explain that she is the one who taught me to write this. This song. I want to show how much I love through the words. Like Mommy does. But she doesn't understand. I love her here, but I also want to be with Aunt Alexia and Uncle Edmond. To stay somewhere. To be safe, away from drugs. With the bunnies and the puppies. And my friends. But I didn't have all the words for the song and I didn't know how to finish. How can I tell her? How can I?

"Sweetie, are you having breathing issues again? Do you need medicine, Pen? Hey! I made a rhyme! Another song, coming up!" She smiles a little and turns back to the TV.

"I need to tell you," I say.

Now Mommy looks at me. "Tell me what?"

"I want—" I bite my lip. I can't do this. I'm shaking. I'm going to make Mommy cry.

"Oh, Hon, c'mere." Mom hugs me tight, putting me in her lap. My legs hang off the chair and one toe touches the floor. "You can tell me. What is it?"

"I—" I take a breath and try to sit up more. "I want to stay with Aunt Alexia and Uncle Edmond."

"What? Are you kidding?" I shake my head. Mom looks me in the face. She stares. "I—" Then she looks away. Not at me. She rubs one hand over her face. "Why?" Mom pushes me off the chair so I'm standing on the ground. She grabs my shoulders, not gently. "Tell me, what's going on? Why would you say something like this?"

I try to say something, but nothing comes out.

"What is making you feel like this, Penny? Did your aunt put you up to this? I'll have a talk with her this very minute!"

"No!" I'm crying now. What can I say? How can I tell her the truth? She's going to hate me for life!

"Why do you want to leave our home, sweetie?"

I don't. I shake my head.

"What?" she says loud and I hear her take a deep breath, just like she's taught us. Then she curses, all those ugly words that she tells us we should never say. She walks back and forth. "How do you think this makes me feel, Penny? I'm doing my best here. For you! I'm working two jobs and spending as much time as I can with you girls. The other day at the park, didn't we have fun together? We can do more of that. But we can't...there's no way..." Her voice keeps coming faster and faster and I take a step back.

She looks at me.

I know she's waiting for me to say something back.

But nothing comes out.

Just a breath.

"C'mon, Penny, I'm so sick of the silent treatment. Just talk! I know you can do it! TELL ME WHAT YOU THINK!"

She's mad at me, I know.

"Fine. If that's what you want. If that's the life you choose. If you want *that* instead of this one. The better life with the perfect people, perfect neighbors, perfect friends. A perfect family, really." She curses again. Probably at me. "Go, Penny. Please. Just go and get ready for bed. I'll come and kiss you goodnight in a little bit." Maybe. Mommy sounds like she is about to cry.

Penny

Present Day.

"Hey, Pen? Are you leaving today?" Kelly drops something made of green material next to the door. I nod and stand up from my desk. My picture drawing falls on the floor and Kelly gets it for me. "I like this one. It's a butterfly? You're getting good." She puts it on top of my desk and grabs a pencil that rolls off. "Ha ha! The magic touch!" She SQUEALS and puts it on top of my picture.

I smile, but it's a sad smile. Mom still isn't happy. I nod at Kelly. "It's time."

Kelly runs at me and hugs me way too tight. I wiggle and push her away. She starts to cry and I want to say something. But before I can, she says, "Here. I have something for you." She grabs the green thing she dropped earlier, a bright green shirt with a winking smiley face on the front. "This is for you. It's to remind you to always keep smiling, even when we can't see each other. We'll remember each other. And then we'll give each other huge hugs when we visit again. When we—"

"Thank you." I don't want her to keep talking. I know what happens. We already talked lots. Mom is moving again in a couple weeks. She works really hard all the time, but can never stay in one place. She calls it a "fresh start." Maybe she misses something. Maybe she is looking for something. I want to be with Kelly and Mommy and the baby soon, but I need to be safe. And Aunt Alexia and Uncle Edmond's house is that safe place. It doesn't move. I don't know how to put this into words, but I need that. I don't even know when the idea came in my head. But I know it's where I want to be. And even though Mom loves me a lot, Aunt Alexia and Uncle Edmond can teach me a lot. Even more than Mommy right now. And even more than Kelly. It's what I want.

I wave at Kelly to help with the green shirt. Since it's hers, it's a little big, but it fits over my other shirt. Yes, I can do this. She grabs my hand and that's how we leave the house. My house. Mom throws my suitcase in the trunk and I know it's really heavy because her eyes get big when she pushes it inside.

I am almost in the car when I go over to Mom. I tell her what I need to. "I love you." I say it really quickly, but I say it loud enough for Mom to hear. I keep expecting her to change her mind.

She bends down and hugs me. "I love you, too, Penny." Her tear falls on my cheek.

"Meow!"

I look for the sound and it is by the bushes again. It's the neighbor cat that doesn't belong to anyone. It paws up to the door, where I keep food out sometimes. It never stays around long, just hangs out under a porch or a tree or bush on different days. I saw it last time after a really big storm.

"Oh!" The word escapes me and I try to go slowly toward the cat. I don't want to scare it where it won't come out. But it hasn't seen me yet. Right when I get close enough to reach out and grab it, it YELPS and HIsssssss ES. I stand quiet.

I know how it feels when someone gets too close.

"Let me." Mom's voice surprises me, and I point over to the bushes. "Here, kitty, kitty." Her voice is soft and quick, and she wiggles her fingers towards where the cat is hiding. She has an orange Cheeto and she holds it out for the cat. She gets it. "Are you sure you want this thing?" Mom says, holding it out to me with one hand while it squirms and MEEEWS. "I don't know if it wants a home with people. It seems to be doing pretty good on its own."

I hold out my hands, but I almost drop the cat.

"Hold it tight," she tells me, "but be careful of the claws." Yeah, I already feel the sting on my arm. I nod and bite my lip. That hurt. And the cat scratches my arm again.

I get in the car, and I don't listen to Kelly when she says she wants to hold the cat. I hug him real tight as Mommy starts driving toward Aunt Alexia's house. After a little while, he stops scratching me.

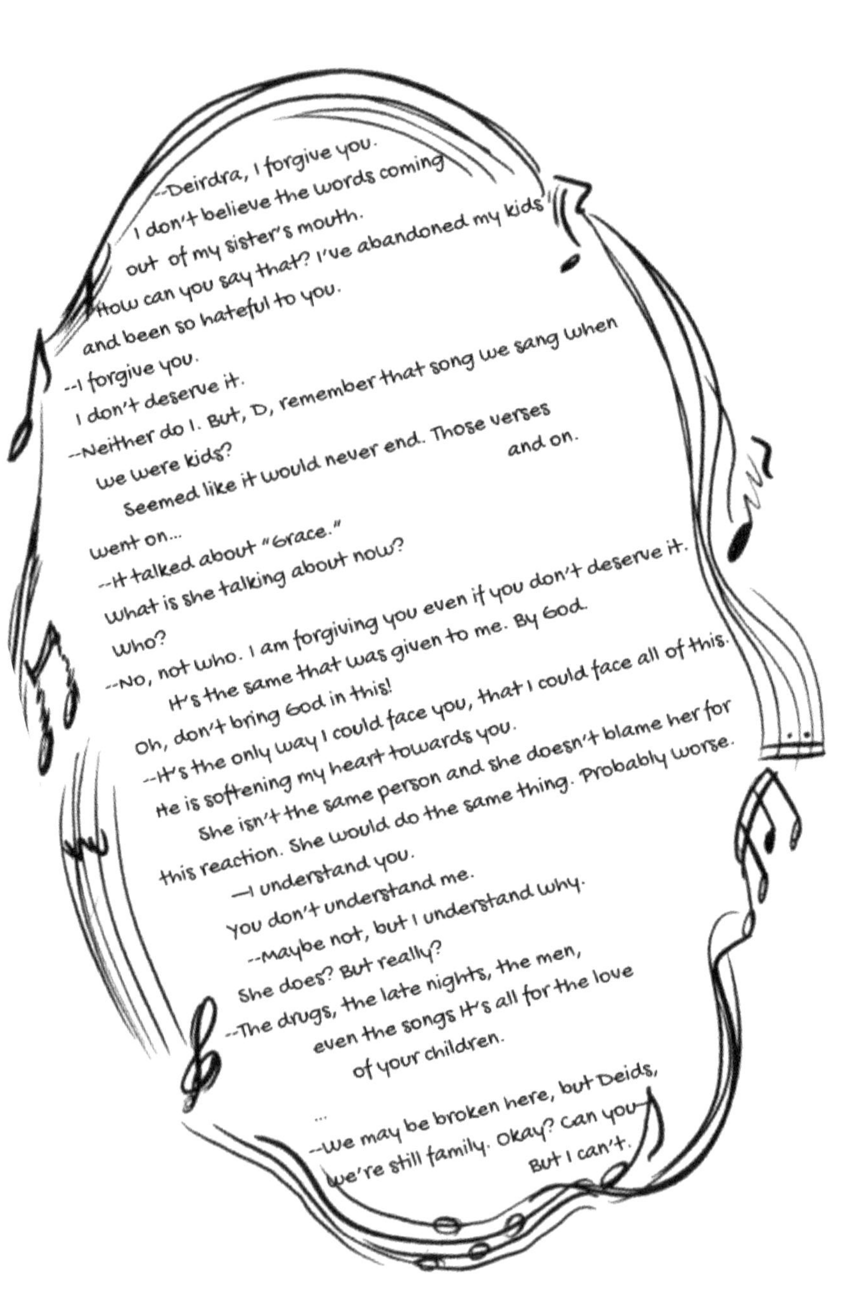
--Deirdra, I forgive you.
I don't believe the words coming
out of my sister's mouth.
How can you say that? I've abandoned my kids
and been so hateful to you.
--I forgive you.
I don't deserve it.
--Neither do I. But, D, remember that song we sang when
we were kids?
Seemed like it would never end. Those verses
and on.
went on...
--It talked about "Grace."
What is she talking about now?
Who?
--No, not who. I am forgiving you even if you don't deserve it.
It's the same that was given to me. By God.
Oh, don't bring God in this!
--It's the only way I could face you, that I could face all of this.
He is softening my heart towards you.
She isn't the same person and she doesn't blame her for
this reaction. She would do the same thing. Probably worse.
—I understand you.
You don't understand me.
--Maybe not, but I understand why.
She does? But really?
--The drugs, the late nights, the men,
even the songs It's all for the love
of your children.
...
--We may be broken here, but Deids,
we're still family. Okay? Can you—
But I can't.

Alexia

Present Day.

It's been a long day. Vici is going to come tomorrow, to help make sure things are ready. She has two kids of her own, so she can make sure I didn't miss anything. Oh, I'm feeling a bit nervous. Okay, more than a bit. Now, that blanket will be perfect for Penny! Hum-de hum-du hummm.

SLAM!

"Oh, Ed, can you do that a little quieter?"

"Hehe, sure, but can you help with these groceries? I bought some stuff for breakfast in the morning, and lots of other goodies for the rest of the week. How are you doing?"

"Um, I'm not sure at the moment. Our niece is coming to live with us! I should be over the moon, but–"

"Hey, hey. Put that down for a second," Ed urges. He grabs a box from me. And my list.

"But I feel like—I feel like I'm taking her away from my sister. I know, I know, it's what she wants. We talked about this. I just wish Deirdra and I were closer, that we could all just get through this and be a normal family." I'm rambling, but Ed still listens.

"Normal? What's normal? Who has a normal family?"

"You know, like together. Everybody where they belong and everyone loving one another."

"Now, Al, don't be so hard on yourself. It's not your job to play God and keep this family together. Every single person makes their own decisions in life and that person has got to live with it. Deirdra has to make up her own mind about where she wants to be, and whether she wants to get better. About what is best for her kids. Right now she can only think about what she needs. She is just surviving. Penny is going to do just fine, with a little help from her auntie."

He always knows how to make me smile. "I—"

"And if you're worried about Kelly, she's made it fine these first nine years of her life, and we'll keep an eye on her. But she's chosen to stay with her mom, and her little brother will need her, too."

Brother, is it?

"Well, sure. I know she made that choice because she's a little caretaker herself. Kelly's worried about her Mommy. Somehow, the two of 'em will figure out how to make it work."

"Mm-hmm." He's right. He usually is. Why doesn't that assure me?

"Let's get this bedroom put together. Now the comforter goes here?"

"Let's move the bed over to the window so it gets more light. Now the blanket can go here." Decorating is a great way to put our minds on future joys. And that Ed is helping—

"This beanbag chair is great. With something to sit on, that corner makes a nice little reading nook."

Just one bit, that's all it will take
I've got to keep a place where I can make a home without all the—
SCRAPE it away and TEARS; watch it through my tears.
    BAKE, STAY awake.
I'm giving in here because I can't ask
I need to be a mom and I'm failing hopelessly at this task.
Now there's another. A little one for my home. How am I going to last?
How am I--

"Sure. Can you help with the bed? It's easier with two people." I motion to my end.

"Ow! Al! Watch it! My fingers are right in between the bedpost and the wall!"

"Are you okay? Do you need Allie to come and kiss it?"

Ed laughs, putting the injured finger in his mouth. "I think so. Maybe that'll make the bleeding stop. Haha, you wouldn't think such a little dot of a wound would hurt so much! Ah, yes, much better. Another kiss?" He kisses me full on the mouth. "There. All better." He grins. "Just one more for good measure."

Mmm. "Thank you. Oh, it's just so..." My emotions are mixed up right now. Big joys and love combined with regret and worry.

"I know this is hard, and it's not fair." Ed wraps his arms around my waist. "I'm not pretending it is. But the Lord has put this child in our lives for a reason. Maybe only He knows why." He begins to pray aloud.

"So, Lord, please help us. We don't know how we're going to do this, but we know you are here to guide this family. Please help us take care of Penny. We pray, too, for Deirdra and Kelly and their new little one. They are doing what they can, Lord, and we pray that you give them wisdom and strength and keep them safe."

I nod and my tears fall on his hands, dripping onto my thumbs.

"Amen. Well, Ed. Here we go."

PENNY
Present Day.

Dear Mom—

ALEXIA

Present Day.

"Al, what are you thinking?" A tense laugh from the other end of my phone. But I still can't say anything. "So? That's a long pause even for you." Vici asks me point blank. And honestly, I don't know. I feel like I'm being tested, but I've got to just keep going, no matter the pricks along the way.

"I...uh," I give a tense. "I think I need to give it a minute. This is what I wanted, but it's not what I wanted. I love those girls and it'll be great to have Penny here, but at the same time, it's not fair."

"I know–"

"It's not fair that this is how I...got...her. But I'm excited, too!" My voice breaks. "And then I feel like a horrible person for saying that because someone needs to love her. And right now it's too hard for Deirdra. I'm worried." Another laugh. "And now I'm a crazy person, answering my own questions. Just call me Gollum!"

"Well, Allie–"

"I mean, I talked to Ed about this and he helped so much, that dear man! But I just keep going over and over it in my head and I can't figure out if this is the best decision for everyone. Would it be better for Penny to stay with Deirdra? I can make her stay and then maybe that would help Deids have some motivation to get better. But then do I really want to keep Penny in that environment? She's getting older and she notices so much. She probably did before, but now she's starting to vocalize it. And Kelly is such a help, but she has a good head on her shoulders, and if she wants to stay, she's going to do it. She has her own opinions and though I've never seen her buck Deid's authority, she's also a little dreamer and knows when to get away."

"Are you ready to listen to me now?" I can hear the grin in Vici's voice, but I know she's serious. I can imagine her tapping her finger quickly on her coffee cup like she does when she means business.

"Yes, what is it? I need some insight."

"I don't know about that, but I can tell you about family. They are not perfect, no matter how much you love them. You also can't force someone to do something they don't want to do. Well, you can, but then they would hold it against you for the rest of your life, or as long as you have a relationship with them. A relationship like that is superficial and it won't last long anyway. What I *can* tell you is that right now, you can help with this one child. You can reach out to Penny because she's reaching out to you. And you're not 'taking her away,' as you call it, from Deidra. She has made her own decisions and she's not being the most attentive mama right now. Can things change in a month? Yes. Can things change in an hour? Absolutely! But for right now, you are trying to keep your family together. Do what you can. And we can work on all the legal jargon together."

"Okay. Thanks, Vici."

"And you know what, Al?"

"What?"

"You're going to make mistakes."

I laugh out loud at that one. "I know…" I groan.

"It might seem like the worst thing to you right now, but it's really making you better. And guess what." She pauses, probably to make sure I'm listening. Nothing can tear me away now. "It is good for Penny to see you fail. She needs to know not just that you love her, but that you are human. She needs some humanity right now. And even for Ed. He wants to be able to help his family. Yes, Deirdra is his family, too! But he has to know that you will let him help you. He loves you too much for you to be upset and so he will let you do it on your own if you insist."

Tears are falling now.

"Please don't shut him out. Let him help you. And let him help Penny in his own way."

"You are so right! Ed has his own ideas about kids, but sometimes they're so much more effective!" Vici laughs with me.

"Al, I don't have many answers. But love. Make sure to love."

I nod, even though she can't see. "Right. Thanks so much. She'll be here in a few minutes, so I've gotta go!"

"Let me know!"

I nod again and hang up, realizing I forgot to say goodbye. Mistakes. Embrace it.

Penny

Present Day.

Dear Kelly,

Hi its Penny. I hope you are doing good. I am here at Aunt Alexia and Uncl Edmonds house, I relly relly miss you! I wanted to draw you a pictur for your room. Say hi to Mommy! I will call you soon.

Penny

It takes me a long time to write it out, and I know some of the words are not spelled right. It still makes me upset when I want to do really good in school and can't figure things out, not without the word wall. I still fold the letter very careful and put the picture inside. I already folded it into about fifty squares but I still wiggle it a lot to make sure that it stays in there. Then I put a stamp from the "knick-knacks" drawer and copy the address that Uncle Edmond wrote on that piece of paper. All ready!

Yeah, it's weird to send letters to my sister instead of going to the next room to talk. Maybe email will be faster, but Aunt Alexia and Uncle Edmond need to help show me how to put my picture in there. And also they'd see what I was writing. I don't know. I'll just do this for now.

Uncle Edmond can flip pancakes exactly right every time. It feels good to be back here, but I miss Mom and Kelly every single day. Here I feel, well, safe. It's like my heart knows that I will be taken care of and won't have to worry about making sure we have food or get to school on time or other stuff like that.

"Hey, Penny," says Uncle Edmond. "Can you go get your aunt? I think she's upstairs." When I go up there, I look in my old room, which looks different now. That seems like a really long time ago when I stayed in there. It's going to be hard to fall asleep in my new room without Kelly next to me.

When I get to the room where Aunt Alexia is, I hear something that is familiar, but I haven't heard for a while. Not since with Mom. When I walk into the room, Aunt Alexia sits on the bed and she's crying. Her hands are up on her face. Then she sees me and wipes her face to get the tears. "I'm sorry, Sweetie," she says. "I'm okay, just a little tired." She tries a smile. I go over and put my hand on top of hers. Then she starts crying again. Did I hurt her?

I pull my hands away. I wish these pants had pockets I could fit my hands into. She looks at me and we have one of those silent eye conversations. I don't understand, but it's going to be okay. Pain. But happiness, too. Both at the same time. And then something else. Maybe I'm just not big enough yet to know.

Out loud, Aunt Alexia says, "When you go through something sad, it makes you have a pain in your gut, right here." She tickles my stomach. "What? You feel it, too? It's right here." She moves her hands all around and makes me laugh. "No, it's here!"

Alexia

Present Day.

A rapid knock on the door rushes me to answer. Deirdra stands there, her hair matted, yet pulled back. She holds a large duffel with several of Penny's toys. She is breathless and immediately starts talking, shaking her head when I motion for her to come in. "I know that I'm the last person that you want to see right now. And I've got an appointment right after this, so I'll make it quick. That's it. There's no need in hiding it from you, but I've still got to make money. Kids and all that."

For a second I'm flabbergasted, so I glance at the items in her hand. "Oh, you've brought some toys."

She nods. "Right. Not a lot, and I know yours are probably better, but she's had these since she was little and I wanted you to still have a...a keepsake, if you need it."

"Thank you." I lean in to try to hug her and she takes a step back. "I...I'm sure she will love having them. I'll make sure to find a special place."

She nods.

"It's not going to be in a closet." Her grin mirrors her relief. "I have a couple shelves in my office that I can move to Penny's room and we can display them there."

She nods again, walking away and giving a little wave without looking back at me.

"I'm in Narcotics Anonymous. For family members." I blurt out. Deirdra turns back to me and stops. "And that helps me to daily lift you up in prayer. It also reminds me that recovery is a step-by-step process. You must be on board with it fully or it will not work. Even then, there are so many stumbling blocks."

"If you're about to give me a lecture about what I should and shouldn't do, now's not a good time—"

"I know!" I catch my sharp tone. I can't do that now. I step toward her. "I know I've made so many mistakes with us, and I know you are doing everything you can to be a good mother. You haven't failed. You're just letting your little girls soar. I get how I can be." I wave away Deirdra's grunt in agreement. "And I will probably keep forgiving you and keep reminding myself that you're only human."

Deirdra's shock shows plainly on her face and she blushes. I put my hands on her arms.

"But, Deids, so am I. I'm just a human here with human bones. I can't do any of this any better than the rest of the people on the planet."

"I guess we've both got to give each other slack, then, right?" She gives me a pale smile.

"Right. And you're welcome to come with me anytime you want. Or I can come with you if you find a group!"

"Baby steps, Al."

Deirdra

Present Day.

"Hey, hon, what is this?" I pass a small box to my girl and she snatches it from me.

"Oh, here. It's not mine, though. Well, I guess it kind of is. It's from–" She doesn't finish, and I tear up and wipe away the moisture just as fast. It's from my daughter, I'm sure of it, though I don't even know if she claims me as her mom anymore. Deep breath. Focus on now. I shake my head at my conflicting emotions, as present as the desire for drugs. This is going to be a long road.

Kelly snatches the package from me, pulls open the top of the box and pinches a cream-colored paper. She unfolds it gingerly and runs her finger across a pencil smudge, probably from the move. I sit on the end of her bed and she glances up, but doesn't make a move to turn away. The page has one of Penny's drawings. The petals on the flower are a bright red, and it looks like the hummingbird is winking because its eye lands in the middle of one of the creases. Then she unfolds the second paper, which it looks like she's kept since Penny moved, more than four months ago.

"What is this?" The dull echo of my question seems to reverberate off the walls and I doubt if Kelly will answer. But she does. She plays with something in the box while she talks. "Penny gave me a bunch of papers before she went away and–" Kelly chokes and pauses. Then she clears her throat and looks me in the eyes. "She said, 'Don't be scared.' I'm the one who's supposed to tell her that!" She sobs, and tears slide down my cheeks. She buries her head against the back of her chair, and I want to hug her, but what can I say? We've just moved. Again. I had to get away from those influences, from the familiar. But I didn't think about what it might do to my kiddos. "What was going to happen to us, apart like this?"

"Can I see that?" I hold out my hand for the page she has in her hand. She nods silently and passes it over, watching for a reaction as I follow the story. I read the paper slowly, savoring the sound of Penny's voice in the handwriting.

Monsters

Monsters can be fond in the giant scary wuds. It is hard to see the monsters sumtims. But monsters are always thir. In your bedroom in your kichin, and in thos durk dark plasis outsid My teacher says that monsters are our fears but I think they are mor. I think they are reel to I have lerned that i need to trust the lord when i am scared but i most just cry miself to sleep. In my dreems i am brav and i can fight them. Kelly alwas helps me. Then monsters are no mor.

It sounds like something that was an assignment at school or something. Things like this never came easily for her. How is my girl doing now?

"Is Penny happy?" Kelly questions.

"I really, really hope so. With everything in me." She scoots over and bends her head against her daughter. "Maybe she gets to swim in a pool every day or maybe she sleds down a hill, screaming her lungs out." Will she remember her? Will Penny keep the bracelet Kelly sent her like she's keeping Penny's pictures?

"Will I ever see her again?"

I close my eyes. I can't answer that. But with everything in me, I hope so. I sincerely hope so. "Here, Kelly, can you do something for me?" Kelly hides the letter in the back of a desk drawer. She nods as if she's curious what I'm going to ask. "I need you to watch Dilly."

Dillon Ryan, Kelly's new little brother. I never quite figured out who his dad was, but Kelly for sure never met him. I quit doing that a long time ago. It wasn't worth it. But man, this little one sure is! "It'll just be for a little bit, but I need to talk with a friend. Can you do that?" Old habits are hard to break.

"Yeah, Mom, I'm a teenager now, remember? I'm not a baby!"

"But Dilly is. Remember, he's been fed, but you can play with him for about half an hour and then put him down. Remember to hold his head and then--"

"Sure, sure. I know how. I can do this, Mom. Then can I sing him to sleep?"

I poke her lightly on the nose. "Of course! We're just going to talk and I'm going to ask a few questions. It's a beginning, but everyone has been trying to tell me that I need to let others in. It's hard, but I'm going to try. Remember that, Kelly. Even if it's hard, promise me that you'll try?"

"Are you talking about me watching Dilly?"

I'm sure it sounds as if I talk in riddles, but there's always a future song in my head, and most of them I'm singing before they even turn into anything.

Kelly wrinkles her nose, something she and her friends do a lot now. "Dilly is just as sweet as a dilly bar, and he smells better."

"Like fresh laundry or a fluffy cloud in human form." She grins. I continue, "Watching Dilly and also all the other decisions you're going to make as you get older. You're growing up, Kelly, and I'm so proud of you." She rolls her eyes, but still has a smile on her face. I nod, turning for the stairs. She hugs me quickly from behind and rushes back into Dilly's room. I watch with a proud smile. Kelly sneaks over to Dilly's crib where he's already looking at her, kicking his feet. His large brown eyes get even bigger when she wiggles her little fingers in his face.

"Hey, baby," she whispers.

PENNY

Present Day.

Home. Now my home is here with Aunt Alexia and Uncle Edmond. I laugh as she tickles me, not even minding Aunt Alexia touching my stomach. She grabs a wad of tissue from by the bed and sniffs. When she stops tickling, I look at her, right in the eyes. "When you let yourself cry, it's like there's this release of pain that has twisted you up inside. It lets out all of those ugly emotions and the angry thoughts wash away." She SHOO-s her hand in front of her face. "I'm not saying, of course, that crying is the answer to everything, but sometimes it reminds your brain to sit in the moment and remember some good memories with the pain. Keep doing this and keep doing that and pretty soon the pain will go far away. Most of the time, you'll still be left with the good memories."

Deep breath. I touch the blanket on the end of the bed. Like mine, but a darker color. "What if I forget?"

"Oh, honey, you won't ever forget your mom. She has helped make you into the person you are today. There might be times when you wish she was with us more. And there might be times when you are just so stinking mad at her that you want to scream, especially as you get older and move into your teenage years. But you won't ever forget how important she is to you, and how much she loves you. She just doesn't know the right way to show it yet."

I start crying and Aunt Alexia hugs me and gives me a tissue. A clean one.

"Let the tears come, Pen. Tears will help bring healing to your heart."

About the Author

Hannah Marie. lives in Texas where she enjoys writing in coffee shops and drinking dirty chai lattes with almond milk. *Reserved* is her debut novel, in addition to *Solivagant: Steps for Solo Travel Around the World* (2024), a guidebook for travel adventures, and *Mama* (2017), a book of short stories. Hannah Marie. was a teacher for almost a decade and received her graduate degree in Curriculum and Instruction with a focus on Language and Literacy and English as a Second Language. In her spare time she runs in her neighborhood and watches procedural dramas. Hannah Marie. always searches for inspiration for future stories and paintings, some of which can be viewed on her website, https://hannahmarieartwork.blog. Previous illustration credits include Heather Dillard's *Flowers for Friends*, Maury Sanders' *The Emergence of Sam Weiss* and Callie M. Walker's *Threads of Thought*.

Research

This book could not have been accomplished without copious research. Dear reader, if you would like to know more, or have questions, look into the following areas, as a start. Find someone who can be your support during hard times.

Berent, Jonathan, L.C.S.W., A.C.S.W. "Toward a Resolution of Selective Mutism: Understanding Obsessive Compulsive." Social-Anxiety.com. Berent Associates, 16 Dec. 2016. Web. 26 Feb. 2017.

Child Welfare Informational Gateway. "Placement of Children With Relatives."Placement of Children With Relatives - Child Welfare Information Gateway. Child Welfare Informational Gateway, July 2013. Web. 04 Apr. 2017.

Davies, Julian, MD. "Prenatal Opiate Exposure." Center for Adoption Medicine. Center for Adoption Medicine, 2017. Web. 19 Apr. 2017.

Dummit, E. Steven, III, MD. "Common Myths – Selective Mutism Foundation." Selective Mutism Foundation. The Therapy Center, 2017. Web. 24 Feb. 2017.

"Samhsa's National Helpline." SAMHSA, June 2023, www.samhsa.gov/find-help/national-helpline.

Selective Mutism Association, 27 June 2024, www.selectivemutism.org/.

"Transforming Children's Lives." Child Mind Institute, 17 July 2024, childmind.org/.

References

Grindley, Sally, and John Butler. Little Elephant Thunderfoot. Atlanta, GA: Peachtree, 1999. Print.

Lindgren, Astrid. Pippi Longstocking. Oxford University Press, 2015

Milne, A. A. 1882-1956. and Ernest H. 1879-1976 Shepard. Winnie-the-Pooh. [1st ed.]. New York, Dutton, 1974.

Montgomery, L. M. (Lucy Maud), 1874-1942. Anne of Green Gables. Boston :Godine, 1989.

Schulman, Janet, ed, et al. *The 20th Century Children's Book Treasury: Celebrated Picture Books and Stories to Read Aloud*. CNIB, 2007.

Silverstein, Shel. A Giraffe and a Half, HarperCollins Publishers, 2004

Silverstein, Shel. The Giving Tree. HarperCollins Publishers, 2014.

Tolkien, J. R. R. The Hobbit. HarperCollins, 2012.

Various. *The Children's Classics Collection*. Arcturus, 2018.

Viorst, Judith. *Alexander and the Terrible, Horrible, No Good, Very Bad Day*. Simon & Schuster, 1987.

White, E.B. *Charlotte's Web*. Hanna Barbera, 1993.